THE RAILROADERS

Armed with grit, daring—and guns—they rode the iron rails into the untamed land. This collection captures the rich flavor of life on the Union Pacific, the Southern Pacific, and the Santa Fe.

THE BEST OF THE WEST

Anthologies of new and old stories written with gusto and realism by your favorite Western authors.

Fawcett Gold Medal Books
by Martin Harry Greenberg & Bill Pronzini:

The Cowboys

The Lawmen

The Outlaws

The Warriors

THE RAILROADERS

Edited by Bill Pronzini and Martin H. Greenberg

FAWCETT GOLD MEDAL • NEW YORK

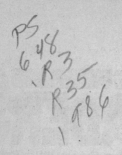

PS
648
.R3
R35
1986

Acknowledgments

"Song of the Steel Rails," Tom W. Blackburn. Copyright 1941 by Popular Publications, New York. First published in *Dime Western*. Reprinted by permission of the author.

"For Want of a Horse," Clay Fisher. Copyright © 1978 by Clay Fisher. From the Bantam anthology *Nine Lives West* by Clay Fisher. Reprinted by permission of Henry W. Allen (Clay Fisher).

"Steel to the West," Wayne D. Overholser. Copyright © 1977 by Western Writers of America, Inc. All rights reserved. First published in *WWA's Silver Anniversary Anthology*. Reprinted by permission of the author.

"Flying Switch," H. L. Davis. From *Team Bells Woke Me and Other Stories* by H. L. Davis. Copyright 1930 by Collier's; renewed 1958 by H. L. Davis. Reprinted by permission of William Morrow and Company.

"Westward Rails," Giles A. Lutz. Copyright © 1977 by Western Writers of America, Inc. First published in *WWA's Silver Anniversary Anthology*. Reprinted by permission of the author.

"The Phantom Train Robbers," Jeffrey M. Wallmann. Copyright © 1972 by Zane Grey Western Magazine. First published in Zane Grey Western Magazine. Reprinted by permission of the author.

"Hell on the High Iron," John Jakes. Copyright 1952 by Popular Publications, Inc.; renewed 1980 by John Jakes. Originally published under the title "The High-Iron Killer" in *Big-Book Western Magazine* for March, 1953. Reprinted by permission of the author.

Contents

Introduction

The Railroaders is the fifth in a series of *Best of the West* anthologies of outstanding short Western fiction that has too long been out of print and unavailable to modern readers. The first four volumes in the series—*The Lawmen*, *The Outlaws*, *The Cowboys*, and *The Warriors*—feature realistic and exciting stories about Old West peace officers, desperadoes, cowpunchers and trail hands, and members of the various American Indian tribes. In *The Railroaders* you will find a dozen of the best tales written during this century about the iron horse—stories of the men who built and operated the great Western railroads, of the men who tried to use them for power and personal gain, of the outlaws such as Jesse James who sought to steal the gold and other valuables they carried.

These stories are rich with the flavor of old-time railroading, authentic in their depiction of life on and around such lines as the Union Pacific, the Southern Pacific, and the Atcheson, Topeka & the Santa Fe, which opened the American West to rapid settlement and growth. We're sure you'll find them every bit as action-packed and memorable as those in the previous four collections.

Future *Best of the West* anthologies will contain stories about the steamboats that plied the rivers and other waterways of the Old West, about the hardy pioneers who led the westward expansion, about the miners and prospectors who searched for precious metals, about the drifters and loners of legend and fact—stories by such major writers as John Jakes, Brian Garfield, Norman A. Fox, A. B. Guthrie, Jr., Jack Schaefer, Dorothy M. Johnson, and many more. We hope these volumes, too, give you many hours of reading pleasure, and that you find

1

them worthy of a permanent place in your Western library.

—Bill Pronzini and Martin H. Greenberg

*The most stirring of all the great railroading songs are
"Casey Jones" and "John Henry." The former provides an
appropriate prologue to this anthology.*

Casey Jones

(ballad)

Come, all you rounders, if you want to hear
A story 'bout a brave engineer.
Casey Jones was the rounder's name
On a six-eight wheeler, boys, he won his fame.
The caller called Casey at a half past four,
Kissed his wife at the station door,
Mounted to the cabin with his orders in his hand
And he took his farewell trip to the promised land:
   *Casey Jones, mounted to the cabin,
   Casey Jones, with his orders in his hand,
   Casey Jones, mounted to the cabin,
   And he took his farewell trip to the promised land.*

"Put in your water and shovel in your coal,
Put your head out the window, watch them drivers roll,
I'll run her till she leaves the rail
'Cause I'm eight hours late with the western mail."
He looked at his watch and his watch was slow,
He looked at the water and the water was low,
He turned to the fireman and then he said,
"We're goin' to reach Frisco but we'll all be dead":

Casey Jones, goin' to reach Frisco,
Casey Jones, but we'll all be dead,
Casey Jones, goin' to reach Frisco,
"We're goin' to reach Frisco, but we'll all be dead."

Casey pulled up that Reno Hill,
He tooted for the crossing with an awful shrill,
The switchman knew by the engine's moan
That the man at the throttle was Casey Jones.
He pulled up within two miles of the place
Number Four stared him right in the face,
He turned to the fireman, said, "Boy, you better jump,
'Cause there's two locomotives that's a-goin' to bump":
    Casey Jones, two locomotives,
    Casey Jones, that's a-goin' to bump,
    Casey Jones, two locomotives,
    "There's two locomotives that's a-goin' to bump."

Casey said just before he died,
"There's two more roads that I'd like to ride."
The fireman said, what could they be?
"The Southern Pacific and the Santa Fe."
Mrs. Casey sat on her bed a-sighin',
Just received a message that Casey was dyin'.
Said, "Go to bed, children, and hush your cryin',
'Cause you got another papa on the Salt Lake Line":
    Mrs. Casey Jones, got another papa,
    Mrs. Casey Jones, on that Salt Lake Line,
    Mrs. Casey Jones, got another papa,
    "And you've got another papa on the Salt Lake Line."

Black Eagle, a bandit who ''infested the Texas border along the Rio Grande,'' is one of three fictional desperadoes created by native Texan O. Henry (William Sydney Porter, 1862–1910). The other two are the Cisco Kid, who appears in ''The Caballero's Way'' (reprinted in The Outlaws), and was transformed into a dashing ''Robin Hood of the Old West'' in the TV series starring Duncan Renaldo; and the Llano Kid, who is featured in ''A Double-Dyed Deceiver'' and in the 1930 Gary Cooper film, The Texan. O. Henry's sure hand with the Western story is readily apparent in these tales and in those found in his superb 1904 collection, Heart of the West.

The Passing of
Black Eagle

O. Henry

*F*or some months of a certain year a grim bandit infested the Texas border along the Rio Grande. Peculiarly striking to the optic nerve was this notorious marauder. His personality secured him the title of ''Black Eagle, the Terror of the Border.'' Many fearsome tales are on record concerning the doings of him and his followers. Suddenly, in the space of a single minute, Black Eagle vanished from earth. He was never heard of again. His own band never even guessed the mystery of his disappearance. The border ranches and settlements feared he would come again to ride and ravage the mesquite flats. He never will. It is to disclose the fate of Black Eagle that this narrative is written.

The initial movement of the story is furnished by the foot of a bartender in Saint Louis. His discerning eye fell upon the form of Chicken Ruggles as he pecked with avidity at the free lunch. Chicken was a "hobo." He had a long nose like the bill of a fowl, an inordinate appetite for poultry, and a habit of gratifying it without expense, which accounts for the name given him by his fellow vagrants.

Physicians agree that the partaking of liquors at meal times is not a healthy practice. The hygiene of the saloon promulgates the opposite. Chicken had neglected to purchase a drink to accompany his meal. The bartender rounded the counter, caught the injudicious diner by the ear with a lemon squeezer, led him to the door, and kicked him into the street.

Thus the mind of Chicken was brought to realize the signs of coming winter. The night was cold; the stars shone with unkindly brilliancy; people were hurrying along the streets in two egotistic, jostling streams. Men had donned their overcoats, and Chicken knew to an exact percentage the increased difficulty of coaxing dimes from those buttoned-in vest pockets. The time had come for his annual exodus to the south.

A little boy, five or six years old, stood looking with covetous eyes in a confectioner's window. In one small hand he held an empty two-ounce vial; in the other he grasped tightly something flat and round, with a shining milled edge. The scene presented a field of operations commensurate to Chicken's talents and daring. After sweeping the horizon to make sure that no official tug was cruising near, he insidiously accosted his prey. The boy, having been early taught by his household to regard altruistic advances with extreme suspicion, received the overtures coldly.

Then Chicken knew that he must make one of those desperate, nerve-shattering plunges into speculation that fortune sometimes requires of those who would win her favor. Five cents was his capital, and this he must risk against the chance of winning what lay within the close grasp of the youngster's chubby hand. It was a fearful lottery, Chicken knew. But he must accomplish his end by strategy, since he had a wholesome terror of plundering infants by force. Once, in a park, driven by hunger, he had committed an onslaught upon a bottle of peptonized infant's food in the possession of an occupant of a baby carriage. The outraged infant had so promptly opened its mouth and pressed the button that communicated with the welkin that help arrived, and Chicken did his thirty days in a snug coop. Wherefore he was, as he said, "leery of kids."

Beginning artfully to question the boy concerning his choice of sweets, he gradually drew out the information he wanted. Mamma said he was to ask the drugstore man for ten cents' worth of paregoric in the bottle; he was to keep his hand shut tight over the dollar; he must not stop to talk to anyone in the street; he must ask the drugstore man to wrap up the change and put it in the pocket of his trousers. Indeed, they had pockets—two of them! And he liked chocolate creams best.

Chicken went into the store and turned plunger. He invested his entire capital in C. A. N. D. Y. stocks, simply to pave the way to the greater risk following.

He gave the sweets to the youngster, and had the satisfaction of perceiving that confidence was established. After that it was easy to obtain leadership of the expedition, to take the investment by the hand and lead it to a nice drugstore he knew of in the same block. There Chicken, with a parental air, passed over the dollar and called for the medicine, while the boy crunched his candy, glad to be relieved of the responsibility of the purchase. And then the successful investor, searching his pockets, found an overcoat button—the extent of his winter trousseau—and, wrapping it carefully, placed the ostensible change in the pocket of confiding juvenility. Setting the youngster's face homeward, and patting him benevolently on the back—for Chicken's heart was as soft as those of his feathered namesakes—the speculator quit the market with a profit of 1,700 percent on his invested capital.

Two hours later an Iron Mountain freight engine pulled out of the railroad yards, Texas bound, with a string of empties. In one of the cattle cars, half buried in excelsior, Chicken lay at ease. Beside him in his nest was a quart bottle of very poor whiskey and a paper bag of bread and cheese. Mr. Ruggles, in his private car, was on his trip south for the winter season.

For a week that car was trundled southward, shifted, laid over, and manipulated after the manner of rolling stock, but Chicken stuck to it, leaving it only at necessary times to satisfy his hunger and thirst. He knew it must go down to the cattle country, and San Antonio, in the heart of it, was his goal. There the air was salubrious and mild; the people indulgent and long-suffering. The bartenders there would not kick him. If he should eat too long or too often at one place they would swear at him as if by rote and without heat. They swore so drawlingly, and they rarely paused short of their full vocabulary, which was copious, so that Chicken had often gulped a good meal during the process of the vituperative prohibition. The season there was always springlike; the plazas were pleasant at night, with music and gayety: except during the slight and infrequent cold snaps one could sleep comfortably out of doors in case the interiors should develop inhospitality.

At Texarkana his car was switched to the I. and G. N. Then still southward it trailed until, at length, it crawled across the Colorado bridge at Austin, and lined out, straight as an arrow, for the run to San Antonio.

When the freight halted at that town Chicken was fast asleep. In ten minutes the train was off again for Laredo, the end of the road. Those empty cattle cars were for distribution along the line at points from which the ranches shipped their stock.

When Chicken awoke his car was stationary. Looking out between the slats he saw it was a bright, moonlit night. Scrambling out, he saw his car with three others abandoned on a little siding in a wild and lonesome country. A cattle pen and chute stood on one side of the track. The railroad bisected a vast, dim ocean of prairie, in the midst of which Chicken, with his futile rolling stock, was as completely stranded as was Robinson with his land-locked boat.

A white post stood near the rails. Going up to it, Chicken read the letters at the top, S. A. 90. Laredo was nearly as far to the south. He was almost a hundred miles from any town. Coyotes began to yelp in the mysterious sea around him. Chicken felt lonesome. He had lived in Boston without an education, in Chicago without nerve, in Philadelphia without a sleeping place, in New York without a pull, and in Pittsburgh sober, and yet he had never felt so lonely as now.

Suddenly, through the intense silence, he heard the whicker of a horse. The sound came from the side of the track toward the east, and Chicken began to explore timorously in that direction. He stepped high along the mat of curly mesquite grass, for he was afraid of everything there might be in this wilderness—snakes, rats, brigands, centipedes, mirages, cowboys, fandangoes, tarantulas, tamales—he had read of them in the story papers. Rounding a clump of prickly pear that reared high its fantastic and menacing array of rounded heads, he was struck to shivering terror by a snort and a thunderous plunge, as the horse, himself startled, bounded away some fifty yards and then resumed his grazing. But here was the one thing in the desert that Chicken did not fear. He had been reared on a farm; he had handled horses, understood them, and could ride.

Approaching slowly and speaking soothingly, he followed the animal, which, after its first flight, seemed gentle enough, and secured the end of the twenty-foot lariat that dragged after him in the grass. It required him but a few moments to contrive the rope into an ingenious nose-bridle, after the style of the Mexican *borsal*. In another he was upon the horse's back and off at a splendid lope, giving the animal free choice of direction. "He will take me somewhere," said Chicken to himself.

It would have been a thing of joy, that untrammeled gallop over the moonlit prairie, even to Chicken, who loathed exertion, but that his mood was not for it. His head ached; a growing thirst was upon him; the "somewhere" whither his lucky mount might convey him was full of dismal peradventure.

And now he noted that the horse moved to a definite goal. Where the prairie lay smooth he kept his course straight as an arrow's toward the east. Deflected by hill or arroyo or impracticable spinous brakes, he quickly flowed again into the current, charted by his unerring instinct. At last, upon the side of a gentle rise, he suddenly subsided to a complacent walk. A stone's cast away stood a little mott of coma trees; beneath it a *jacal* such as the Mexicans erect—a one-room house of upright poles daubed with clay and roofed with grass or tule reeds. An experienced eye would have estimated the spot as the headquarters of a small sheep ranch. In the moonlight the ground in the nearby corral showed pulverized to a level smoothness by the hoofs of the sheep. Everywhere was carelessly distributed the paraphernalia of the place—ropes, bridles, saddles, sheep pelts, wool sacks, feed troughs, and camp litter. The barrel of drinking water stood in the end of the two-horse wagon near the door. The harness was piled, promiscuous, upon the wagon tongue, soaking up the dew.

Chicken slipped to earth and tied the horse to a tree. He halloed again and again, but the house remained quiet. The door stood open, and he entered cautiously. The light was sufficient for him to see that no one was at home. He struck a match and lighted a lamp that stood on a table. The room was that of a bachelor ranchman who was content with the necessaries of life. Chicken rummaged intelligently until he found what he had hardly dared hope for—a small brown jug that still contained something near a quart of his desire.

Half an hour later, Chicken—now a gamecock of hostile aspect—emerged from the house with unsteady steps. He had drawn upon the absent ranchman's equipment to replace his own ragged attire. He wore a suit of coarse brown ducking, the coat being a sort of rakish bolero, jaunty to a degree. Boots he had donned, and spurs that whirred with every lurching step. Buckled around him was a belt full of cartridges with a six-shooter in each of its two holsters.

Prowling about, he found blankets, a saddle, and a bridle with which he caparisoned his steed. Again mounting, he rode swiftly away, singing a loud and tuneless song.

Bud King's band of desperadoes, outlaws, and horse and cattle thieves were in camp at a secluded spot on the bank of the Frio. Their depredations in the Rio Grande country, while no bolder than usual, had been advertised more extensively, and Captain Kinney's company of rangers had been ordered down to look after them. Consequently, Bud King, who was a wise general, instead of cutting out a hot trail for the upholders of the law, as his men wished to do, retired for the time to the prickly fastnesses of the Frio valley.

Though the move was a prudent one, and not incompatible with Bud's well-known courage, it raised dissension among the members of the band. In fact, while they thus lay ingloriously *perdu* in the brush, the question of Bud King's fitness for the leadership was argued, with closed doors, as it were, by his followers. Never before had Bud's skill or efficiency been brought to criticism; but his glory was waning (and such is glory's fate) in the light of a newer star. The sentiment of the band was crystallizing into the opinion that

Black Eagle could lead them with more luster, profit, and distinction.

This Black Eagle—subtitled the "Terror of the Border"—had been a member of the gang about three months.

One night while they were in camp on the San Miguel water hole a solitary horseman on the regulation fiery steed dashed in among them. The newcomer was of a portentous and devastating aspect. A beaklike nose with a predatory curve projected above a mass of bristling, blue-black whiskers. His eye was cavernous and fierce. He was spurred, sombreroed, booted, garnished with revolvers, abundantly drunk, and very much unafraid. Few people in the country drained by the Rio Bravo would have cared thus to invade alone the camp of Bud King. But this fell bird swooped fearlessly upon them and demanded to be fed.

Hospitality in the prairie country is not limited. Even if your enemy passes your way you must feed him before you shoot him. You must empty your larder into him before you empty your lead. So the stranger of undeclared intentions was set down to a mighty feast.

A talkative bird he was, full of most marvelous loud tales and exploits, and speaking a language at times obscure but never colorless. He was a new sensation to Bud King's men, who rarely encountered new types. They hung, delighted, upon his vainglorious boasting, the spicy strangeness of his lingo, his contemptuous familiarity with life, the world, and remote places, and the extravagant frankness with which he conveyed his sentiments.

To their guest the band of outlaws seemed to be nothing more than a congregation of country bumpkins whom he was "stringing for grub" just as he would have told his stories at the back door of a farmhouse to wheedle a meal. And, indeed, his ignorance was not without excuse, for the "bad man" of the Southwest does not run to extremes. Those brigands might justly have been taken for a little party of peaceable rustics assembled for a fish-fry or pecan gathering. Gentle of manner, slouching of gait, soft-voiced, unpicturesquely clothed; not one of them presented to the eye any witness of the desperate records they had earned.

For two days the glittering stranger within the camp was feasted. Then, by common consent, he was invited to become a member of the band. He consented, presenting for enrollment the prodigious name of "Captain Montressor." This was immediately overruled by the band, and "Piggy" substituted as a compliment to the awful and insatiate appetite of its owner.

Thus did the Texas border receive the most spectacular brigand that ever rode its chaparral.

For the next three months Bud King conducted business as usual, escaping encounters with law officers and being content with reasonable profits. The band ran off some very good companies of horses from the ranges, and a few bunches of fine cattle which they got safely across the Rio Grande and disposed of to fair advantage. Often the band would ride into the little villages and Mexican settlements, terrorizing the inhabitants and plundering for the provisions and ammunition they needed. It was during these bloodless raids that Piggy's ferocious aspect and frightful voice gained him a renown more widespread and glorious than those other gentle-voiced and sad-faced desperadoes could have acquired in a lifetime.

The Mexicans, most apt in nomenclature, first called him the Black Eagle, and used to frighten the babes by threatening them with tales of the dreadful robber who carried off little children in his great beak. Soon the name extended, and Black Eagle, the Terror of the Border, became a recognized factor in exaggerated newspaper reports and ranch gossip.

The country from the Nueces to the Rio Grande was a wild but fertile stretch, given over to the sheep and cattle ranches. Range was free; the inhabitants were few; the law was mainly a letter, and the pirates met with little opposition until the flaunting and garish Piggy gave the band undue advertisement. Then Kinney's ranger company headed for those precincts, and Bud King knew that it meant grim and sudden war or else temporary retirement. Regarding the risk to be unnecessary, he drew off his band to an almost inaccessible spot on the bank of the Frio. Wherefore, as has been said, dissatisfaction arose among the members and impeachment proceedings against Bud were premeditated, with Black Eagle in high favor for the succession. Bud King was not unaware of the sentiment, and he called aside Cactus Taylor, his trusted lieutenant, to discuss it.

"If the boys," said Bud, "ain't satisfied with me, I'm willin' to step out. They're buckin' against my way of handlin' 'em. And 'specially because I concludes to hit the brush while Sam Kinney is ridin' the line. I saves 'em from bein' shot or sent up on a state contract, and they up and says I'm no good."

"It ain't so much that," explained Cactus, "as it is they're plum locoed about Piggy. They want them whiskers and that nose of his to split the wind at the head of the column."

"There's somethin' mighty seldom about Piggy," declared Bud, musingly. "I never yet see anything on the hoof that he exactly grades up with. He can shore holler aplenty, and he straddles a hoss from where you laid the chunk. But he ain't never been smoked yet. You know, Cactus, we ain't had a row since he's been with us. Piggy's all right for skearin' the greaser kids and layin' waste a crossroads store. I reckon he's the finest canned oyster buccaneer and cheese pirate that ever was, but how's his appetite for fightin'? I've knowed some citizens you'd think was starvin' for trouble get a bad case of dyspepsy the first dose of lead they had to take."

"He talks all spraddled out," said Cactus, " 'bout the rookuses he's been in. He claims to have saw the elephant and hearn the owl."

"I know," replied Bud, using the cow-puncher's expressive phrase of skepticism, "but it sounds to me!"

This conversation was held one night in camp while the other members of the band—eight in number—were sprawling around the fire, lingering over their supper. When Bud and Cactus ceased talking they heard Piggy's formidable voice holding forth to the others as usual while he was engaged in checking, though never satisfying, his ravening appetite.

"Wat's de use," he was saying, "of chasin' little red cowses and hosses 'round for t'ousands of miles? Dere ain't nuttin' in it. Gallopin' t'rough dese bushes and briers, and gettin' a t'irst dat a brewery couldn't put out, and missin' meals! Say! You know what I'd do if I was main finger of dis bunch? I'd stick up a train. I'd blow de express car and make hard dollars where you guys get wind. Youse makes me tired. Dis sook-cow kind of cheap sport gives me a pain."

Later on, a deputation waited on Bud. They stood on one leg, chewed mesquite twigs and circumlocuted, for they hated to hurt his feelings. Bud foresaw their business and made it easy for them. Bigger risks and larger profits was what they wanted.

The suggestion of Piggy's about holding up a train had fired their imagination and increased their admiration for the dash and boldness of the instigator. They were such simple, artless, and custom-bound bush-rangers that they had never before thought of extending their habits beyond the running off of livestock and the shooting of such of their acquaintances as ventured to interfere.

Bud acted "on the level," agreeing to take a subordinate place in the gang until Black Eagle should have been given a trial as leader.

After a great deal of consultation, studying of timetables, and discussion of the country's topography, the time and place for carrying out their new enterprise was decided upon. At that time there was a feedstuff famine in Mexico and a cattle famine in certain parts of the United States, and there was a brisk international trade. Much money was being shipped along the railroads that connected the two republics. It was agreed that the most promising place for the contemplated robbery was at Espina, a little station on the I. and G. N., about forty miles north of Laredo. The train stopped there one minute; the country around was wild and unsettled; the station consisted of but one house, in which the agent lived.

Black Eagle's band set out, riding by night. Arriving in the vicinity of Espina, they rested their horses all day in a thicket a few miles distant.

The train was due at Espina at 10:30 P.M. They could rob the train and be well over the Mexican border with their booty by daylight the next morning.

To do Black Eagle justice, he exhibited no signs of flinching from the responsible honors that had been conferred upon him.

He assigned his men to their respective posts with discretion and coached them carefully as to their duties. On each side of the track four of the band were to lie concealed in the chaparral. Gotch-Ear Rodgers was to stick up the station agent. Bronco Charlie was to remain with the horses, holding them in readiness. At a spot where it was calculated the engine would be when the train stopped, Bud King was to lie hidden on one side, and Black Eagle himself on the other. The two would get the drop on the engineer and fireman, force them to descend and proceed to the rear. Then the express car would be looted, and the escape made. No one was to move until Black Eagle gave the signal by firing his revolver. The plan was perfect.

At ten minutes to train time every man was at his post, effectually concealed by the thick chaparral that grew almost to the rails. The night was dark and lowering, with a fine drizzle falling from the flying gulf clouds. Black Eagle crouched behind a bush within five yards of the track. Two six-shooters were belted around him. Occasionally

An Easterner who had a lifelong fascination with the West, Clarence E. Mulford (1883–1956) created one of the most enduring characters in all of Western fiction—Hopalong Cassidy. Hoppy first appeared in Bar-20 Days in 1907, and along with his Bar-20 pards he appeared in numerous novels and stories for more than forty years. "The Holdup" was first published in 1913, and pits Hoppy and the boys against a band of train robbers.

The Holdup

Clarence E. Mulford

*T*he herd delivered at Sandy Creek had traveled only halfway, for the remaining part of the journey would be on the railroad. The work of loading the cars was fast, furious fun to anyone who could find humor enough in his makeup to regard it so. Then came a long, wearying ride for the five men picked from the drive outfit to attend the cattle on the way to the cattle pens of the city. Their work at last done, they "saw the sights" and were now returning to Sandy Creek.

The baggage smoking-car reeked with strong tobacco, the clouds of smoke shifting with the air currents, and dimly through the haze could be seen several men. Three of these were playing cards near the baggage-room door, while two more lounged in a seat halfway down the aisle and on the other side of the car. Across from the cardplayers, reading a magazine, was a fat man, and near the water cooler was a dyspeptic-looking individual who was grumbling about the country through which he was passing.

The first five, as their wearing apparel proclaimed, were not of the kind usually found on trains, not the drummer, the tourist, or the farmer. Their heads were covered with heavy sombreros, their coats were of thick, black woolens, and their shirts were also of wool. Around the throat of each was a large handkerchief, knotted at the back; their trousers were protected by "chaps," of which three were of goatskin. The boots were tight-fitting, narrow, and with high heels, and to them were strapped heavy spurs. Around the waist, hanging loosely from one hip, each wore a wide belt containing fifty cartridges in the loops, and supporting a huge Colt's revolver, which rested against the thigh.

They were happy and were trying to sing, but, owing to different tastes, there was noticeable a lack of harmony. "Oh Susanna" never did go well with "Annie Laurie," and as for "Dixie," it was hopelessly at odds with the other two. But they were happy, exuberantly so, for they had enjoyed their relaxation in the city and now were returning to the station where their horses were waiting to carry them over the two hundred miles which lay between their ranch and the nearest railroad station.

For a change the city had been pleasant, but after they had spent several days there it lost its charm and would not have been acceptable to them even as a place in which to die. They had spent their money, smoked "topnotcher" cigars, seen the "shows," and feasted each as his fancy dictated and as behooved cowpunchers with money in their pockets. Now they were glad that every hour reduced the time of their stay in the smoky, jolting, rocking train, for they did not like trains, and this train was particularly bad. So they passed the hours as best they might and waited impatiently for the stop at Sandy Creek, where they had left their horses. Their trip to the "fence country" was now a memory, and they chafed to be again in the saddle on the open, windswept range, where miles were insignificant and the silence soothing.

The fat man, despairing of reading, watched the card-players and smiled in good humor as he listened to their conversation, while the dyspeptic, nervously twisting his newspaper, wished that he were at his destination. The baggage-room door opened and the conductor looked down on the cardplayers and grinned. Skinny moved over in the seat to make room for the genial conductor.

"Sit down, Simms, an' take a hand," he invited. Laughter arose continually and the fat man joined in it, leaning forward more closely to watch the play.

Lanky tossed his cards facedown on the board and grinned at the onlooker. "Billy shore bluffs more on a variegated flush than any man I ever saw."

"Call him once in a while and he'll get cured of it," laughed the fat man, bracing himself as the train swung around a sharp turn.

"He's too smart," growled Billy Williams. "He tried that an' found I didn't have no variegated flushes. Come on, Lanky, if yo're playing cards, put up."

Farther down the car, their feet resting easily on the seat in front of them, Hopalong and Red puffed slowly at their large, black cigars and spoke infrequently, both idly watching the plain flit by in wearying sameness, and both tired and lazy from doing nothing but ride.

"Blast th' cars, anyhow," grunted Hopalong, but he received no reply, for his companion was too disgusted to say anything.

A startling, sudden increase in the roar of the train and a gust of hot, sulphurous smoke caused Hopalong to look up at the brakeman, who came down the swaying aisle as the door slammed shut.

"Phew!" he exclaimed, genially. "Why in thunder don't you fellows smoke up?"

Hopalong blew a heavy ring, stretched energetically, and grinned. "Much farther to Sandy Creek?"

"Oh, you don't get off for three hours yet," laughed the brakeman.

"That's shore a long time to ride this bronc train," moodily complained Red as the singing began. "She shore pitches a-plenty," he added.

The train-hand smiled and seated himself on the arm of the front seat. "Oh, it might be worse."

"Not this side of Hades," replied Red with decision, watching his friend, who was slapping the cushions to see the dust fly out. "Hey, let up on that, will you! There's dust a-plenty without no help from you!"

The brakeman glanced at the cardplayers and then at Hopalong. "Do your friends always sing like that?" he inquired.

"Mostly, but sometimes it's worse."

"On the level?"

"Shore enough; they're singing 'Dixie,' now. It's their bes' song."

"That ain't 'Dixie!' "

"Yes, it is—that is, most of it."

"Well, then, what's the rest of it?"

"Oh, them's variations of their own," remarked Red, yawning and stretching. "Just wait till they start something sentimental; you'll shore weep."

"I hope they stick to the variations. Say, you must be a pretty nifty gang on the shoot, ain't you?"

"Oh, some," answered Hopalong.

"I wish you fellers had been aboard with us one day about a month ago. We was the wrong end of a holdup, and we got cleaned out proper, too."

"An' how many of 'em did you get?" asked Hopalong quickly, sitting bolt upright.

The fat man suddenly lost his interest in the card game and turned an eager ear to the brakeman, while the dyspeptic stopped punching holes in his time-card and listened. The cardplayers glanced up and then returned to their game, but they, too, were listening.

The brakeman was surprised. "How many did we get! Gosh, we didn't get none! They was six to our five."

"How many cards did you draw, you Piute?" asked Lanky.

"None of yore business; I ain't dealing, an' I wouldn't tell you if I was," retorted Billy.

"Well, I can ask, can't I?"

"Yes—you can, an' did."

"You didn't get none?" cried Hopalong, doubting his ears.

"I should say not!"

"An' they owned th' whole train?"

"They did."

Red laughed. "Th' cleaning-up must have been sumptuous an' elevating."

"Every time I holds three's he allus has better," growled Lanky to Simms.

"On th' level, we couldn't do a thing," the brakeman ran on. "There's a water tank a little farther on, and they must 'a' climbed aboard there when we stopped to connect. When we got into the gulch the train slowed down and stopped, and I started to get up to go out and see what was the matter; but I saw *that* when I looked down a gun barrel. The man at the throttle end of it told me to put up my hands, but they were up as high then as I could get 'em without climbin' on the top of the seat."

"Can't you listen and play at th' same time?" Lanky asked Billy.

"I wasn't countin' on takin' the gun away from him," the brakeman continued, "for I was too busy watchin' for the slug to come out of the hole. Pretty soon somebody on the outside whistled and then another feller come in the car—he was the one that did the cleanin' up. All this time there had been a lot of shootin' outside, but now it got worse. Then I heard another whistle and the engine puffed up the track, and about five minutes later there was a big explosion, and then our two robbers backed out of the car among the rocks, shootin' back regardless. They busted a lot of windows.''

"An' you didn't git none," grumbled Hopalong, regretfully.

"When we got to the express car, what had been pulled around the turn," continued the brakeman, not heeding the interruption, "we found a wreck. And we found the engineer and fireman standin' over the express messenger, too scared to know he wouldn't come back no more. The car had been blowed up with dynamite, and his fighting soul went with it. He never knowed he was licked.''

"An' nobody tried to help him!" Hopalong exclaimed, wrathfully now.

"Nobody wanted to die with him," replied the brakeman.

"Well," cried the fat man, suddenly reaching for his valise, "I'd like to see anybody try to hold me up!" Saying which he brought forth a small revolver.

"You'd be praying out of your bald spot about that time," muttered the brakeman.

Hopalong and Red turned, perceived the weapon, and then exchanged winks.

"That's a fine shootin'-iron, stranger," gravely remarked Hopalong.

"You bet it is," purred the owner proudly. "I paid six dollars for that gun.''

Lanky smothered a laugh and his friend grinned broadly. "I reckon that'd kill a man—if you stuck it in his ear.''

"Pshaw!" snorted the dyspeptic scornfully. "You wouldn't have time to get it out of that grip. Think a train-robber is going to let you unpack? Why don't you carry it in your hip pocket, where you can get at it quickly?''

There were smiles at the stranger's belief in the hip-pocket fallacy, but no one commented upon it.

"Wasn't there no passengers aboard when you was stuck up?" Lanky asked the conductor.

"Yes, but you can't count passengers in on a deal like that."

Hopalong looked around aggressively. "We're passengers, ain't we?"

"You certainly are."

"Well, if any misguided maverick gets it into his fool head to stick *us* up, you see what happens. Don't you know th' fellers outside have all th' worst o' th' deal?"

"They have not!" cried the brakeman.

"They've got all the best of it," asserted the conductor emphatically. "I've been inside, and I know."

"Best nothing!" cried Hopalong. "They are on th' ground, watching a danger-line over a hundred yards long, full of windows and doors. Then they brace th' door of a car full of people. While they climb up the steps they can't see inside, an' then they go an' stick their heads in plain sight. It's an even break who sees th' other first, with th' men inside training their guns on th' glass in th' door!"

"Darned if you ain't right!" enthusiastically cried the fat man.

Hopalong laughed. "It all depends on th' men inside. If they ain't used to handling guns, 'course they won't try to fight. We've been in so many gun festivals that we wouldn't stop to think. If any coin collector went an' stuck his ugly face against th' glass in that door he'd turn a back-flip off'n th' platform before he knowed he was hit. Is there any chance for a stick-up today, d'y think?"

"Can't tell," replied the brakeman. "But this is about the time we have the section-camps' pay on board," he said, going into the baggage end of the car.

Simms leaned over close to Skinny. "It's on this train now, and I'm worried to death about it. I wish we were at Sandy Creek."

"Don't you go worryin' none, then," the puncher replied. "It'll get to Sandy Creek all right."

Hopalong looked out of the window again and saw that

there was a gradual change in the nature of the scenery, for the plain was becoming more broken each succeeding mile. Small woods occasionally hurtled past and banks of cuts flashed by like mottled yellow curtains, shutting off the view. Scrub timber stretched away on both sides, a billowy sea of green, and miniature valleys lay under the increasing number of trestles twisting and winding toward a high horizon.

Hopalong yawned again. "Well, it's none o' our funeral. If they let us alone I don't reckon we'll take a hand, not even to bust up this monotony."

Red laughed derisively. "Oh, no! Why, you couldn't sit still nohow with a fight going on, an' you know it. An' if it's a stick-up! Wow!"

"Who gave you any say in this?" demanded his friend. "Anyhow, you ain't no angel o' peace, not nohow!"

"Mebby they'll plug yore new sombrero," laughed Red.

Hopalong felt of the article in question. "If any two-laigged wolf plugs my war-bonnet he'll be some sorry, an' so'll his folks," he asserted, rising and going down the aisle for a drink.

Red turned to the brakeman, who had just returned. "Say," he whispered, "get off at th' next stop, shoot off a gun, an' yell, just for fun. Go ahead, it'll be better'n a circus."

"Nix on the circus, says I," hastily replied the other. "I ain't looking for no excitement, an' I ain't paid to amuse th' passengers. I hope we don't even run over a track-torpedo this side of Sandy Creek."

Hopalong returned, and as he came even with them the train slowed. "What are we stopping for?" he asked, his hand going to his holster.

"To take on water, the tank's right ahead."

"What have you got?" asked Billy, ruffling his cards.

"None of yore business," replied Lanky. "You call when you gets any curious."

"Oh, th' devil!" yawned Hopalong, leaning back lazily. "I shore wish I was on my cayuse pounding leather on th' home trail."

"Me, too," grumbled Red, staring out of the window. "Well, we're moving again. It won't be long now before we gets out of this."

The card game continued, the low-spoken terms being interspersed with casual comment. Hopalong exchanged infrequent remarks with Red, while the brakeman and conductor stared out of the same window. There was noticeable an air of anxiety, and the fat man tried to read his magazine with his thoughts far from the printed page. He read and reread a single paragraph several times without gaining the slightest knowledge of what it meant, while the dyspeptic passenger fidgeted more and more in his seat, like one sitting on hot coals, anxious and alert.

"We're there now," suddenly remarked the conductor, as the bank of a cut blanked out the view. "It was right here where it happened—the turn's farther on."

"How many cards did you draw, Skinny?" asked Lanky.

"Three, drawin' to a straight flush," laughed the dealer.

"Here's the turn! We're through all right," exclaimed the brakeman.

Suddenly there was a rumbling bump, a screeching of air brakes, and the grinding and rattle of couplings and pins as the train slowed down and stopped with a suddenness that snapped the passengers forward and back. The conductor and brakeman leaped to their feet, where the latter stood quietly during a moment of indecision.

A shot was heard and the conductor's hand, raised quickly to the whistle rope, sent blast after blast shrieking over the land. A babel of shouting burst from the other coaches and, as the whistle shrieked without pause, a shot was heard close at hand and the conductor reeled suddenly and sank into a seat, limp and silent.

At the first jerk of the train the cardplayers threw the

board from across their knees, scattering the cards over the floor, and, crouching, gained the center of the aisle, intently peering through the windows, their Colts ready for instant action. Hopalong and Red were also in the aisle, and when the conductor had reeled, Hopalong's Colt exploded and the man outside threw up his arms and pitched forward.

"Good boy, Hopalong!" cried Skinny.

Hopalong wheeled and crouched, watching the door, and it was not long before a masked face appeared on the farther side of the glass. Hopalong fired and a splotch of red stained the white mask as the robber fell against the door and slid to the platform.

"Hear that shooting?" cried the brakeman. "They're at the messenger. They'll blow him up!"

"Come on, fellers!" cried Hopalong, leaping toward the door, closely followed by his friends.

They stepped over the obstruction on the platform and jumped to the ground on the side of the car farthest from the robbers.

"Shoot under the cars for legs," whispered Skinny. "That'll bring 'em down where we can get 'em."

"Which is a good idea," replied Red, dropping quickly and looking under the car.

"Somebody's going to be surprised, all right," exulted Hopalong.

The firing on the other side of the train was heavy, being for the purpose of terrifying the passengers and to forestall concerted resistance. The robbers could not distinguish between the many reports and did not know they were being opposed, or that two of their number were dead.

A whinny reached Hopalong's ears and he located it in a small grove ahead of him. "Well, we know where th' cayuses are in case they make a break."

A white and scared face peered out of the cab window and Hopalong stopped his finger just in time, for the inquisitive man wore the cap of fireman.

"You idiot!" muttered the gunman angrily. "Get back!" he ordered.

A pair of legs ran swiftly along the other side of the car and Red and Skinny fired instantly. The legs bent, their owner falling forward behind the rear truck, where he was screened from sight.

"They had it their own way before!" gritted Skinny. "Now we'll see if they can stand th' iron!"

By this time Hopalong and Red were crawling under the express car and were so preoccupied that they did not notice the faint blue streak of smoke immediately over their heads. Then Red glanced up to see what it was that sizzled, saw the glowing end of a three-inch fuse, and blanched. It was death not to dare and his hand shot up and back, and the dynamite cartridge sailed far behind him to the edge of the embankment, where it hung on a bush.

"Good!" panted Hopalong. "We'll pay 'em for that!"

"They're worse than rustlers!"

They could hear the messenger running about over their heads, dragging and upending heavy objects against the doors of the car, and Hopalong laughed grimly.

"Luck's with this messenger, all right."

"It ought to be—he's a fighter."

"Where are they? Have they tumbled to our game?"

"They're waiting for the explosion, you chump."

"Stay where you are, then. Wait till they come out to see what's th' matter with it."

Red snorted. "Wait nothing!"

"All right, then. I'm with you. Get out of my way."

"I've been in situations some peculiar, but this beats 'em all," Red chuckled, crawling forward.

The robber by the car truck revived enough to realize that something was radically wrong, and shouted a warning as he raised himself on his elbow to fire at Skinny, but the alert puncher shot first.

As Hopalong and Red emerged from beneath the car and rose to their feet, there was a terrific explosion and they were knocked to the ground, while a sudden, heavy shower of stones and earth rained down over everything. The two punchers were not hurt and they arose to their feet in time to see the engineer and fireman roll out of the cab and crawl along the track on their hands and knees, dazed and weakened by the concussion.

Suddenly, from one of the day-coaches, a masked man looked out, saw the two punchers, and cried, "It's all up! Save yourselves!"

As Hopalong and Red looked around, still dazed, he fired at them, the bullet singing past Hopalong's ear. Red smothered a curse and reeled as his friend grasped him. A wound over his right eye was bleeding profusely and Hopalong's face cleared of its look of anxiety when he realized that it was not serious.

"They creased you! Blamed near got you for keeps!" he cried, wiping away the blood with his sleeve.

Red, slightly stunned, opened his eyes and looked about confusedly. "Who done that? Where is he?"

"Don't know, but I'll shore find out," Hopalong replied. "Can you stand alone?"

Red pushed himself free and leaned against the car for support. "Course I can! Git that cuss!"

When Skinny heard the robber shout the warning, he wheeled and ran back, intently watching the windows and doors of the car for trouble. "We'll finish yore tally right here!" he muttered.

When he reached the smoker he turned and went toward the rear, where he found Lanky and Billy lying under the platform. Billy was looking back and guarding the rear, while his companion watched the clump of trees where the second herd of horses was known to be. Just as they were joined by their foreman, they saw two men run across the track, fifty yards distant, and into the grove, both going so rapidly as to give no chance for a shot at them.

"There they are!" shouted Skinny, opening fire on the grove.

At that instant Hopalong turned the rear platform and saw the brakeman leap out of the door with a Winchester in his hands. The puncher sprang up the steps, wrenched the rifle from its owner, and, tossing it to Skinny, cried, "Here, this is better!"

"Too late," grunted the puncher, looking up, but Hopalong had become lost to sight among the rocks along the right of way. "If I only had this a minute ago!" he grumbled.

The men in the grove, now in the saddle, turned and opened fire on the group by the train, driving them back to shelter. Skinny, taking advantage of the cover afforded, ran toward the grove, ordering his friends to spread out and surround it; but it was too late, for at that minute galloping was heard and it grew rapidly fainter.

Red appeared at the end of the train. "Where's th' rest of the coyotes?"

"Two of 'em got away," Lanky replied.

"Ya-ho!" shouted Hopalong from the grove. "Don't none of you fools shoot! I'm coming out. They plumb got away!"

"They near got *you*, Red," Skinny cried.

"Nears don't count," Red laughed.

"Did you ever notice Hopalong when he's fighting mad?" asked Lanky, grinning at the man who was leaving the woods. "He allus wears his sombrero hanging on one ear. Look at it now!"

"Who touched off that cannon some time back?" asked Billy.

"I did. It was an antigravity cartridge what I found sizzling on a rod under th' floor of th' express car," replied Red.

"Why didn't you pinch out th' fuse 'stead of blowing everything up, you half-breed?" Lanky asked.

"I reckon I was some hasty," grinned Red.

"It blowed me under th' car an' my lid through a windy,"
cried Billy. "An' Skinny, he went up in th' air like a shore
'nough grasshopper."

Hopalong joined them, grinning broadly. "Hey, reckon
ridin' in th' cars ain't so bad after all, is it?"

"Holy smoke!" cried Skinny. "What's that a-popping?"

Hopalong, Colt in hand, leaped to the side of the train and
looked along it, the others close behind him, and saw the fat
man with his head and arm out of the window, blazing away
into the air, which increased the panic in the coaches. Hopalong grinned and fired into the ground, and the fat man
nearly dislocated parts of his anatomy by his hasty disappearance.

"Reckon he plumb forgot all about his fine, six-dollar
gun till just now," Skinny laughed.

"Oh, he's making good," Red replied. "He said he'd
take a hand if anything busted loose. It's a good thing he
didn't come to life while me an' Hoppy was under his windy
looking for laigs."

"Reckon some of us better go in th' cars an' quiet th'
stampede," Skinny remarked, mounting the steps, followed
by Hopalong. "They're shore *loco*."

The uproar in the coach ceased abruptly when the two
punchers stepped through the door, the inmates shrinking
into their seats, frightened into silence. Skinny and his companion did not make a reassuring sight, for they were grimy
with burned powder and dust, and Hopalong's sleeve was
stained with Red's blood.

"Oh, my jewels, my pretty jewels," sobbed a woman,
staring at Skinny and wringing her hands.

"Ma'am, we shore don't want yore jewelry," replied
Skinny, earnestly. "Ca'm yoreself. We don't want nothin'."

"*I* don't want that!" growled Hopalong, pushing a wallet
from him. "How many times do you want us to tell you we
don't want nothin'? We ain't robbers. We licked the robbers."

Suddenly he stooped and, grasping a pair of legs which protruded into the aisle obstructing the passage, straightened up and backed toward Red, who had just entered the car, dragging into sight a portly gentleman, who kicked and struggled and squealed, as he grabbed at the stanchions of seats to stay his progress. Red stepped aside between two seats and let his friend pass, and then leaned over and grasped the portly gentleman's coat collar. He tugged energetically and lifted the frightened man clear of the aisle and deposited him across the back of a seat, facedown, where he hung balanced, yelling and kicking.

"Shut yore face, you cave-hunter!" cried Red in disgust. "Stop that infernal noise! You fat fellers make all yore noise after th' fighting is all over!"

The man on the seat, suddenly realizing what a sight he made, rolled off his perch and sat up, now more angry than frightened. He glared at Red's grinning face and sputtered:

"It's an outrage! It's an outrage! I'll have you hung for this day's work, young man!"

"That's right," grinned Hopalong. "He shore deserves it. I told him more'n once that he'd get strung up some day."

"Yes and you, too!"

"Please don't," begged Hopalong. "I don't want t' die!"

Tense as the past quarter of an hour had been, a titter ran along the car and, fuming impotently, the portly gentleman fled into the smoker.

"I'll bet he had a six-dollar gun, too," laughed Red.

"I'll bet he's calling hisself names right about now," Hopalong replied. Then he turned to reply to a woman. "Yes, ma'am, we did. But they wasn't real badmen."

At this a young woman, who was about as pretty as any young woman could be, arose and ran to Hopalong and, impulsively throwing her arms around his neck, cried, "You brave man! You hero! You dear!"

"Skinny! Red! Help!" cried the embarrassed puncher, struggling to get free.

She kissed him on the cheek, which flamed even more red as he made frantic efforts to keep his head back.

"Ma'am!" he cried, desperately. "Leggo, ma'am! Leggo!"

"Oh! Ho! Ho!" roared Red, weak from his mirth and, not looking to see what he was doing, he dropped into a seat beside another woman. He was on his feet instantly. Fearing that he would have to go through the ordeal his friend was going through, he fled down the aisle, closely followed by Hopalong, who by this time had managed to break away. Skinny backed off suspiciously and kept close watch on Hopalong's admirer.

Just then the brakeman entered the car, grinning, and Skinny asked about the condition of the conductor.

"Oh, he's all right now," the brakeman replied. "They shot him through the arm, but he's repaired and out bossin' the job of clearin' the rocks off the track. He's a little shaky yet, but he'll come around all right."

"That's good. I'm shore glad to hear it."

"Won't you wear this pin as a small token of my gratitude?" asked a voice at Skinny's shoulder.

He wheeled and raised his sombrero, a flush stealing over his face. "Thank you, ma'am, but I don't want no pay. We was plumb glad to do it."

"But this is not pay! It is just a trifling token of my appreciation of your courage, just something to remind you of it. I shall feel hurt if you refuse."

Her quick fingers had pinned it to his shirt while she spoke, and he thanked her as well as his embarrassment would permit. Then there was a rush toward him and, having visions of a shirt looking like a jeweler's window, he turned and fled from the car, crying, "Pin 'em on the brakeman!"

He found the outfit working at a pile of rocks on the track, under the supervision of the conductor, and Hopalong looked up apprehensively at Skinny's approach.

"Lord!" he ejaculated, grinning sheepishly. "I was some scairt you was a woman."

Red dropped the rock he was carrying and laughed derisively. "Oh, yo're a brave man, you are! Scared to death by a purty female girl! If I'd 'a' been you I wouldn't 'a' run, not a step!"

Hopalong looked at him witheringly. "Oh, no! You wouldn't 'a' run! You'd dropped dead in your tracks, you would!"

"You was both of you a whole lot scared," Skinny laughed. Then, turning to the conductor: "How do you feel, Simms?"

"Oh, I'm all right, but it took the starch out of me for a while."

"Well, I don't wonder, not a bit."

"You fellows certainly don't waste any time getting busy," Simms laughed.

"That's the secret of gun-fightin'," replied Skinny.

"Well, you're a fine crowd, all right. Any time you want to go any place when you're broke, climb aboard my train and I'll see't you get there."

"Much obliged."

Simms turned to the express car. "Hey, Jackson! You can open up now if you want to."

But the express messenger was suspicious, fearing that the conductor was talking with a gun at his head. "You go to hell!" he called back.

"Honest!" laughed Simms. "Some cowboy friends o' mine licked the gang. Didn't you hear that dynamite go off? If they hadn't fished it out from under your feet you'd be communing with the angels 'bout now."

For a moment there was no response, and then Jackson could be heard dragging things away from the door. When he was told of the cartridge and Red had been pointed out to him as the man who had saved his life, he leaped to the ground and ran to where that puncher was engaged in carrying the ever-silenced robbers to the baggage car. He shook hands with Red, who laughed deprecatingly, and then turned and assisted him.

Hopalong came up and grinned. "Say, there's some cayuses in that grove up th' track. Shall I go up an' get 'em?"

"Shore! I'll go an' get 'em with you," replied Skinny.

In the grove they found seven horses picketed, two of them pack-animals, and they led them forth and reached the train as the others came up.

"Well, here's five saddled cayuses, an' two others," Skinny grinned.

"Then we can ride th' rest of th' way in th' saddle instead of in that blamed train," Red eagerly suggested.

"That's just what we can do," replied Skinny. "Leather beats car seats any time. How far are we from Sandy Creek, Simms?"

"About twenty miles."

"An' we can ride along th' track, too," suggested Hopalong.

"We shore can," laughed Skinny, shaking hands with the train crew. "We're some glad we rode with you this trip. We've had a fine time."

"And we're glad you did," Simms replied, "for that ain't no joke, either."

Hopalong and the others had mounted and were busy waving their sombreros and bowing to the heads and handkerchiefs which were decorating the car windows.

"All aboard!" shouted the conductor, and cheers and good wishes rang out and were replied to by bows and waving of sombreros. Then Hopalong jerked his gun loose and emptied it into the air, his companions doing likewise. Suddenly five reports rang out from the smoker and they cheered the fat man as he waved at them. They sat quietly and watched the train until the last handkerchief became lost to sight around a curve, but the screeching whistle could be heard for a long time.

"Gee!" laughed Hopalong as they rode on after the train, "won't th' fellers home on th' ranch be a whole lot sore when they hears about the good time they missed!"

Frank H. Spearman (1859–1937) is best known today as the author of Whispering Smith, *the classic 1906 novel about a soft-spoken, quick-shooting railroad detective in the Old West. Spearman also wrote numerous other novels and stories about Western railroading; among the best of his shorter works is "The Yellow Mail," a rousing tale of a test run of the transcontinental mail set on the Union Pacific at the turn of the century.*

The Yellow Mail

Frank H. Spearman

There wasn't another engineer on the division that dared talk to Doubleday the way Jimmie Bradshaw talked.

But Jimmie had a grievance, and every time he thought about it, it made him nervous.

Ninety-six years. It seemed a good while to wait; yet in the regular course of events on the Mountain Division there appeared no earlier prospect of Jimmie's getting a passenger run.

"Got your rights, ain't you?" said Doubleday, when Jimmie complained.

"I have and I haven't," grumbled Jimmie, winking hard; "there's younger men than I am on the fast runs."

"They got in on the strike; you've been told that a hundred times. We can't get up another strike just to fix you out on a fast run. Hang on to your freight. There's better men than you in Ireland up to their bilt in the bog, Jimmie."

"It's a pity they didn't leave you there, Doubleday."

38

"You'd have been a good while hunting for a freight run if they had."

Then Jimmie would get mad and shake his finger and talk fast: "Just the same, I'll have a fast run here when you're dead."

"Maybe; but I'll be alive a good while yet, my son," the master mechanic would laugh. Then Jimmie would walk off very warm, and when he got into the clear with himself, he would wink furiously and say friction things about Double-day that needn't now be printed, because it is different. However, the talk always ended that way, and Jimmie Bradshaw knew it always would end that way.

The trouble was, no one on the division would take Jimmie seriously, and he felt that the ambition of his life would never be fulfilled; that he would go plugging to gray hairs and the grave on an old freight train; and that even when he got to the right side of the Jordan there would still be something like half a century between him and a fast run. It was funny to hear him complaining about it, for everything, even his troubles, came funny to him, and in talking he had an odd way of stuttering with his eyes, which were red. In fact, Jimmie was nearly all red: hair, face, hands—they said his teeth were sandy.

When the first rumors about the proposed Yellow Mail reached the mountains Jimmie was running a new ten-wheeler; breaking her in on a freight "for some fellow without a lick o' sense to use on a limited passenger run," as Jimmie observed bitterly. The rumors about the mail came at first like stray mallards, opening signs of winter, and as the season advanced flew thicker and faster. Washington never was very progressive in the matter of improving the transcontinental service, but once by mistake they put in a postmaster general down there who wouldn't take the old song. When the bureau fellows that put their brains up in curl papers told him it couldn't be done, he smiled softly and sent for the managers of the crack lines across the continent, without suspecting how it bore incidentally on Jimmie Bradshaw's grievance against his master mechanic.

The postmaster general called the managers of the big lines, and they had a dinner at Chamberlain's, and they told him the same thing. "It has been tried," they said in the old, tired way; "really it can't be done."

"California has been getting the worst of it for years on the mail service," persisted the postmaster general moderately. "But Californians ought to have the best of it. We don't think anything about putting New York mail in Chicago in twenty hours. It ought to be simple to cut half a day across the continent and give San Francisco her mail a day earlier. Where's the fall down?" he asked, like one refusing "no" for an answer.

The general managers looked at our representative sympathetically and coughed cigar smoke his way to hide him.

"West of the Missouri," murmured a Pennsylvania swell, who pulled indifferently at a fifty-cent cigar. Everybody at the table took a drink on the exposé, except the general manager who sat at that time for the Rocky Mountains.

The West End representative was unhappily accustomed to facing the finger of scorn on such occasions. It has become with our managers a tradition. There was never a conference of transcontinental lines in which we were not scoffed at as a weak link in the chain of everything: mail, passenger, specials, whatnot—the trouble was invariably laid at our door.

This time a new man was sitting for the line at the Chamberlain dinner; a youngish man with a face that set like cement when the West End was trod on.

The postmaster general was inclined, from the reputation we had, to look on our man as one looks at a dog without a pedigree or at a dray horse in a bunch of standard-breds. But something in the mouth of the West End man gave him pause; since the Rough Riders, it has been a bit different with verdicts on things Western. The postmaster general suppressed a rising sarcasm with a sip of Chartreuse, for the dinner was ripening, and waited; nor did he mistake, the West Ender was about to speak.

"Why west of the Missouri?" he asked, with a lift of the face not altogether candid. The Pennsylvania man shrugged his brows; to explain might have seemed indelicate.

"If it is put through, how much of it do you propose to take yourself?" inquired our man, looking evenly at the Allegheny official.

"Sixty-five miles, including stops from the New York post office to Canal Street," replied the Pennsylvania man, and his words flowed with irritating ease.

"What do you take?" continued the man with the jaw, turning to the Burlington representative, who was struggling, belated, with an artichoke.

"About seventy from Canal to Tenth and Mason. Say, seventy," repeated the "Q" manager, with the lordliness of a man who has miles to throw at almost anybody, and knows it.

"Then suppose we say sixty-five from Tenth and Mason to Ogden," suggested the West Ender. There was a well-bred stare the table round, a lifting of glasses to mask expressions that might give pain. Sixty-five miles an hour? Through the Rockies?

The postmaster general struck the table quick and heavily: he didn't want to let it get away. "Why, hang it, Mr. Bucks," he exclaimed with emphasis, "if you will say sixty, the business is done. We don't ask you to do the Rockies in the time these fellows take to cut the Alleghenies. Do sixty, and I will put mail in Frisco a day earlier every week in the year."

"Nothing on the West End to keep you from doing it," said General Manager Bucks. He had been put up then only about six months. "But—"

Everyone looked at the young manager. The Pennsylvania man looked with confidence, for he instantly suspected there must be a string to such a proposition, or that the new representative was "talking through his hat."

"But what?" asked the Cabinet member, uncomfortably apprehensive.

"We are not putting on a sixty-five-mile schedule just because we love our country, you understand, nor to heighten an already glorious reputation. Oh, no," smiled Bucks faintly, "we are doing it for 'the stuff.' You put up the money; we put up the speed. Not sixty miles; sixty-five—from the Missouri to the Sierras. No; no more wine. Yes, I will take a cigar."

The trade was on from that minute. Bucks said no more then; he was a good listener. But next day, when it came to talking money, he talked more money into the West End treasury for one year's running than was ever talked before on a mail contract for the best three years' work we ever did.

When they asked him how much time he wanted to get ready, and told him to take plenty, three months was stipulated. The contracts were drawn, and they were signed by our people without hesitation because they knew Bucks. But while the preparations were being made for the fast schedule, the government weakened on signing. Nothing ever got through a Washington department without hitch, and they said our road had so often failed on like propositions that they wanted a test. There was a deal of wrangling; then a test run was agreed on by all the roads concerned. If it proved successful, if the mail was put to the Golden Gate on the second of the schedule, public opinion and the interests in the Philippines, it was concluded, would justify the heavy premium asked for the service.

In this way the dickering and the figuring became, in a measure, public, and keyed up everybody interested to a high pitch. We said nothing for publication, but under Buck's energy sawed wood for three whole months. Indeed, three months goes as a day getting a system into shape for an extraordinary schedule. Success meant with us prestige; but failure meant obloquy for the road and for our division chief who had been so lately called to handle it.

The real strain, it was clear, would come on his old, the

Mountain Division; and to carry out the point, rested on the Motive Power of the Mountain Division; hence, concretely, on Doubleday, master mechanic of the hill country.

In thirty days, Neighbor, superintendent of the Motive Power, called for reports from the division master mechanics on the preparations for the Yellow Mail run, and they reported progress. In sixty days he called again. The subordinates reported well except Doubleday. Doubleday said merely, "Not ready"; he was busy tinkering with his engines. There was a third call in eighty days, and on the eighty-fifth a peremptory call. Everybody said, "Ready," except Doubleday. When Neighbor remonstrated sharply, he would say only that he would be ready in time. That was the most he would promise, though it was generally understood that if he failed to deliver the goods he would have to make way for somebody that could.

The Plains Division of the system was marked up for seventy miles an hour, and, if the truth were told, a little better; but, with all the help they could give us, it still left sixty for the mountains to take care of, and the Yellow Mail proposition was conceded to be the toughest affair the Motive Power at Medicine Bend had ever faced. However, forty-eight hours before the mail left the New York post office, Doubleday wired to Neighbor, "Ready"; Neighbor to Bucks, "Ready"; and Bucks to Washington, "Ready"— and we were ready from end to end.

Then the orders began to shoot through the mountains. The best run was of especial importance, because the signing of the contract was believed to depend on the success of it. Once signed, accidents and delays might be explained; for the test run there must be no delays. Dispatchers were given the eleven, which meant Bucks; no lay-outs, no slows for the Yellow Mail. Roadmasters were notified: no track work in front of the Yellow Mail. Bridge gangs were warned, yard masters instructed, section bosses cautioned, track walkers spurred—the system was polished like a bar-keeper's diamond and swept like a parlor car for the test flight of the Yellow Mail.

Doubleday, working like a boiler washer, spent all day Thursday and all Thursday night in the roundhouse. He had personally gone over the engines that were to take the racket in the mountains. Ten-wheelers they were, the 1012 and the 1014, with fifty-six-inch drivers and cylinders big enough to sit up and eat breakfast in. Spick and span both of them, just long enough out of the shops to run smoothly to the work; and on Friday, Oliver Sollers, who, when he opened a throttle, blew miles over the tender like feathers, took the 1012, groomed like a Wilkes mare, down to Piedmont for the run up to the Bend.

Now Oliver Sollers was a runner in a thousand, and steady as a clock; but he had a fireman who couldn't stand prosperity—Steve Horigan, a cousin of Johnnie's. The glory was too great for Steve, and he spent Friday night in Gallagher's place celebrating, telling the boys what the 1012 would do to the Yellow Mail. Not a thing, Steve claimed after five drinks, but pull the stamps clean off the letters the minute they struck the foothills. But when Steve showed up at 5:00 A.M. to superintend the movement, he was seasick. The minute Sollers set eyes on him he objected to taking him out. Mr. Sollers was not looking for any unnecessary chances on one of Bucks's personal matters, and for the general manager the Yellow Mail test had become exceedingly personal. Practically everybody East and West had said it would fail; Bucks said no.

Neighbor himself was on the Piedmont platform that morning, watching things. The McCloud dispatchers had promised the train to our division on time, and her smoke was due with the rise of the sun. The big superintendent of Motive Power, watching anxiously for her arrival, and planning anxiously for her outgoing, glared at the bunged fireman in front of him, and, when Sollers protested, Neighbor turned on the swollen Steve with sorely bitter words. Steve swore mightily he was fit and could do the trick—but what's the word of a railroad man who drinks? Neighbor spoke wicked words, and while they poured on the guilty Steve's crop there was a shout down the platform. In the east the sun was breaking over the sandhills, and below it a haze of black thickened the horizon. It was McTerza with the 808 and the Yellow Mail. Neighbor looked at his watch: she was, if anything, a minute to the good, and before the car tinks could hustle across the yard, a streak of gold cut the sea of purple alfalfa in the lower valley, and the narrows began to smoke with the dust of the race for the platforms.

When McTerza blocked the big drivers at the west end of the depot, every eye was on the new equipment. Three standard railway mail cars, done in varnished buttercup, strung out behind the sizzling engine, and they looked pretty as cowslips. While Neighbor vaguely meditated on their beauty and on his boozing fireman, Jimmie Bradshaw, just in after a night run down from the Bend, walked across the yard. He had seen Steve Horigan making a "sneak" for the bath-house, and from the yard gossip Jimmie guessed the rest.

"What are you looking for, Neighbor?" asked Jimmie Bradshaw.

"A man to fire for Sollers—up. Do you want it?"

Neighbor threw it at him cross and carelessly, not having any idea Jimmie was looking for trouble. But Jimmie surprised him; Jimmie did want it.

"Sure, I want it. Put me on. Tired? No. I'm fresh as rainwater. Put me on, Neighbor; I'll never get fast any other way. Doubleday wouldn't give me a fast run in a hundred years.

"Neighbor," cried Jimmie, greatly wrought, "put me on, and I'll plant sunflowers on your grave."

There wasn't much time to look around; the 1012 was being coupled on to the mail for the hardest run on the line.

"Get in there, you blamed idiot," roared Neighbor presently at Jimmie. "Get in and fire her; and if you don't give

Sollers two hundred and ten pounds every inch of the way I'll set you back wiping."

Jimmie winked furiously at the proposition while it was being hurled at him, but he lost no time climbing in. The 1012 was drumming then at her gauge with better than two hundred pounds. Adam Shafer, conductor for the run, ran backward and forward a minute examining the air. At the final word from his brakeman he lifted two fingers at Sollers; Oliver opened a notch, and Jimmie Bradshaw stuck his head out of the gangway. Slowly, but with swiftly rising speed, the yellow string began to move out through the long lines of freight cars that blocked the spurs; and those who watched that morning from the Piedmont platform thought a smoother equipment than Bucks's mail train never drew out of the mountain yards.

Jimmie Bradshaw jumped at the work in front of him. He had never lifted a pick in as swell a cab. The hind end of the 1012 was big as a private car; Jimmie had never seen so much play for a shovel in his life, and he knew the trick of his business better than most men even in West End cabs, the trick of holding the high pressure every minute, of feeling the drafts before they left the throttle; and as Oliver let the engine out very, very fast, Jimmie Bradshaw sprinkled the grate bars craftily and blinked at the shivering pointer, as much as to say, "It's you and me now for the Yellow Mail, and nobody else on earth."

There was a long reach of smooth track in front of the foothills. It was there the big start had to be made, and in two minutes the bark of the big machine had deepened to a chest tone full as thunder. It was all fun for an hour, for two hours. It was that long before the ambitious fireman realized what the new speed meant: the sickening slew, the lurch on lurch so fast the engine never righted, the shortened breath along the tangent, the giddy roll to the elevation and the sudden shock of the curve, the roar of the flight on the car, and, above and over it all, the booming purr of the maddened steel. The canoe in the heart of the rapid, the bridge of a liner at sea, the gun in the heat of the fight, take something of this—the cab of the mail takes it all.

When they struck the foothills, Sollers and Jimmie Bradshaw looked at their watches and looked at each other like men who had turned their backs on every mountain record. There was a stop for water—speed drinks so hard—an oil round, an anxious touch on the journals; then the Yellow Mail drew reeling into the hills. Oliver eased her just a bit for the heavier curves, but for all that the train writhed frantically as it cut the segments, and the men thought, in spite of themselves, of the mountain curves ahead. The worst of the run lay ahead of the pilot, because the art in mountain running is not alone or so much in getting uphill; it is in getting downhill. But by the way the Yellow Mail got that day uphill and down, it seemed as if Steve Horigan's dream would be realized, and the 1012 actually would pull the stamps off the letters. Before they knew it they were through the gateway, out into the desert country, up along the crested buttes, and then, sudden as eternity, the wheel-base of the 1012 struck a tight curve, a pentdown rail sprang out like a knitting-needle, and the Yellow Mail shot staggering off track into a gray borrow-pit.

There was a crunching of truck and frame, a crashing splinter of varnished cars, a scream from the wounded engine, a cloud of gray ash in the burning sun, and a ruin of human effort in the ditch. In the twinkle of an eye the mail train lay spilled on the alkali; for a minute it looked desperate bad for the general manager's test.

It was hardly more than a minute; then like ants out of a trampled hill men began crawling from the yellow wreck. There was more—there was groaning and worse, yet little for so frightful a shock. And first on his feet, with no more than scratches, and quickest back under the cab after his engineer, was Jimmie Bradshaw, the fireman.

Sollers, barely conscious, lay wedged between the tank and the footboard. Jimmie, all by himself, eased him away from the boiler. The conductor stood with a broken arm directing his brakeman how to chop a crew out of the head mail car, and the hind crews were getting out unaided. There was a quick calling back and forth, and the cry, "Nobody killed!" But the engineer and the conductor were put out of action. There was, in fact, only one West End man unhurt—Jimmie Bradshaw.

The first wreck of the fast mail—there have been worse since—took place just east of Crockett's siding. A westbound freight lay at that moment on the passing track waiting for the mail. Jimmie Bradshaw, the minute he righted himself, cast up the possibilities of the situation. Before the freight crew had reached the wreck, Jimmie was hustling ahead to tell them what he wanted. The freight conductor demurred, and when they discussed it with the freight engineer, Kingsley, he objected. "My engine won't never stand it; it'll pound her to scrap," he argued. "I reckon the safest thing to do is to get orders."

"Get orders!" stormed Jimmie Bradshaw, pointing at the wreck. "Get orders! Are you running an engine on this line and don't know the orders for those mail bags? The orders is to move 'em! That's orders enough. Move 'em! Uncouple three of those empty box-cars and hustle 'em back. By the Great United States!—any man that interferes with moving this mail will get his time, that's what he'll get. That's Doubleday, and don't you forget it. The thing is to move the mail, not to stand here chewing about it!"

"Bucks wants the stuff hustled," put in the freight conductor, weakening before Jimmie's eloquence, "everybody knows that."

"Uncouple there!" cried Jimmie, climbing into the mogul cab. "I'll pull the bags, Kingsley; you needn't take any chances. Come back there, every mother's son of you, and help on the transfer."

He carried his points with a gale. He was conductor and engineer and general manager all in one. He backed the boxes to the curve below the spill, and set every man at work piling the mail from the wrecked train to the freight cars.

The wounded cared for the wounded, and the dead might have buried the dead; Jimmie moved the mail. Only one thing turned his hair gray; the transfer was so slow, it threatened to defeat his plan. As he stood fermenting, a stray party of Sioux bucks on a vagrant hunt rose out of the desert passes, and halted to survey the confusion. It was Jimmie Bradshaw's opportunity. He had the blanket men in council in a trice. They talked for one minute; in two, he had them regularly sworn in and carrying second-class. The registered stuff was zealously guarded by those of the mail clerks who could still hobble—and who, head for head, leg for leg, and arm for arm, can stand the wrecking that a mail clerk can stand? The mail crews took the registered matter; the freight crews and Jimmie, dripping sweat and anxiety, handled the letter-bags; but second- and third-class were temporarily hustled for the Great White Father by his irreverent children of the Rockies.

Before the disabled men could credit their senses the business was done, they made as comfortable as possible, and, with the promise of speedy aid back to the injured, the Yellow Mail, somewhat disfigured, was heading again westward in the box-cars. This time Jimmie Bradshaw for once in his life had the coveted fast run, and till he sighted Fort Rucker he never for a minute let up.

Meantime, at Medicine Bend, there was a desperate crowd around the dispatcher. It was an hour and twenty minutes after Ponca station reported the Yellow Mail out, before Fort Rucker, eighteen miles west, reported the box-cars and Jimmie Bradshaw in, and followed with a wreck report from the Crockett siding. When that end of it began to tumble into the Wickup office Doubleday's face turned hard; fate was against him, the contract gone glimmering, and he didn't feel at all sure his own head and the roadmaster's wouldn't follow it. Then the Rucker operator began again to talk about Jimmie Bradshaw, and "Who's Bradshaw?" asked somebody; and Rucker went on excitedly with the story of the mogul and of three box-cars, and of a war party of Sioux squatting on the brake-wheels; it came so mixed that Medicine Bend thought everybody at Rucker Station had gone mad.

While they fumed, Jimmie Bradshaw was speeding the mail through the mountains. He had Kingsley's fireman, big as an ox and full of his own enthusiasm. In no time they were flying across the flats of the Spider Water, threading the curves of the Peace River, and hitting the rails of the Painted Desert, with the mogul sprinting like a Texas steer, and the box-cars leaping like yearlings at the joints. It was no case of scientific running, no case of favoring the road-bed, of easing the strain on the equipment; it was simply a case of galloping to a Broadway fire with a Silsby rotary on a 4-11 call. Uphill and down, curve and tangent, it was all one. There was speed made on the plains with that mail, and there was speed made in the foothills with the fancy equipment, but never the speed that Jimmie Bradshaw made when he ran the mail through the gorges in three box-cars; and frightened operators and paralyzed station agents all the way up the line watched the fearful and wonderful train, with Bradshaw's red head sticking out of the cab window, shiver the switches.

Medicine Bend couldn't get the straight of it over the wires. There was an electric storm in the mountains, and the wires went bad in the midst of the confusion. They knew there was a wreck, and understood there was mail in the ditch, and, with Doubleday frantic, the dispatchers were trying to get the track to run a train down to Crockett's. But Jimmie Bradshaw had asked at Rucker for rights to the Bend, and in an unguarded moment they had been given; after that it was all off. Nobody could get action on Jimmie Bradshaw. He took the rights, and stayed not for stake nor stopped not for stone. In thirty minutes the operating department were wild to kill him, but he was making such time it was concluded better to humor the lunatic than to hold him up anywhere for a parley. When this was decided, Jimmie and his war party were already reported past Bad Axe, fifteen miles below the Bend, with every truck on the box-cars smoking.

The Bad Axe run to the Bend was never done in less than fourteen minutes until Bradshaw that day brought up the mail. Between those two points the line is modeled on the curves of a ram's horn, but Jimmie with the mogul found every twist on the right of way in eleven minutes; that particular record is good yet. Indeed, before Doubleday, then in a frenzied condition, got his cohorts fairly on the platform to look for Jimmie, the hollow scream of the big freight engine echoed through the mountains. Shouts from below brought the operators to the upper windows; down the Bend they saw a monster locomotive flying from a trailing horn of smoke. As the stubby string of freight cars slewed quartering into the lower yard, the startled officials saw them from the Wickiup windows wrapped in a stream of flame. Every journal was afire, and the blaze from the boxes, rolling into the steam from the stack, curled hotly around a bevy of Sioux Indians, who clung sternly to the footboards and brake-wheels on top of the box-cars. It was a ride for the red men that is told around the council fires yet. But they do not always add in their traditions that they were hanging on, not only for life, but likewise for a butt of plug tobacco promised for their timely aid at Crockett siding.

By the time Jimmie slowed up his astounding equipment, the fire brigade was on the run from the roundhouse. The Sioux warriors climbed hastily down the fire escapes, a force of bruised and bare-headed mail clerks shoved back the box-car doors, the car tinks tackled the conflagration, and Jimmie Bradshaw, dropping from the cab with the swing of a man who has done a trick, waited at the gangway for the questions to come at him. For a minute they came hot.

"What the blazes do you mean by bringing in an engine in that condition?" choked Doubleday, pointing to the blown machine.

"I thought you wanted the mail?" winked Jimmie.

"How the devil are we to get the mail with you blocking the track two hours?" demanded Callahan, insanely.

"Why, the mail's here, in these box-cars," answered Jimmie Bradshaw, pointing to his bobtail train. "Now don't look daffy like that; every sack is right here. I thought the best way to get the mail here was to bring it. Hm? We're forty minutes late, ain't we?"

Doubleday waited to hear no more. Orders flew like curlews from the superintendent and the master mechanic. They saw there was a life for it yet. Before the fire brigade had done with the trucks a string of new mail cars was backed down beside the train. The relieving mail crews waiting at the Bend took hold like cats at a pudding, and a dozen extra men helped them sling the pouches. The 1014, blowing porpoisewise, was backed up just as Benedict Morgan's train pulled down for Crockett's siding, and the Yellow Mail, rehabilitated, rejuvenated, and exultant, started up the gorge for Bear Dance, only fifty-three minutes late, with Hawksworth in the cab.

"And if you can't make that up, Frank, you're no good on earth," sputtered Doubleday at the engineer he had put in for that especial endeavor. And Frank Hawksworth did make it up, and the Yellow Mail went on and off the West End on the test, and into the Sierras for the coast, ON TIME.

"There's a butt of plug tobacco and transportation to Crockett's coming to these bucks, Mr. Doubleday," wheezed Jimmie Bradshaw uncertainly, for with the wearing off of the strain came the idea to Jimmie that he might have to pay for it himself. "I promised them that," he added, "for helping with the transfer. If it hadn't been for the blankets we wouldn't have got off for another hour. They chew Tomahawk, rough and ready preferred, Mr. Doubleday. Hm?"

Doubleday was looking off into the yard.

"You've been on a freight run some time, Jimmie," said he tentatively.

The Indian detachment was crowding in pretty close on

the red-headed engineer. He blushed. "If you'll take care of my tobacco contract, Doubleday, we'll call the other matter square. I'm not looking for a fast run as much as I was."

"If we get the mail contract," resumed Doubleday reflectively, "and it won't be your fault if we don't—hm?—we may need you on one of the runs. Looks to me as if you ought to have one."

Jimmie shook his head. "I don't want one, don't mind me; just fix these gentlemen out with some tobacco before they scalp me, will you?"

The Indians got their leaf, and Bucks got his contract, and Jimmie Bradshaw got the pick of the runs on the Yellow Mail, and ever since he's been kicking to get back on a freight. But they don't call him Bradshaw anymore. No man in the mountains can pace him on a run. And when the head brave of the hunting party received the butt of tobacco on behalf of his company, he looked at Doubleday with dignity, pointed to the sandy engineer, and spoke freckled words in the Sioux.

That's the way it came about. Bradshaw holds the belt for the run from Bad Axe to Medicine Bend; but he never goes anymore by the name of Bradshaw. West of McCloud, everywhere up and down the mountains, they give him the name the Sioux gave him that day—Jimmie the Wind.

"C. P. R." stands for Canadian Pacific Railroad and tells the salty, amusing tale of a legendary drinking bout between a steel-gang boss and a French-Canadian trapper on the night before the first trans-Canadian train is due to arrive in Vancouver. Its authenticity is typical of the work of James Stevens (1892–1971), who wrote numerous stories and two novels—Brawny-Man and Big Jim Turner—about life in the Pacific Northwest. He also penned the first and most famous book-length version of that "Big Woods" legend, Paul Bunyan (1925).

C. P. R.

James Stevens

I

It was three in the morning before Shot McCune had the Metis villain, Johnny Flemmand, so blarneyed with whiskey and words that he was agreeable to quitting the dance for the rough company of celebrating railway-builders in the barroom of the Coronet Hotel. The feat was something of a miracle. The dance was the most festive one Vancouver had ever known. All of the Vancouver belles and boys were out for the affair. Tomorrow there would be a more ceremonious celebration of the coming of the first trans-Canadian train to the city. Tonight youth cheered. And Johnny Flemmand no less, though the railway was an enemy of his life and kind. With his brilliant black eyes, flashing teeth and vivid clothes he glittered through the dance. Only one man

54

cared when it was seen what an easy conquest he was having with Essie Creel, the slim, freckle-nosed, soft-eyed waitress of the Coronet Hotel.

But that man was Shot McCune, a veteran of the building of the U. P. and the N. P. and for five years a steel-gang boss on the building of the C. P. R. He had his own stubborn notions concerning the man who should finally triumph with Essie Creel. Shot McCune knew that as a romantic lover he wouldn't have a look-in with Johnny Flemmand. But he had guile, he could plot and scheme, and so at three in the morning he was leading Johnny Flemmand into the Coronet's barroom. Johnny Flemmand was already talking in his boasting style.

"Talk all ye like, me fine buck," thought Shot McCune. "Talk away—just so ye pour down the redeye!"

The two found a place at the lower end of the bar. There was a roaring crowd above them, and Sandy McBeath, the landlord of the Coronet, grinned through his scraggly beard as he watched the bottles emptying and heard silver and gold clinking into the till. He was usually a solemn and dour Scotchman, but not tonight, with a big crowd celebrating and a railway coming to his city tomorrow. His eyebrows, which were like two rusty tufts of moss, seemed to wave and glow as the gray eyes under them gazed from the lower end of the bar, where Shot McCune and Johnny Flemmand were drinking whiskey straight, to the upper end, where six sailors from a Glasgow windjammer were drinking ale. The midnight bell had run three hours ago. In a few more hours the sun would rise on a great celebration which had already begun. It would bring many dollars to the Coronet. Hark, now!

"Fill 'em up again!" ordered Shot McCune.

As he drank with Johnny Flemmand he looked with yearning upon the gang of railroaders—dynamiters, dirt-movers, gandy-dancers, spike-maulers—who were drinking together halfway up the bar. His ears caught snatches of bawled brags and arguments. His tongue ached to join the battle. But he must listen to Johnny Flemmand.

"You have ask' w'y I come to Vancouv'. M'sieu', my frien', me, I don' know. Eh, bien, I nevaire give wan tamn w'ere I go, w'at I do, any tam. I jus' come down to de railway wit' de gol' I tol' you I fin' on de Saskatchewan and me, I say to Jean Hercule Flemmand, 'Johnny, you go to Montreal, Kebec, Trois Rivières, w'ere you' père's people live or you see new countree Canayen. W'ich, you don' give wan tamn!' Dat's me, Jean Hercule Flemmand. Sacree mo'jee! W'at is anyt'ing now to me w'en Louis Riel, dat gran' man, is beat by l'Anglaise? I tell you of dat some tam, m'sieu', my frien'. You don't know de Metis, de Bois Brulés, de fur trade, les coureurs de bois, de voyageurs. You are railway man. You know not'ing true Canayen. Me, I t'ink you' tamn' railway she's spoil ever'ting."

"I expect yer right, Johnny," said Shot McCune, twisting his mouth into a grin. "Have another snort." To himself he relieved his feelings. Let the black villain brag all he wanted. Just so he poured the redeye down. "You may think yer slick with yer oglin' and sashayin' in a quadrille," thought Shot McCune, "but I'll show ye who's boss at this bar, me fine buck!"

"You was bon Irlandais," said Johnny Flemmand. "So I tell you many t'ings you don' know."

But he fell silent just then, having caught an enchanting reflection of himself in the bar mirror. Two moist curls dangled rakishly over his forehead from under the back-tipped felt hat. His black eyes, under thin level brows that had just the smallest devilish turn toward his temples at their ends, were glowing with a handsome shine. His glossy mustaches were widened in such a smile that they made a hairy canopy for his snowy teeth. The black silk handkerchief set off his shoulders beautifully. His chest bulged a red wool shirt with green buttons between the lapels of his coat. A row of bottles on the back bar shut off most of the reflection of the high top of his l'Assomption belt, but a few crimson, orange and purple checks flashed from the narrow gaps between the colored labels and the fat brown sides of the bottles.

II

Shot McCune was more than ever disgusted with Johnny Flemmand, as a man who could be so brazenly stuck on himself. He turned away for a minute to refresh himself with the pleasantly familiar sights and smells of the barroom. The glow from hanging kerosene lamps swam down through troubled clouds of smoke drifting from many pipes, it shone over the wide mirror and made gold splashes on the stacks of polished glasses. The mellow light made a pretty sparkle in the redeye wherever it trickled from bottle neck to whiskey glass. Before the six sailors the bar blossomed with the foam of ale. Knotty hands waved up, down, and around in the smoky light; and now and again one of the hands would land with a lusty whack where a suspender crossed a wool-shirted shoulder. Shouted brags, bawled laughs and once in a while boozy songs rolled along the bar. There were always arguments over the glasses. . . .

"Vancouver'll be a good town now, if we run out the Chinks." "Man, yer Yankee contractorrs br'ught 'em here, the puir haythen." "Yes, and we brought yer damn railroad here too, Scotty. Hadn't been for Van Horne, Shaugnessey and the rest of us from the States . . ." "I'm headin' for St. Paul to help Jim Hill shove his road to the Coast. No C. P. R. gandy-dancin' for your Uncle Dudley! Me for the States and the big job!" ". . . and I'm tellin' you straight, you dog-face' omadhaun, I drove the first drill in the rock of the Kickin' Horse Pass—" "Ye're tellin' me nothin', man! I wurrked in the rock from Lake Sooperior to the Selkirks. I doot if ye were near the Kickin' Horse—" "Here, you two, drink up and fergit yer argyments. I guess Van Horne and the rest of us from the States could never have built the road without you two!'' ''You and yer Chinks from the States be damn'!''

Shot McCune's ears quivered and his tongue ached for that talk. But he had business on hand and he returned to it with a sigh. Johnny Flemmand was talking again.

''Have another snort,'' coaxed Shot McCune.

Johnny Flemmand poured with such recklessness that he slopped liquor over the rim of the glass. The little pool of redeye shone on the polished wood of the bar until the bartender wiped it away. The wet towel left trails of liquid beads behind. Johnny Flemmand stared down at them as he drank and so did Shot McCune. The steel-gang boss was a little troubled after this drink. For the first time tonight he felt heat in his head and smoke around his eyes. His heart bubbled so with alcoholic sentiment that for a minute he felt almost brotherly toward Johnny Flemmand. But that passed as Johnny talked on.

''You would say, m'sieu', a countree she's not mak' until she have de railway, she do not live till dis tamn' injinne she snort, w'istle, smoke, rattle de cars from town to town. Mais for me, Jean Hercule Flemmand, I say not so. I'm dog-drive', me, M'sieu' McCune, and voyageur. De railway come, I go. She's come Sout', I'm gone Nor'. She's no tamn' good, you' railway, M'sieu' McCune!''

''Now you looky here, old settler—what the hell!'' Then Shot McCune remembered what he was after and shut up. But Johnny Flemmand had caught fire. He thumped the bar and growled.

''You was get mad, m'sieu'? Me, I don' give tamn' for dat too. Jean Hercule Flemmand was fight many tams. Wit' w'at you lak!''

''Ca'm yerself, Frenchy,'' said Shot McCune, though his knuckles throbbed. ''Ca'm yerself and have another snort.''

Johnny Flemmand drank, but he still sneered.

''You was from de States, m'sieu'. You don' know Canadaw. You t'ink you' railway mak her gran' countree? Non,

m'sieu'. Canadaw was mak long tam ago by trapper, fur
trade', voyageur. W'at you know of dis, my frien'? You are
big and strong, you t'ink. Oui, m'sieu', but lak wan ox.
W'at would you do wit' canoe? Spill him quick, by gor!
You' big neck she's ben' and ache wit' de head strap on portage. You feet would break in de bottes sauvage, trackin' de
boat up de river—you' feet would break on de stone of de
shore. You' legs would swell and burn w'en de snowshoes
get heavy lak rock behin' de dogteam. You don' know de ot-
ter from de mink. And how would you mak you'self wit' de
Injun and de Metis gal? I have see you dance lak de duck and
I t'ink you sing lak de frog. You don' care I spik w'at my
min' she's t'ink, M'sieu' McCune?''

"Oh, hell no," mumbled Shot McCune. "Just have another snort."

It was all he could say. He was about to choke. He felt
like caving this black Metis's head in and being done with
him. But he'd started with the idea of putting him to bed paralyzed drunk at the dawn of the celebration day, and he still
stuck to it. He bought another drink.

"You is de bes' Yankee Irlandais I evaire see, by gor!"
Johnny Flemmand exclaimed. "W'en you see un homme
you know he's un homme! Sacree mo'jee, I lak you tamn
moche! I tell you more t'ings you don' know, my bon
frien'.''

He drank his redeye down and now his black eyes got a
softer shine. And a kind of singing came into his voice. Shot
McCune listened with a satisfied smile.

"De men who mak Canadaw were de voyageurs,
m'sieu'. I know how she was of ol' from mon père. His
père was big voyageur for de ol' Nor'west companee,
w'at fight wit' l'Anglaise of Hudson's Bay. You know,
m'sieu', how de Nor'westers would go from Montreal
wit' goods to trade for beaverskin wit' de Iroquois and de
Cree? No. Well, de canoes was fill' wit' blanket, beads,
musket, powder, shot, tabac, w'iskey blanc, and wit'
pemmican for eat de voyageurs. Me, I have heard and I

can see and know how dey sing and paddle away. Out dey go from Lachine, up Lac Saint Louis, w'ere de Saint Lawrence is grow fat and big; all a singin' de chanson, 'En Roulant ma Boule.' ''

Johnny Flemmand went to singing it himself in French, and Shot McCune said to himself:

"Praise all the saints! Sing yerself to sleep, me fine blackbird!" Then he called to the bartender. "Fill 'em up again!"

"Ah, m'sieu', dem ol' chansons!" Johnny Flemmand's voice was husky and it throbbed with feeling as he lifted his glass. He drank. "Ah, my friend, I have dream' moche of de ol' tams. I have nevaire seen de Saint Lawrence but from mon père on de Red River I have hear'. De voyageurs would swing de paddles, keepin' tam wit' de singin', and on to w'ere de brown water of de Ottawa flow in de green Saint Lawrence, aroun' wes' side de Isle of Montreal. De Ottawa she's boil and roar into de Saint Lawrence, so dere is canal by de rapide. De voyageurs paddle to de village of Saint Anne and moor at de ol' wharf. At church de priest mak long prayer to le bon Dieu and many saints for de voyageurs. And it is paddle on, up to lac of de two mountains. It is not all paddle and sing, m'sieu'. Dere is hard portage by many rapide—Carillion, Long Sault and Chute au Blondeau. It is hardes' work you can nevaire know, my frien', goin' by paddlin', trackin' and portage up to de gran' Chaudiere.'

"I was know well, me, Jean Hercule Flemmand. Not on de Ottawa and de Saint Lawrence but on de Red River, de Assiniboine and de Saskatchewan. To dem we was drive', us Metis, mon père, me, Jean Hercule Flemmand. So my people mak Canadaw gran' countree, mak de posts of de Nor'west traders, mak de posts for l'Anglaise of Hudson's Bay. Wit' Louis Riel us Metis was nation and we would have de Saskatchewan for ourselves; but you' railway she's bring de queen's soldiers so quick—zzt!—flyin' so over de prairie, swoopin' on de fores'.

"Me, I don' lak de railway. I lak go by canoe to de free beaver meadow, and wit' de carriole and de dogteam. I am son of de voyageurs. But I am same as de exile. I could cry for myself, de exile, m'sieu'. I could cry, my frien', for de ol' tams, w'en de voyageur was king, w'en beaverskin was gol'. It is ruin, dis bon Canadaw. You' railway has mak her so—a ruin' countree for Jean Hercule Flemmand, son of de voyageurs and de Bois Brulés. I am sad, my frien'."

Johnny Flemmand pushed back his hat and shoved his fingers through his hair like he was about to tear it out in sorrow for the voyageurs. Sandy McBeath drew near and eyed him solemnly.

"I'll take care of this lad," said Shot McCune, whispering behind his hand. "A few more shots and he'll be paralyzed. Then I'll cart the black bum up to bed."

III

Johnny Flemmand had dropped both hands to the bar, and now he was swinging from side to side, bowing his head and staring down between his arms with swimmy eyes. He certainly appeared to be nearly gone. But it was mainly from the effect of his orating and singing. Shot McCune was overheard and Johnny Flemmand straightened up with a snort and his palm smacked the bar.

"I trink no more as you, M'sieu' McCune!" he roared. "And you say I am paralyze'? Me, I can trink w'iskey blanc by de gallone! Evaire tam I stay on my feet, me, by gor, de las' man! You say you cart Jean Hercule Flemmand to bed? Sapree maudit! We see, m'sieu'! It is you who will trink off de feet. Garçon! W'iskey encore!"

Shot McCune exploded at this challenge. His romantic purpose went up in red fire and blue smoke. He was all Irish wrath.

"Ye never saw the day ye could do ut, ye black-eyed lynx!" he bawled. "Sure, come on with the redeye and I'll pay for every snort! We'll see how big ye talk in aynother hour!'' And then his jealousy broke out in words. ''And I'll be showin' ye who's to take Essie Creel to the celebration today too, ye Metis villain! Ye were cute enough with yer dancin', smirkin', oglin' and sashayin', but I'll get ye foul with the redeye, me hot-footed buck!''

''I don' boas' of my dance,'' sneered Johnny Flemmand. ''She is not so moche. It is jus' you dance lak de duck is mak my waltz look so fine. And you sing lak de frog, M'sieu' McCune. De same t'ing you fight wit' de tongue, my frien'?''

''Come out back and I'll show ye how I fight!'' yelled Shot.

''Eh, you don' trink me off de feet, no? I t'ink you was goin' cartin' me to bed?''

''We drink or we fight. Anything ye like, damn yer black eyes!''

''Eh, bien. We trink. Garçon! W'iskey encore!''

The news grapevined through the crowd. Glasses were held in midair as all eyes looked down the bar to where the rivals faced each other. Shot McCune's back was to the crowd. His left foot was on the rail and his left elbow was on the bar. Johnny Flemmand's right foot was on the rail and he leaned on his right elbow. He poured with his left hand. Glare answered glare as both men lifted their glasses. The back of Shot McCune's head tipped toward the watchers; Johnny Flemmand's chin pointed toward the lights over their heads; and then the two emptied glasses tinkled dully on the wooden surface of the bar together.

''Another snort,'' ordered Shot McCune.

Many of the railroaders recognized the voice.

''That bully'll drink a dozen frog-eaters off their feet, ta-kin' 'em one at a time!'' declared a Yankee spike-mauler.

''Ye don't know the Metis, if ye say that, man,'' pro-tested a burry voice. ''I'm bettin' on the black un mysel'.''

''How much?''

''Five—'twas enou'.''

"Ah, ye close thistle! Well, put up or shut up!"

The betting spread. Sandy McBeath held the stakes. At the sixth round there were five hundred dollars in his hands. He began to feel the importance of the event and he motioned the bartender aside and lorded it over the rivals' bottle himself. As they drank it empty and called for another a smile began to shine through his scraggly beard. Between his rusty bunch of hair and the mossy tufts of his eyebrows his forehead got warm and damp; it shone like a rose after a heavy dew. This was certain to be a famous drinking bout and the story of it would make gr-rand advertising for his hotel. Sandy McBeath scowled as the noise of an argument rose among the gang of railroaders.

"You couldn't fill this steel-boss with redeye if you poured it down him with a funnel, I'm tellin' you! I know this bully and I know what I'm talkin' of!"

"Ye don't know whuskey blanc and ye don't know the Metis, who lap it down like a pig guzzlin' clabber," the burry voice growled. "I'm tellin ye, man, this Frenchy tuk whuskey as a baby instead of milk!"

"Hush yer-r-sels," ordered Sandy McBeath. "Dinna distur-rb th' perfoormance."

The battle was getting hot. Before long, as glass after glass of the red liquor was poured down, the noisy talk of the watchers settled into a buzz of whispers. As the second quart neared its bottom there was silence, except for pipe-puffs and heavy breaths. The crowd stared, and waited. Surely one of the men would soon slide to the floor. . . .

Two glasses were left in the second bottle. . . .

IV

Shot McCune set his empty glass down with tremendous care. And just as carefully he lifted the bottle. Slowly he tilted it—but the mouth waved and shook over the glass. Shot squinted his left eye shut. He raised his right eyebrow until he sighted down the bottle neck with a straight one-eyed stare. That steadied his aim. He poured, and then he pushed the bottle toward Johnny Flemmand. Johnny's eyelids were bearing down heavily as he cocked his head to the left, gazed woozily at the bottle and closed the fingers of his left hand around it. He had forgotten to wipe his mustaches after the last few rounds and they hung, wet and limp, over his mouth. His chin was hanging so loosely that it wobbled with the motions of his arm. But he aimed fairly well. The last drop trickled from the bottle's mouth. Now Johnny Flemmand's fingers closed around his glass. Shot McCune followed his motion. Both glasses were brimming. The redeye twinkled and sparkled. It twinkled and sparkled from the light that swam down through the drifts of pipe smoke. Sandy McBeath's hands rested on the bar. Their backs were matted with rusty hairs. The two white-aproned bartenders stood above him, their hands on their hips. Nobody in the barroom drew a breath as Shot McCune and Johnny Flemmand lifted their glasses. Then one windy sigh rose from the crowd as the emptied glasses were returned to the bar.

The second quart was gone.

"Set up another," ordered Shot McCune.

When he had poured his first glass from the third quart of redeye, Shot McCune's left foot slipped off the rail and his right foot skidded out a yard. His backers groaned. But he hauled his feet back into place. He drank. And poured again. So did Johnny Flemmand.

The third quart was going.

When it was half empty Johnny Flemmand started to pour, then his hand slid away from the bottle, and his eyelids slowly dragged themselves shut. His head sank to the bar, then he half lifted it and it wagged and rolled on his thick neck. He waved his hand around at nothing. And he spoke in a choked voice.

"I know w'y all so dark—lak twilight—she's chasse galerie—phantome is Jean Hercule Flemmand—in de phantome canoe I am come—from Saskatchewan—to de gran' fête and de people of mon père—lak of ol'—phantome voya-

geur at de fête—Noël, is no? And de gal—Essie, la belle
sauvage—la belle sauvage—avec w'iskey blanc—hooraw!
hooraw!''

"The Frenchy's goin'!" somebody yelled.

At that yell Johnny Flemmand straightened up with a
jerk. He grabbed the bottle, splashed his glass full, then
gulped the redeye down.

"Mais non!" he roared.

"Ah!" groaned Shot McCune.

When he thought he was winning the smoke had cleared
from his eyes. But now there was a hot smothery fog of it
wherever he looked, even when he used his one-eyed stare.
Three glasses appeared in the heat and smoke—three bottle
necks—three red hands—and all jiggered and danced—but
he poured. . . . The two drank again—again—again—and
they were down to the bottom of the third quart. The two
lifted their glasses, slopping out most of the liquor, and
drank. With every one of the last few drinks the smoke had
thickened around Shot McCune's head. Now it began to
burn and roar. Out of the fiery fog a monster face showed
itself, and shoved close to his own. . . .

"I tak—I tak her—to de—I tak—"

"Shu'll liksh 'ell—Metish shuzza—"

"They're goin'!" "Both to onct!" "Ketch 'em!" Excited
bawls broke from the crowd as Shot McCune and Johnny
Flemmand slid toward each other, growling and spluttering
until their faces met. Their feet began to slide; their elbows
slipped; face to face and chest to chest, their heads hung low
and their bodies sloped as they sagged in the middle, as their
knees buckled and their elbows slid off the bar—they went
down as one man and sprawled in one heap over the foot
rail.

Then the crowd whooped and roared and jammed about
the fallen. Sandy McBeath lumbered around the bar.

"Carry 'em to theer rooms—7 and 12." Then he bawled
at the crowd, "It was a draw! No man wins a bet!"

A big bell rang as Shot McCune and Johnny Flemmand

were being carried upstairs. It was breakfast time. The red rays of sunrise broke through the curtained windows of the Coronet's bar. . . .

Essie Creel carried steaming platters of ham and eggs and pots of coffee to the dining-room table. She wondered once or twice about Johnny Flemmand, but that was all. There was a new man at the table this morning, a redheaded railroad brakeman who had come over from Seattle to look for work on the C. P. R. He was young and the devil was in his blue eyes. He sat at the table till the other men were gone. Wouldn't she like to take in the big celebration today with a sporty young feller?

"Oh, yes! . . ."

Upstairs, dead to the world, lay Johnny Flemmand. Three doors below him and across the hall lay the bulk of Shot Mc-Cune. . . .

V

Some time after darkness had driven Vancouver's celebrators to their homes, to the dance halls and the saloons, Wing Moy was busy in the kitchen of the Coronet Hotel. He was wrapping up a roasted duck so that he could carry it under his blouse. Up in Chinatown there was a blossom who loved roast duck. Wing Moy heard the dining-room doors swing open and he chucked the duck under a down-turned pot. Then he turned and gazed calmly through the darkness. Eyes stared blearily at him through a tangle of hair.

"Where's Essie?" a hoarse voice asked.

"She gone."

"Where she go?"

"She gone all day celumblation led-headed man. Af' supp' she settem on lap by po'ch. Gone now dance." Wing Moy was anxious for this big Irish devil to get out. He wanted to hurry with the roast duck to his blossom. "Whassa malla you? Get dlunk all samee damn fool! No ketchum gal now. Somebody else ketchum. Go 'way. I got wo'k. Whassa malla?''

The door closed.

"What th' hell!" groaned Shot McCune, as he tramped up the stairs. "What th' hell!"

There was hot lead in his innards and cold lead in his head. He couldn't think. Hardly realizing what he was doing he pushed open Johnny Flemmand's door. The son of the voyageurs was awake. His eyelids looked like a dozen bees had stung them, his black eyes were dull, and his fine mustaches were all bedraggled and limp.

Shot told the news.

"Sacree mojee!" moaned Johnny Flemmand. "We was miss celebratione, gal, ever'ting, by gor! We was mak tamn' fine fools of us, M'sieu' McCune. I'm sick Vancouv'. Me, I t'ink I go quick by railway to Calgary and home to Saskatchewan. Back to de dogteam, de canoe and de beaver meadow for Jean Hercule Flemmand! Back to Metis gal and w'iskey blanc. Dis waitress gal don' give wan tamn' for me, you, redhead, no tamn' man. We was bot' fools, my frien'. I don' be some more, by gor!''

Shot McCune heaved a sad, sick sigh. Johnny was right. He'd been a fool. Had to admit it. Yep. Past the time for copping women. Getting too old for such stuff. Well, he'd go on to Seattle. Then to a tracklaying job on Jim Hill's new road. Seattle. He'd never performed in that town. High and handsome tales had traveled from it over the N. P. . . . There was still plenty of gold in his money belt. The gloom lifted a little. That performance last night would be something to talk about anyway. He shook hands with Johnny Flemmand and dragged down to the bar.

"Say, Sandy, which of us win last night?" he asked hopefully.

"It was a draw; ye both passed out together," said Sandy McBeath.

"Well, hell!" said Shot, sadder than ever. "A reg'lar fizzle all through. Damn Vancouver anyway!" A shot of redeye made him feel better. ''Well, Sandy,'' he sighed on, ''that drunk last night wasn't much to brag about, maybe, though I feel like I'll never get over it. But if I do''—and Shot McCune's bloodshot eyes had some of their old glitter now—''I'll get on a *good* one!''

Song of the Steel Rails

Tom W. Blackburn

*T*here were windows around all four sides of the little room. Along the west, overlooking the night gleam of the rails, were a row of shining metal switching levers. There was a stool for a man to sit on. And a lamp for dim light when the shadows came down out of the mountains which hung above the road.

All this was inside a cubicle atop a cleat-latticed pole, forty feet above the ground. But there were no wheels to sing against the ringing steel of mountain curves; no cindered smoke to sting a man's eyes and taste good in his mouth. Nor any roar of swiftly passing distance, or piston thunder to keep a man big and swelled up and proud.

Just the silent whisperings of night in the canyon, the

three-times repeated hammer of a passing train each shift, and the clacking of the telegraph sounder every hour as the distant dispatcher checked the passing trains along the line. But it was Ben Sutton's world from dusk to daylight again.

Ben Sutton was born when the road through the Paiutes was yet a dream on paper. As a kid he had carried water for the construction crews which drove in a grade to tap the mines then flourishing in these hills. He had been married less than a year when he braked the first ten-car mill train through the cuts.

His daughter was five when they put him in the cab of a shining new mountain Mallet, gave him a schedule, and told him to keep it. And she was in her first long dress at a high school dance when they carried her word that old Ben had been caught between the coupling bars of a train making up in the yards, and that he was dead.

But Ben wasn't dead. He'd lost a leg, that was all. So he was just half dead, and his nerves shot to pieces. He was a long time healing; a longer time finding a leg that would work on the stump the doctors had left him.

They had to eat, and the girl went to work. It was hard sledding and it cost old Ben a lot to watch his daughter come home thin and weary, while he bobbed helplessly about the little house on crutches he could never seem to catch the knack of managing.

Then she fell in love with the strapping youngster they had put in the cab of Ben's Mallet. They were married when Ben wouldn't have it any other way. And things began to work out.

A whiskered boomer stopped off at Ben's shack and ate his food and slept in his blankets for a week. And before he left, he whittled in payment a brass-studded leg of pine. It was a leg Ben could use.

The road heard he could walk again, and that old Ben was faced with starvation or the humiliation of loading down his girl and her husband with his care. And the super came out on a noon train and gave him the tower in the canyon.

It was a fit job for a one-legged man. The three sidings spurred off to the old mines in the hills, all of them along a quarter-mile of the canyon floor, rusty with long disuse. But they'd never taken the switches out or lifted the rails, so they had to have a watchman to set the lights and check the trains on the main tracks, and to be sure that the stiff old switch dogs were never moved.

Ben's grandson was born when he had been in the tower a year. He used to sit there through the long nights, watching the subtlely growing palsy of his hands, cringing at the way sudden sounds and swift occurrences left him sort of unhinged, but he'd got satisfaction from thinking of and seeing that baby in the town across the divide. For everyone said the youngster was the image of old Ben.

That sort of thing let a feller break up slowly without too heavy a regret, clinging to the thought that as he went down this last long grade, his grandson was pulling up the other side just as swiftly.

It had been his comfort. But now, well—everything came to an end in time, he supposed. . . .

They'd made him go down to the doctor's yesterday for a check-up. And the doctor had shaken his head. The baby's father—his daughter's big, strapping husband who tooled the Mallet through the canyon in these days—he said he'd see what he could do for Ben when he hit headquarters at the end of this run.

Tonight he'd be coming back from the north, rolling a special express. . . .

But when a man's nerves are gone, the road can't use him at all—not even for the tower in the canyon. So tomorrow Ben Sutton would be done with the road, with the little old tower above the rusty rails. And with life.

At ten o'clock the Fruit Express came grinding up out of the valley, engine front and rear, hammering the night with the staccato exhausts of their laboring pistons.

The man in the front cab gave Ben a breath of a whistle, and Ben waved from his window.

Later, when the northbound was around the first turn, he set the lights for a cattle-train down out of Wyoming. Hardly finished with this, he listened to the clacking box on his little table that was the distant dispatcher checking the passage of the fruit string. Ben depressed his signal key in acknowledgment, and in Division Headquarters Ben could imagine the dispatcher moving the green pin of the fruit train. . . . "On time."

This done, he set the lights carefully once more.

Now time for the big express, running special tonight, thirty minutes behind, and on a schedule which would draw steam from the very heart of her Mallet and keep Ben's son-in-law tense in the cab the entire length of the run.

This was the long wait, from twelve-thirty until after four. It was the time Ben ate his midnight lunch and read a bit and took his ease. He was pouring his second cup of coffee when he saw men on the floor of the canyon. But his mind skipped over them, and the cup was half empty again before old Ben's hand began to tremble with sudden interpretation of what he had seen.

The first two men were down on the main line, hunkered on the rails just below the spur-switches that Ben controlled from his tower. They were doing something there. Later, half a dozen more men came down the old Caroline spur out of the little hidden side canyon, into which rails had been run almost a mile to serve the once-famous mine.

This group mingled with the others on the main line for a moment or two. Then they all moved on across the canyon and climbed a ridge on the other side. There, a decrepit box-car still sat, having been left years ago at the top of the hundred-foot drop of the Timothy-Lad spur from this other abandoned mine off the main road on the canyon floor. For a while, the men worked around the old car. Then most of them climbed into it, and one man started back down the spur. Ben eased down onto his stool, every muscle of his body trembling. There was ice in his belly. There could be no doubt of these men and their purpose. Something was shipped on the big express, and they wanted it!

He swore bitterly at himself. It wasn't that he was afraid—not afraid inside, that was. It was just that his body was afraid, that his nerves were no bulwark between what he dared in his mind and the physical punishment which might come of it. . . .

This was what the doctor had seen in the examination. It was for this reason they'd put old Ben on the permanent record in the company's offices. It made him sick that he couldn't will steadiness into his shaking hands, that he couldn't get up on two good feet and set his body and mind whirring into activity.

He was sweating when the ladder up the shaft of the tower began to creak.

There was no thought in old Ben—just ridiculous things, like trying to stand on top of the trap door without even asking the fellow's business. Just planting a good foot and a brass-bound peg atop the little trap, and keeping breathlessly still while the man below hailed for admittance . . .

The man on the ladder lost patience. He rapped insistently with some hard instrument.

A galling new tide of reaction from his shattered nerves shook Ben so that he had to put a hand to the wall to steady himself when he realized the rapping was done with a gunmuzzle.

Then something splintered up through the planking of the trap door and dumped Ben dazedly on the back of his neck in a corner. There was gun sound, and Ben knew he had been shot. He was surprised this was all there was to it—a crash of sound; a hard, quick blow. Then you're sitting against the wall with your good leg out before you, and the peg one twisted crazily to one side, because the shock has jarred it loose from its stump and you're shaken up bad. But you don't hurt. You've even got time to wonder what your girl's husband is bringing down tonight on the big express that these men should want.

The trap door raised slowly. A gun-muzzle, yet trailing a faint wisp of smoke, poked in first, swung around like a snake's head until it located Ben in the corner. And after it, coming up swiftly and banging the door behind him, came the man.

In the close confines of the tower the man looked huge, but his size would have made no difference. It was his eyes. Nothing in them but one thing—a plan. No concern. No anger. No consideration. Just something to be done.

He jerked the gun at Ben. "Get up, Pop!" he said.

But men who have been shot can't get up. That thought must have shown on Ben's face, yet the man's stony expression did not change.

Ben looked down. A long furrow was plowed in the wood between bindings. And near the top was wedged the bullet which had come through the floor to dump him where he lay.

He twisted the peg-leg around with his hands and set his stump down in the socket where it belonged, and came unsteadily to his feet.

"If you're thinking, Pop—quit it!" the big man said slowly. "Just listen. The express is due by here at four-ten. It's carrying a shipment of new bills for the banks at San Francisco. And we're going to get them. Open the switch into that spur up the little canyon on the west side. The one you seen us come out of!"

Ben hobbled slowly across to his row of controls before the window above the roadbed. His hand brushed across the handle which would open the old Caroline spur—which was the one the man had meant. His fingers hesitated on it for a fractional moment, then slid to another lever.

This one he yanked back solidly. The big man grunted.

"Now, Pop," he went on carefully, "you do this: You set them switches so that when the express shoots off the main line up into that west canyon, we can roll that old box-car on the other spur down across the main line and up that same west canyon right *behind* the train. Once the express gets up in that old cut, we don't want it backing out. And the box-car'll anchor it. Savvy?''

It could easily be done. Get that old car on the Timothy-Lad siding off the blocking it had rested against so long and turn the wheels over to break the rust free, and it would be going at a good clip when it hit the main line. Shunt it down the main roadbed a little way and leave the Caroline spur open. Then it would follow the express into the little side canyon with its own momentum.

It could be derailed, then, and the express penned in. It would work well . . . if Ben pulled the right handles.

Well, a man couldn't keep nerves steady that were beyond his control. But a switchman could handle his switches.

The first lever he had pulled had set a caution light against the express, up at the end of the section, up around the first turn on the main line. His daughter's husband, driving in the cab, would know something strange was afoot in the quiet canyon when he caught that light, and he'd be looking for trouble.

The second one he pulled opened the switch at the Y on the spur where the old box-car sat, so that it would be derailed before it ever hit the main line, and effectively blocking the express. He tugged also on the handle of the Caroline spur switch—the one which the gunman had told him at first to open, to divert the express. Thus he was certain for himself that it was tightly closed. Then he backed to his stool and hunched up on it.

It wasn't right that a man who has lived an active life for so long should be abandoned in his old age with a lawless renegade and killer. Not when that man's greatest test of loyalty to his employer must come in his last night of duty. And that grim thought was quite barren of comfort.

At four o'clock, the man with the gun ground a cigarette out on the floor and stood solidly before Ben.

"Look, Pop," he asked. "You sure you got things set the way they should be?"

Ben nodded.

The big man let a little smile across his face for the first time—a little smile of dry malevolence.

"I hope you have," he agreed flatly. "You saw us working out some business on the main track down there? That was a safety move. If the express doesn't take the spur up that side canyon like it's supposed to, there's fifty pounds of dynamite under the rails of the main line, and a man hid in a culvert with a battery to blow the train sky high. We aim to stop the express, come high water or low. How much of a mess we make in doing it sits right in *your* lap, and which of those levers you pull!"

Ben Sutton came to his feet, his peg-leg thudding heavily. Dynamite under the main line—enough to lift even a giant Mallet in a dust of debris! Enough to wedge the canyon floor with tangled steel and broken bodies.

And he had flagged the express through!

But he couldn't stop it, either. He had worked too long for the road to do that. Express or freight, the road carried its shipments through the hills. It was part of a law by which Ben Sutton had governed his entire life. He couldn't change that now. Not when he was through in the morning. Not when it was his son-in-law's train. Hell, that was a government express! It had to be in San Francisco morning after tomorrow. That was the pledge of the road.

He looked at the big man appraisingly. Time was when Ben Sutton could have cut at a man like this, cut and fought and stood a chance of coming out on top. But that was out, now, too. The pendulum of the wall clock swung back and forth, and Ben Sutton's mind ticked with it.

Too, there wasn't just this one man to count. There was one in a culvert with a ready battery wired to dynamite under his hand. And a pack more men hiding in the box-car on the

Timothy-Lad siding, waiting to coast down and shuttle across after the express when he shunted it up the little canyon toward the old Caroline mine. But if he didn't shunt the train, they'd tumble out and race down on the express car before the dust had settled from the explosion which would rip the big Mallet wide open.

There was just one way out. And Ben thought about it perilously long while the big man waited.

Far up the line a whistle sounded. That was his daughter's man talking, telling Ben that he was homeward bound to his wife and son, that tomorrow he would see Ben.

Ben's face tightened. If he was in that cab, now, expecting what was coming, he'd figure his chances were worth taking. He'd warn his fireman so he could duck. And maybe they'd come out all right when they hit.

But he wasn't in that cab. The husband of Ben Sutton's daughter was there—father to Ben Sutton's grandson. As important a man as ever had come into Ben Sutton's world.

Too important a life to risk. . . .

And whatever way he threw the switches, the big man would still be there in the tower facing Ben. . . .

So it was, that even after the light at the head of the Mallet was a brilliant, onrushing beacon inside his own section, and the gunman was beginning to fret, Ben Sutton held on with his thinking to the beat of the clock. . . .

Ben's hands were steady, now; clenched tightly at his sides. His breath came evenly, his face somber and motionless. The roar of the train was in his ears. He could see his son-in-law leaning from the cab in which the brakes were already set down halfway, wondering in sharp concern over the caution signal against which he was running.

And then Ben Sutton made his choice.

Both of them worked for the road. It was the price of having grown old that he could not be in that cab now to make what sacrifice was necessary. But he knew that his daughter's husband would choose it the same way. For the road was in his blood, too. Shutting his daughter and her baby from his mind, thinking only of the man in the cab and of the road, Ben Sutton moved.

He caught two switch handles, setting them firmly. One closed the open "Y" below the waiting box-car. The other shunted the slowing express from the main line—*not* toward the canyon of the Caroline, but onto the rising Timothy-Lad spur, straight toward the old box-car crouching there before its onrushing weight.

For a moment Ben thought the Mallet would leave the rusty rails of the curving spur, but the man in the cab slammed on more air, and it held. Fire streamed from screaming brake shoes along the whole train. The Mallet rocked and bucked on the old roadbed, dragging its cars roughly after it. And it was on the old box-car so swiftly not one outlaw within its ramshackle shelter could leap to safety.

With every nerve of his body screaming to watch that smashing collision, to measure the damage to the heavy engine and the occupants of its cab, Ben leaped back from the windows, spun, and plunged awkwardly into the big man.

He caught the man's thick gun-wrist with one skinny hand, jerked it above his head, and came down hard with his pegged leg on the man's foot as the first shot tore from the weapon.

Stunned by the sudden course of the express, agonized by the grinding of Ben's peg on his foot, the big man fell back across the desk. Then the daze slid from him. He roared and kicked Ben across the room so savagely that glass fell from some of the windows.

Ben fought to his feet, sickened and reeling, then fell again. The straps of his peg-leg had slipped once more and it rolled free. This second fall saved him the crushing impact of the big man's charge. The man went over him, brought up thunderously against the wall. Somehow, Ben Sutton clawed upright once more, his peg gripped in both hands. And he swung it.

It was neither a hard blow nor a murderous one, but it caught the big man full in the face as he turned. He staggered back, tripped over the stool, and rolled half under the table.

Frantic to know what had happened on the old spur when the Mallet hit the waiting car, Ben pried up the trap-door with his fingers. He hung himself through the squared opening, found a foothold for his one foot, and dropped the portal after him.

Above him, the big man clawed at the door, and, clinging desperately to the shaft of the tower, Ben was afraid for a moment that he could not close the hasp before the door lifted. Then it snapped. The big man was a prisoner, and Ben started down, lowering himself awkwardly, step by step. It was grueling work, without his peg. And when it seemed he could go no farther, the man above made it easy.

Leaning from a broken window, the man emptied his gun. Splinters flew from the cleated pole to which Ben clung. But twice they didn't fly. So it was easy then for Ben to loosen his grip to drop on down to the ground.

It hurt when he landed. But the hurt passed swiftly and he grew too weary to wonder about anything more. One thing clung to him a moment longer. . . He knew now—really knew—exactly how a man feels who has been shot.

You just get tired and go to sleep. That's all. . . .

But they wouldn't let him sleep long on the hammering express—the conductor and a doctor from the passenger coaches, and a Treasury man from the express car. They wanted to tell him about it.

"Killed six of them in that old car! And we caught another when he jumped out of a culvert and headed for the brush. Even the one you locked in the tower came out easy when we went after him!"

The conductor nodded.

"Busted up the catcher on the front of the engine," he

said, "but that car wasn't much more than so much paper! The headlight of this locomotive got smashed, and the fireman bent some teeth when we hit it. Nobody else even got jarred."

"And your son, when we got you settled down in here and he had to go back to the cab to roll us, he says to me, 'Tell Ben I can get him a rehearing on his retirement after this, and almost anything else he wants from the road.' Which don't make sense to me. Of course he can . . . What I want to know, Ben, is how come you figgered out shunting us off like you did."

But Ben wasn't paying any attention. He was thinking quietly how it was that there was a time and a place for every man to quit. And how he'd come to his—a time when his hands were steady and his luck was good and he'd done something the road would remember him for.

He was thinking, too, how lonesome an old man can get in a half-forgotten watchtower, and how many things there were which he must teach that grandson across the divide before the youngster went to work for the road. . . .

Beginning in 1913 and spanning four decades, Charles W.
Tyler wrote hundreds of mystery, Western, and railroading
stories for the pulps. Some seventy of these were published
in Railroad Man's Magazine and its successors, Railroad
Stories and Railroad Magazine; all of the stories reflect
Tyler's firsthand knowledge of his subject matter, for he
worked as an engine wiper and fireman on a large East
Coast railroad. "The Angel of Canyon Pass" is the legendary account of an engineer named Bill Carnegan and a miracle that takes place high above a mighty southwestern
mountain gorge "shackled by steel but never fully conquered."

The Angel of
Canyon Pass

Charles W. Tyler

*T*he Sangre del Salvadors rise from the high desert floor
of the Llanos Pintado like a wavy purple barrier on a flaming
carpet. Far to the east of Del Rosa, serrated rims trace their
hazy outlines against the horizon.

Of these, one deep slash stands out between towering
peaks like the notched V of a gun sight. Clearly defined, the
eye finds it, a full seventy miles distant. They call it Canyon
Pass.

A mighty gorge, with bold ramparts hewn when the world
was in the making, Canyon Pass has been shackled by steel
but never fully conquered. Ceaseless warfare is forever

waged there. Many pages in the history of the Pacific Coast & Transcontinental's Canyon Division are today written in red, grim entries in the ledger of life.

Stories of Canyon Pass have been told and retold wherever railroad men gather. In sandhouse and switch shanty and dispatcher's office; in engine cab and caboose, even in those stiff sanctuaries where heavy-jowled brass hats sit on their mahogany thrones.

Of these tales one has become legend. It concerns Bill Carnegan and "the Angel of Canyon Pass."

Just over the hump, in the Sangre del Salvadors, are six miles of track that railroad men consider the most dangerous on the division. Long ago the P. C. & T. built a shanty at Milepost 104, on a little flat an eighth of a mile east of the trestle over Big Stormy Canyon, and stationed a track-walker there.

A tiny hut, far from the nearest habitation and surrounded by jagged peaks. It was almost a place of exile. Men called that job "the sheepherder's trick."

Now and then the section boss and his Mexican crew from Paraje had work to do in the vicinity. At intervals a freight stopped to leave supplies. Occasionally wandering Indians broke the monotony. Sometimes folks waved from observation platforms of speeding trains, or there was a shout and a hand raised in salute from cab or caboose. Perhaps a late paper came fluttering off, or a magazine.

Always there were Frowsy Head and Thunder Mountain scowling down from their lofty heights, as though debating what particular kind of hell they would hurl next at Canyon Pass.

Bill Carnegan was big, clean-cut and fine-looking. Superintendent McCuen eyed the man speculatively. Something stamped him as a railroader. McCuen judged him to be about thirty-two.

"Well? What is it?" There was scant encouragement in the flat, hard tone.

Bill said, a hint of desperation in his voice: "I'm looking for a job"—he hesitated—"any kind."

"Jobs are scarce," McCuen announced briefly. "What can you do?"

"I—I was an engineer."

The super shook his head. "We got a list as long as your arm of men set back firing."

"I know," said Bill despondently. "I've tried every roundhouse between here and Trinidad. But I've *got* to get something. Can't you fit me in anywhere? Wages don't matter, just as long as there is enough for my wife and me to get by on."

"So you're married, eh?"

Bill nodded. "We had to come West for her health. I had rights on the Central Valley, back in New England. She had a bad attack of flu and her lungs are affected."

"Kind of tough, wasn't it—quitting back there when you had seniority?"

The other smiled, his eyes lighting. "Not for me," he said. "Anything I could do for her wouldn't be half enough. Ann's the finest woman in the world. It was mighty hard for her to leave friends and relatives and the home we fixed up."

"Humph!" McCuen stared out of the window and far away toward that purple line of the Sangre del Salvadors and the V-shaped cleft of Canyon Pass. At length he asked:

"What's your name?"

"Carnegan. Bill Carnegan."

"Well, Carnegan, there's just one job I know of." The super drummed on his desk. "I doubt if that job would interest you. A Mex had it last, and he went cuckoo."

"What is it?" the hogger inquired with instant hope. So often he had carried back to Ann a discouraging, "Nothing doing today, sweetheart. But tomorrow I'll find something." There had been a lot of tomorrows.

"Track-walker," McCuen said gruffly, "out on the hump." After a pause he added: "Men don't stay in Canyon

Pass long. The solitude gets inside of their skulls and they do queer tricks.''

''But I wouldn't be alone,'' Bill hastened to point out.

''You mean you'd take your wife?''

''Sure. I couldn't leave her here. Where I go, Ann goes. Mountain air is just what she needs to help her get well. And it won't be forever. Things will be picking up after a while. Then I'll get something better.''

''How long you been married, Carnegan?''

''Eight years.''

McCuen's eyes softened under shaggy brows. He stroked his chin thoughtfully. Here was a big husky fellow from engine service stepping down from the cab to walk the ties—and offering no complaint.

The superintendent's mouth twitched a little. Such devotion to a woman was something to think about, in this cockeyed age. He wrote a brief note and handed it to Bill.

''Take this to the roadmaster—Mr. Godett. The last office at the end of the corridor. I guess he'll fix you up.''

And so Bill Carnegan went to Canyon Pass. Bill and Ann.

It was spring. The mountains were cool. Traces of snow lingered in the deeper clefts of the high peaks. They made a wild, unfriendly world, those Sangre del Salvadors. It took Ann Carnegan a long time to get used to their untamed majesty.

The ever-changing vistas—dawns that poured gold over the high rims, flaming sunsets, the quickly descending curtain of night, the blasting winds that poured eternally through the pass—all filled the woman with awe and consternation.

The vastness of this bold, raw country was a far cry from the friendly life that had been hers back there on Elm Street in old New England.

Though she fought it with all her might, Ann was terribly homesick. But she never let Bill know. Nights when the dread wind trumpeted through the canyons, her pillow would be wet with tears. And then when morning came she would be ashamed.

Life and health were here. After all, she could do no less than match the gallantry, deed for deed, of the man who had given up much for her. And so Bill saw only a brave, smiling face.

Never once did the man hint of his own tragedy. But Ann sensed the hunger that haunted his eyes when the trains went roaring by. She knew that Bill missed sitting at the throttle with drivers pounding under him. By comparison it was a dull existence, this walking the ties with a wrench and a maul.

And yet Canyon Division had never had a track-walker as faithful and untiring as Bill Carnegan. It seemed, having been at the throttle himself, he realized the importance of his task. The Sangre del Salvadors were filled with constant menace. Slides, falling rocks, washouts—all went to make the place a railroad man's nightmare.

Summer came, the season of torrential rains. And when Frowsy Head and Thunder Mountain wore trailing veils of black, they gave ominous hint of cloudbursts. The Big Stormy, dry at other times, would become a swollen torrent, rolling down boulders and debris.

Bill was anxious about the trestle over the canyon. And when thunderstorms sounded their booming war drums at night, he would dress, take his lantern and go out to make sure that all was well at the gorge.

And always when he returned, chilled and wet, Ann would be up and have a fire going and a pot of coffee on. That light gleaming in the window stirred strange emotions in his heart. He would slip an arm around Ann's waist, saying, "You're a grand sweetheart," and kiss her.

"I have to be," she'd answer, "to keep up with you, Bill."

Crews reported to Del Rosa that Carnegan's lantern was always there to greet them when the weather was bad. Its twinkling assurance lifted the burden of responsibility for those whose business it was to see that the trains went through safely. McCuen and Godett spoke of it more than once.

Too, the men on the trains came to watch for the slender form of the woman in the door of the little shanty at Mile-post 104. She was as much a part of Canyon Pass as Carne-gan himself.

And when the section foreman's wife was sick, Ann went to the section house at Paraje to be of such service as she could. When a freight went off the iron at the Narrows, Ann attended to the injuries of the fireman and a brakeman, and made coffee for the crew while they waited for the wrecker.

Now and then a hungry 'bo was fed, or the coat of a Mexican gandy dancer was patched. Or they were expecting a new arrival at Pedro's house, and Ann would make a baby dress. So they began to call her the Angel of Canyon Pass.

The young lady from New England found plenty to occupy her time, and busy hands helped her forget. From a shanty beside the tracks she lent her magic touch to the making of a home. Curtains framed the windows. A flower garden took shape. Stones were set in a neat border and whitewashed. The garden was bright and vivid, for Ann loved gay colors—especially red.

The section boss and his men always had a little spare time for landscaping when they were in the vicinity, and it was a good excuse to visit the friendly Mrs. Carnegan.

Vines climbed the drab sides of the little yellow building. A red rose unfolded its petals on a bit of trellis. Geraniums added color. There were hollyhocks and wild verbenas. Passengers on the trains looked from Pullman windows and marveled that a workman's hut could be so lovely.

The general superintendent said it only showed what could be done, and advocated that stations along the line follow the example set for them by the track-walker and his wife in Canyon Pass.

McCuen, coming in from a tour of inspection, spoke to Roadmaster Godett, suggesting that a small addition to the one-room structure at Milepost 104 would add materially to the comfort and convenience of the Carnegans.

"That bridge gang at Wagon Tire are tearing down a couple of shanties," said the roadmaster. "There's the material, and we've got a work train going to Rag River the first of the week. It wouldn't be much of a job, and Mrs. Carnegan ought to have a kitchen."

"You're damn right!" McCuen agreed. "Why, that shack out there attracts more attention now than the scenery. They tell me that half the women on the trains complain because they can't stop and look at that garden, and maybe get some slips."

One day an old Indian named Maggie came to Milepost 104. She had been gathering piñon nuts in the vicinity, and decided to visit the white man's home as a possible new trade outlet.

It was Ann's first woman visitor, and she could have offered no warmer welcome to a neighbor dropping in for a call back on Elm Street.

Maggie said, "How!"

And Ann, proud of a little Spanish taught her by the Mexican section hands, replied: *"Como está!"*

The squaw knew Mex, and her stolid face brightened. "Me Maggie," she said. "Indian name Na-va-wi."

"Me Ann. I call you Na-va-wi. I am so glad you called."

And the lady from New England served lunch, just as she would have done for a visitor at home.

Old Maggie dug down into a pocket of her voluminous skirt and produced a number of desert stones—tourmalines, agates and bits of brightly colored petrified wood. Ann's eyes sparkled. She loved these jewels of the wasteland.

She bought two or three stones, and asked Maggie to come again. Later she sent to Del Rosa and Amargosa for gay pieces of calico and other articles that she felt might find favor with the Indian squaw. It was lots of fun sitting out there on the stoop and bartering with Maggie.

Ann Carnegan's health improved. There was a healing

tonic in the rarefied air of these desolate mountains. Slowly she was rebuilding—winning her fight to live.

A great weight lifted from Bill's heart. He went whistling about his work. Life was good after all. A track-walker's job was better than the best run in the world—so long as he just had Ann.

Too, the roadmaster had hinted there was a better position in store for him. Ann had heard a great deal about the old Indian pueblo at Nunez, where Maggie lived. In time, circumstances made it possible for her to visit it. When she returned to Canyon Pass she was enthusiastic about the bit of ancient world she had seen. It had been like turning back the pages of an old book, she told Bill.

For a long interval Maggie did not come to Canyon Pass, and Ann missed her. One of the Mexican section hands finally told her that the trader at Paraje said the Indian squaw was sick. So Ann went to Nunez, taking along such homely remedies as were at hand, together with presents for Maggie's grandchildren.

She rode in a caboose to Paraje, and from there was driven to Nunez in a shaky flivver owned by one of the section men. She stayed away from home several days.

When Mrs. Carnegan took her departure, old Maggie, now on the road to recovery, said: "You *bueno*! Good! Padre say Great White Father got um heap fine angel. Show picture. You angel. Na-va-wi never forget."

And old Maggie never did.

In June of the second summer that Bill Carnegan and Ann had been in Canyon Pass, tragedy laid its dread finger on Milepost 104.

Ann caught cold. She told Bill it didn't amount to anything, just a case of sniffles. But suddenly it settled on her chest. That night there were chills and fever. Bill flagged a westbound freight and sent for a doctor. The doctor came from Del Rosa the next morning on No. 2. A nurse was with him.

They fought valiantly to save her, but it just wasn't in the cards for Ann to live. The patient died two days later, her hand in Bill's.

She smiled up into his face, and whispered: "Good-by, Bill. It—it's all—been so wonderful—with you. . . ."

The former hoghead was never the same again. After that first stunning, tearing blow had eased a little, he faced things with a strange, vacant fixedness that made men shake their heads.

They spoke awkwardly of sorrow, of sympathy, while Bill stared at them with eyes that looked beyond, toward that far horizon and a woman smiling at him through the mists.

They asked Carnegan where he wanted Ann buried—in the cemetery at Del Rosa, or back East.

Superintendent McCuen was there, and Roadmaster Godett, and the section boss and others. They awaited his answer, grave, troubled. They saw here a man under strain, moving as one who walked in his sleep. Where did he want her buried?

The lines that creased his face softened at last. "Why, bury her here," he said slowly, as though there could be no other course. "I want her close, because I'll be keeping watch in the pass."

McCuen, grizzled railroad veteran, found a lump in his throat. Godett fumbled for his handkerchief and blew his nose. The section boss swore under his breath.

The husband wanted her buried here! Hardened men of the high desert looked from one to the other.

"Out there on that knoll across the canyon," Bill was saying, "where she can see her garden, and look down to the foothills. . . ."

Thus they laid poor Ann Carnegan to rest at Milepost 104, just west of the Big Stormy.

The section men erected a wooden cross, and bordered the mound with white stones from Ann's garden. And Bill set out a red rose, her favorite color.

The first thing that enginemen on eastbound trains saw as

they rounded the long curve at the summit of the Sangre del Salvadors was that white cross on Mrs. Carnegan's grave.

The Angel of Canyon Pass no longer waved from the little house down the track, but the train crews somehow felt that she was still there—watching for them. More than one veteran of the throttle lifted his hand in solemn salute as his engine pounded past.

Bill continued to walk his beat to Milepost 110—out and back each day. He cared for the garden, and smoked his pipe on the stoop in the evening, with the stars looking down.

When thunderstorms crashed off Frowsy Head at night, Bill followed his usual procedure. He dressed, took his lantern and walked to the trestle over the Big Stormy, to be sure that all was well. Before going out he would light the lamp. He liked to see the yellow glow of it when he returned, and would tell himself that *surely* Ann was there waiting for him.

Old Maggie came to Canyon Pass again one day. She brought a beautiful piece of polished chalcedony. The wrinkled old squaw had, in truth, stolen it from the curio store at Paraje. She could have sold it to tourists. But Maggie had not taken the agate for profit, but for love. She put it on the Angel's grave.

Then there was the bottle, dyed a rich purple by long exposure to the sun, that Bill discovered at the foot of the cross. Ann had been very fond of glass thus colored. Also, in the course of time, a cluster of sparkling rock crystals found their way to that mound of earth.

And there was a round piece of grained ruby glass, snuggling in the dirt—a safety reflector, lost from some car or truck down on the highway. Old Maggie had remembered that Ann was fond of red.

One day Bill saw the Indian gathering piñon nuts down beyond the Narrows, and he called to her.

"You still bring Ann pretty stones," he said. *"Gracias! Mucho gracias!"*

"Na-va-wi love white sister," the squaw replied. "She

good woman. She good to old Maggie. She wake up from long sleep some time. See presents Indian bring.''

''Yes, God bless you, Maggie, she will know. She's watching all the time.'' A tender smile lighted Bill's face. ''I can feel her close—walking with me.''

A few days afterward, Bill came home late. Clouds were gathering around Thunder Mountain and Frowsy Head. Black veils threw their long streamers over the higher peaks of the Sangre del Salvadors.

All afternoon squalls had been snarling far off on the desert rim, with lightning playing on the horizon at half a dozen points. Distant thunder had kept up an almost constant grumble.

The former hogger prepared and ate his supper, and sat for a time on the stoop. In the fading light he walked up the track and across the trestle and on to that bit of raised ground where the grave was. He never missed a night. He knelt beside the cross and breathed a prayer.

Then he lingered for a little, tenderly rearranging the stones of the border, smoothing the earth. The rose Bill had put there was unfolding a blossom, a beautiful bud that had opened to smile at him.

Each of the presents that old Maggie had brought he picked up, wiped off carefully and returned to their places.

A freight came roaring over the summit from the west. The whistle moaned under the easy drag of the engineer at the cord. The fireman and brakeman both crossed the cab to look from the gangway. Bill waved at them.

Faces in the cab of the pusher and in the caboose saw the track-walker, and men shook their heads. A strange picture here in the dusk—a lonely figure, a grave, a cross.

A storm was centering around Frowsy Head. The lightning was sharp and frequent. Thunder boomed through the mountains with jarring reverberations. A large proportion of the run-off from the eastern watershed of Frowsy Head spilled into the Big Stormy.

A new storm moved up from the south toward Thunder

Mountain. Bill stood in the door of the shanty watching. It looked bad.

Thunder Mountain and Jawbone dumped water from their rocky slopes into the Narrows. There was always danger of slides and falling boulders.

Bill donned oilskins and boots. "Guess I'd better go down to the Narrows," he told himself.

He lighted the lamp on the table near the window. Ann's picture was near the lamp. It showed her waving her hand and smiling.

The track-walker took his lantern and went out. On the threshold he paused to look back. His eye went to every familiar object that she had touched—and again to the picture.

"Good-by, Ann!" he said. "I'll be back in a little while."

He went out to the trestle over the Big Stormy. There was very little water in the canyon. It seemed that the storm had moved over to the western slope of the divide, there back of Frowsy Head.

Bill started down the track toward the Narrows. It had begun to rain as he reached Milepost 105. A squall was coming off Jawbone.

No. 1, the crack westbound limited, came doubleheading up the grade from Paraje. Her two big Mountain type locomotives roared full-throated in the night. Rain slanted across the headlight of the first engine in gusty sheets. Gray rivulets spewed from the rocky slopes.

The flicker of a lantern near Milepost 106 announced that Carnegan, keeper of the pass, was guarding the rail.

Two brief whistle blasts cracked the salute of No. 1. Blurred faces in the cabs looked down and muffled voices shouted greetings at him. Bill yelled and waved his lantern.

He started back. He had gone perhaps a mile when he detected a new note menacing the night. He stopped for a minute to listen, then went on with a quickened pace.

He had felt so sure that all danger was past, there at the

Big Stormy. But now a grim premonition laid hold of him. A quarter of a mile farther on, he paused again.

Faintly a dull roar came to his ears above the noise of wind and rain. It was an ominous sound. He had heard it before. It was not unlike the rumble of an approaching freight train, drifting down the grade.

Bill broke into a run. A cloudburst was coming down Big Stormy Canyon. Frequent squalls had softened the approaches to the trestle. Only the day before some section men had worked there, filling in those little gullies cut by coursing rivulets. It wasn't the structure itself for which trackmen felt concern, but those fills behind the concrete abutments.

The rain was slackening now. And yet the thunder of tumbling water grew louder. There were, too, the crash and grind of trees and boulders against cut-bank canyon walls, gouging brittle earth, as the increasing accumulation of debris was hurled along in the teeth of the mounting flood.

Somewhere sodden clouds had emptied themselves high in the mountains—the last mad caprice of the storm. Even now stars were peeping through around Frowsy Head.

When at last he neared the Big Stormy, Bill was close to exhaustion. He had long since discarded his cumbersome raincoat and boots. His feet were cut and bruised from the rock ballast.

He glanced at the light in the window of his home as he stumbled on past the little building beside the track. It seemed to give him renewed strength. He felt that Ann was close beside him.

As Bill approached the trestle he was met by muddy water. It was coming down the right-of-way ditches, creeping over the ties. A wide sweep of it spread before him, a veritable river, flowing, gurgling about the steelwork.

Minutes were precious. Every second that ticked away was a step toward eternity. If No. 6 were on time, she was already getting close. Not a month before, the schedule to

Chicago had been cut two hours, while newspaper and magazine advertisements boasted of this new fast service.

Water poured across the rails like a mill-race. Its power was terrific. It clutched at his legs with devilish ferocity, trying to drag him down. A foot dropped between the unseen ties. Already the earth was crumbling. The fill had started to go.

Bill pitched forward. Something in his leg snapped. Blinding pain stabbed him. He felt himself being swept away. He caught at the submerged rail, now a foot beneath the coursing flood. The lantern and a fusee he had gripped in his left hand were lost.

Death held no dread for Bill Carnegan. Life offered little since Ann had gone. And yet tonight a grim determination filled his heart. It was not himself of whom he thought, but the railroad and the men and women whose lives he guarded.

He was going to cross the Big Stormy, in spite of hell and high water. A fighting Irish heart carried him forward, foot by foot.

Smashed and buffeted by muddy water that tried to drag him downstream, Bill struggled on. Ever in his ears sounded the roar of the torrent.

His right leg dragged uselessly. He advanced on hands and knees. A tree came floating down the gorge, its torn roots writhing, flailing like the menacing arms of an octopus. The trunk swung toward him in the gloom. He sought to get clear, but a jagged limb stub struck him on the head, opening an ugly gash.

In desperation, Bill wedged his knee against the guardrail and clung there for a little gasping. He fought dizziness, almost utter exhaustion. Then once more he crawled, refusing to surrender.

Gone were lantern and fusee. Every last match had long been soaked past all usefulness. Even if the former hoghead could reach that west bank of the Big Stormy and solid ground, he had no means of attracting the attention of the engineer at the throttle of No. 6. They'd never see him in time.

And yet in the brain of Bill Carnegan there burned one spark that would not die. In his ears, above the din of waters, he thought he heard the low, sweet voice of the girl he'd wooed and won back in old New England.

Now he was going to keep a rendezvous with her—there by that mound, and the cross, ahead. Something carried him on, something that lifted him across those last flood-torn rail-lengths to solid ground across the Big Stormy.

No. 6 was on time. Two engines over the Sangre del Salvadors, and fourteen all-steel cars—mail, express and Pullmans. Crazy Creek Canyon reverberated to the staccato bark of the exhausts and the drumming of steel on steel.

Light rain was falling, the fringe of the storm that had swung toward Thunder Mountain earlier. Charley Donaldson, a veteran runner of the Canyon Division, was at the throttle. He had been watching the lightning flashes out ahead.

"They been getting hell in Canyon Pass," he called to the fireman.

The latter ceased his labor on the deck for a little and stood beside the engineer.

"Anyhow, it ain't like the old days," he said, "when there was a wooden trestle over the Big Stormy, and the Mex track-walker was more likely than not pounding his ear in the shanty."

"That's right, my boy," the hogger responded fervently. "Carnegan is out there now looking after the track. When we bat 'em over the hump and start rolling down the mountain, we know that everything's O.K."

"It was mighty tough, Carnegan losing his wife the way he did."

Donaldson sighed. "It sure was."

"You know, Charley, that grave kind of gives a man a funny feeling. Don't it you?"

"Why, I dunno. I sort of think of Mrs. Carnegan as being

there beside the track," Donaldson said, "just watching over things."

The fireman agreed. "Yeah, that's right. Bill and her. My God, it must be awful lonesome for him."

No. 6 swung at last over the high rim of the Sangre del Salvadors. Lights shone from the windows, warm, inviting. Life on the train flickered past with cinemalike rapidity. A few travelers lingered in the dining cars. Men and women lounged at ease in club car and observation. Porters were busy making up the berths. An old man dozed in a section, a gray-haired woman beside him. A mother smiled down into a baby's face. A honeymoon couple sat holding hands, their heads close.

Charley Donaldson leaned across the padded armrest, his keen eyes squinting past the glass weather-wing along the track ahead. Two emerald dots hung like a pendant against a black velvet curtain.

He turned his head toward the left and sang out, "Green eye!"

And the fireman called back, "Green on the block!"

A stubby granite post whipped past. Milepost 103. The beat of the exhausts had quickened to a hurried mutter. Drivers and side-rods were but a clashing blur. Fast-rolling wheels were checking off the miles with a singsong clickety-click that measured the rail-lengths as one counts heartbeats.

Heavy cars cradled with gentle undulations that indicated smooth, swift flight. No. 6 was right on the advertised. Speed the watchword.

The big passenger haulers heeled to the curve west of Milepost 104. The silver beam of the electric headlight washed the steep slope to the right of the track in swift review.

Juniper and piñon sprang out of the raven blackness, crouching shadows of boulder and gully, sharp-drawn striations in a red bank hewn by erosion.

On swept the far-reaching finger, like a spotlight hunting for figures on a darkened stage. And then, for just an instant, it seemed to pause, as though that which it sought had been found.

A gently swelling knoll, back somewhat from the right-of-way, with a softening background of piñon. There was a cross, in that dim distance, like a tiny ornament hung on the swelling bosom of the mountain. Gleaming white.

Charley Donaldson never failed to watch for it, as his train swept over the rim of the Sangre del Salvadors. His eyes were on it now in narrowed focus. Suddenly he became rigidly intent.

There was something moving close beside the mound. It was uncanny. The distance was yet too great to vision detail.

Then came a sudden flash of red—a dull-glowing crimson eye. It moved back and forth. The gleam of the headlight swept on around the curve, and it was lost.

Cold fingers clutched at the engineer's heart. The thing was weird, spectral.

The hogger lost not one instant in making his decision. He closed the throttle and snapped one short blast from the whistle, signaling the second engine to shut off. Then his fingers closed over the shiny, brass handle of the ET equipment. He swung it full to the right, *the big hole*.

It would take emergency air to stop them. Charley Donaldson sensed that if anything had gone wrong here in Canyon Pass, it was at the Big Stormy. Rain had been pouring hard out on the divide. There was always the possibility of a cloudburst.

The engineer answered the strange smoldering eye of red with two quick blasts.

Bill's heart swelled almost to the bursting point as he heard the acknowledgment. They had seen his signal. No. 6 was stopping.

The track-walker forgot the agony of his tortured body as he saw that parade of fire-rimmed wheels on the curve. His soul soared to undreamed-of heights. He gasped a prayer of thanksgiving.

The Angel, indeed, had walked with him tonight, her

spirit buoying him up, carrying him on, when it seemed that the best he gave would not be enough. She was here with him now.

Bill slumped onto the grave. "Ann!" he choked. "My own dear sweetheart! Through the power and the glory—and you—we have saved a trainload of people."

The fireman, peering ahead, yelled: "It's a washout! There's hell to pay in the Big Stormy."

"My God, look at it!" Awe was in Donaldson's voice. "The flood has cut around both abutments."

His headlight revealed the devastation of the foaming torrent. The big engines of No. 6 ranged on past a little. Then, with a last buckling surge, the train came to a stop, not a hundred yards from the Big Stormy and its murky death trap!

Charley Donaldson lighted his torch and swung hurriedly down, the roar of mad water in his ears. A miracle had saved them—a miracle, and Bill Carnegan.

Moisture that was not rain trickled down the hogger's seamed cheeks as he walked back and his flaring torch revealed the figure of Carnegan slumped down beside the cross.

Others came stumbling toward the spot—engineer and fireman from the helper, uniformed trainmen, men to whom the booming roar in the blackness meant that they had been riding into the valley of eternal shadow.

The waving tongue from Donaldson's smoky torch laid its yellow illumination over the scene. Faces were white, strained, as the group of veterans of the rail found themselves witnessing a scene that would linger in their minds on through the years.

Carnegan! That was the name framed by their lips. Carnegan, here beside the grave of the wife he had loved so much.

Charley Donaldson handed his torch to his fireman and dropped down to slip his strong arm about Carnegan's shoulder.

"What happened, Bill?"

The track-walker told them. He spoke with effort, slow-worded phrases that told of the storm and the sudden onslaught that had trapped him there to the east of the Big Stormy. He made small mention of his desperate fight against the turbulent waters of the flood.

"I lost my lantern and fusee," he said. "But I knew I had one chance. Long ago, old Maggie, the Indian woman who came so often to see Ann, brought this—"

He still clutched in his hand the ruby-grained safety reflector, and he held it out.

"This piece of red glass," he went on, "and those other things there. Treasures, they were, tokens of love. God bless her faithful old heart! It wasn't much, this piece of glass. But Maggie knew that Ann loved red, so she put it there. I—I—well, I figured you'd see the red, Charley." He looked at the engineer.

Donaldson slowly shook his head. "I did, clear as a bell." There was a catch in his voice. "I couldn't have missed it."

The Canyon Division wanted to erect a memorial—the Canyon Division, and the passengers who were on No. 6 that night. And so a beautiful white shaft was placed where the cross had been. On it was put a bronze tablet with the name *Carnegan* in bold letters, as a tribute for all to read, to a railroad man and his wife.

And thus they remain today, eternally on guard in the high rims of the Sangre del Salvadors—Bill Carnegan and the Angel of Canyon Pass.

*Henry Wilson Allen (and his alter egos, Will Henry and Clay
Fisher) need no introduction to fans of high-quality Western
fiction. He has won four Western Writers of America Spur
Awards, more than any other writer: two for Best Historical
Novel,* From Where the Sun Now Stands *(1960) and* Gates
of the Mountains *(1963); and a pair for Best Short Story,
"Isley's Stranger" (1962, reprinted in* The Cowboys*) and
"The Tallest Indian in Toltepec" (1965, reprinted in* The
Warriors*). "For Want of a Horse" is his memorable account
of the James gang's attempt to rob Missouri & Western's
train number 1608 in the little town of Hatpin, Kansas.*

For Want of a Horse

Clay Fisher

Through the prairie dusk the five riders approached Hatpin, Kansas. Hatpin was a waterstop on the Missouri &
Western main line between Kansas City and Denver. The
mounted men were wary but confident, old professionals
all: Clell Miller, Charlie Pitts, Bill Chadwell, Frank and
Jesse James. These were the Missourians, the raiders of
Lawrence and Centralia, Kansas, and the latter state was enemy territory to them. But the stakes were high this
night—$35,000 in unsigned banknotes aboard train number
1608, due through Hatpin at twelve midnight.

The plan to take number 1608 was Jesse's, naturally.

The blinking-eyed killer maintained there was no risk
whatever, in the hard terms by which he and his men defined
the word, and that it would be the perfect job.

There was no law worth worrying about within a hundred miles. Escape lay open to every point of the prairie compass. Their matchless Missouri thoroughbreds were fresh and eager to run. The beautiful animals moved impatiently beneath them, wanting to go, to race the wind and beat it. But Frank James was nervous nonetheless, and was beginning to show it. He kept looking around through the gusty twilight. Licking his lips repeatedly. Shifting in the saddle every few rods of their advance. His uneasiness got to the watchful Jesse.

"You turning hunchy on us again, Frank?" he demanded. "Why, this here rube town is as easy to kick over as a dry buffler chip. Now, slack off. I've got her all figured."

"Could be," admitted Frank, glancing around once more. "I remain saying she's too still all about. I don't trust these jawhawk farmers. It smells to me like they've got us spotted. I mean it, Jess."

"Sure you do." Jesse nodded. "But quit your squinching around, will you? You're getting the others edgy. Besides, Buck, who do we know in Hatpin, Kansas?"

"Ain't the question, Dingus." Frank frowned, returning the exchange of boyhood nicknames. "Question is, who might know *us* in Hatpin, Kansas?"

"Hell," said Jesse softly. "That could hold for any town in a thousand miles. Keep moving easy."

They were into the deep dust of Main Street now, only a hundred yards out from the town's first buildings. "Bill," said Jesse to Chadwell, "start whistling. You, Charlie, you and Clell get to talking out loud enough to be heard. We don't want anybody thinking we're dishonest."

They were among the buildings. The street, ahead and behind, seemed deserted. Here and there a cracked window reflected a greasy halo of inner lamplight. But no soul was on Main Street. It was spooky. Only the faint jingle of their own bit and spur chains, the squeak of their saddle fenders, the snuffling and blowing of their slender thoroughbreds, accompanied their passage of the town heading out for the railway depot at street's end.

"Damn!" muttered Jesse. "We'd best spread out."

Frank nodded and threw a hand signal to the three men behind. The latter unbooted their carbines, reined mounts wide to cover the station as flankers, Frank and Jesse riding on in to the hitchrail below the raised baggage platform. Halting their horses, they narrowed keen eyes. Within, they saw only the night telegraph operator at his desk beneath a solitary oil lamp. The man was sound asleep. Jesse gritted a word to his older brother. Frank turned in the saddle and waved the three flankers forward. The men swung their horses in, slid off them at the rail.

Chadwell, the horse-holder, gathered all the reins and crouched below the platform behind a trash barrel. Clell Miller and Charlie Pitts joined Frank and Jesse on foot. The four men stepped up on the platform, drew guns, glided toward the station door and the lone telegrapher.

The horses became nervous as their riders departed.

They began to hipshift and to step around on Chadwell. "Be still, blast you!" the latter hissed at them. "There ain't nothing here to turn you jumpy." But the sensitive animals were pricking their ears and rolling dark eyes toward the now-impenetrable dusk blanketing the railway station. Chadwell cursed them again. But his own eyes joined theirs in probing the darkness of the windy night, and it was not the prowling gusts which stirred his neck hairs. Could be old Buck was right. Maybe these rubes had spotted them outside town. Wait a minute. Was that something moving toward him and the horses from behind that stack of empty chicken crates and hogshead barrels yonder? No, it must be only wind shadows. Nightspots. The fantods pure and simple. But why were the horses so itchy?

The telegrapher in the Hatpin depot was awakened from his drowsy after-supper nap by the kiss of steel lips behind his left ear.

"Don't touch the key," advised Jesse, cocking the big Colt for emphasis.

"Yeah," noted Frank. "If we want any messages sent, we'll compose same."

The telegrapher, a man of peace, bobbed his pate in eager assent. Ducking his head gingerly out from in front of Jesse's revolver muzzle, he swiveled in his creaking chair to peer beneath green eyeshade up at his accosters. What he saw decided him in his determinations for love and brotherhood.

Frank James was a sadly handsome man, with clear gray eyes, drooping, sun-faded moustache, the look more of a preacher than a train and bank robber. Young brother Jesse was also a fine-looking man. Not so tall and spare as Frank, his face was more square-cut, with a black spade beard, the eyes a bright blue, albeit bloodshot and continually blinking, and the general outlook that of a cattle buyer or fine horse broker, both of which he indeed was in those areas of his time not blocked out for armed assault and the swifter gains of gun and mask.

No, it wasn't Frank and Jesse that worried a man.

It was those two abysmal brutes who stood behind the brothers James waiting to be loosed upon any such innocent and defenseless citizens as Cyril Peebles, Hatpin's telegraph operator, railroad agent, baggageman, and night clerk for the old reliable M&W's main line for Denver, Colorado.

Those two looked to Peebles as if they would enjoy slitting their own mothers' throats, or kicking crippled children, or, for the present matter, gut-shooting important railroad employees. The telegrapher cleared his throat to announce his love for all men. Before he could get this philosophy, inspired in the main by the Neanderthal glares of Clell Miller and Charlie Pitts, enunciated, a sudden neighing of the outlaws' horses carried in from the outside.

Frank and Jesse traded dark looks.

Jesse was crouching like a big cat about to spring, the blue eyes twitching. Brother Frank spoke first.

"Ding," he said. "I don't care for that. I had best see to the horses. We got to get us a new holder one of these days. Since he's got married, Bill ain't steady."

Clell Miller, the primal brute among them, literally slobbered at the mention of Chadwell's new status. "Hell." He grinned. "Iffen any one of us had us a witch-bodied woman like old Bill to think on, we'd all be worried about getting back home without no lead in our ramrods. Ha! Ha!"

"Wait a minute, Buck." Jesse ignored the crudity of Clell. "Chadwell's all right." He did not want to show indecision or doubt in front of his men, much less to demonstrate uncertainty of purpose to the Hatpin night clerk. He spun about now on the latter. "Friend," he said in his high-pitched voice, "you had better discover whereat is your tongue, and gulp out fast what's going on around here." He slid the long, cold Colt barrel about four inches into the gaping mouth of Cyril Peebles. "Did we walk into something, or not, neighbor?"

The telegrapher commenced to sputter around the Colt barrel. Jesse removed the obstruction.

"You can do better than that." He nodded. "And if you don't, we'll teach you how in a hurry." At his words, the bestial Pitts and Miller slunk in behind the Jameses, each pulling, not a gun, but a glittering eight-inch knife. In his skinny belly, Cyril Peebles knew a fearful chill.

"Wait, wait!" he cried. "I'll tell it all!"

Outside the Hatpin depot, the troubles of horse-holder Chadwell multiplied. "Whoa-up, whoa-up!" he snarled at the head-tossing Missouri thoroughbreds. But the horses saw what they saw, the shadows moving swiftly in toward the man who held them, and they renewed their snorting and rearing.

Now suddenly the holder heard the creaking behind him

of a sun-dried station-platform board. He whirled in time to find the shadowed figure of a large assailant almost upon him. The latter held a sawed-off shotgun. Chadwell, nonetheless, went for his holstered Colt. But it was an off-balance draw, demanded by the fact that he held the reins of five powerful saddle mounts in the left hand, while attempting to pull and fire with the right. In the fraction of time so lost, a second shotgun-armed figure ran up out of the night behind Chadwell. The second man did not shoot the horse-holder, but instead struck him in the back of the head with the butt-stock of the shotgun. Chadwell's jaw went slack, his body sagged, the hand holding the reins of the horses loosened.

But now half a dozen new figures raced up through the darkness. Some took Chadwell's slumping body, hand-and-foot, and carried him off. The others seized the horses before they might escape, but the Missouri-bred animals kicked and reared anew, neighing sharply in alarm.

Inside the depot, the sound carried to Jesse and the others, breaking off the interrogation of the telegrapher. As one, the gang ran for the stationhouse door. Bursting out upon the loading platform, they were in time to see their prized horses disappearing down Main Street and around its far dusty corner into the endless night beyond Hatpin, Kansas.

"Jess," said Frank James. "What will we do?"

It was a moment to try the nerves of any outlaw band. In the quiet way that the older brother had shown the instinctive trust in the judgments of Jesse James, he had also demonstrated the source of the gang's great strength. But before Jesse could reply to Frank's question, they all distinctly heard a loud groaning emanating from the stack of empty barrels on the far side of the loading platform.

Carbines and Colts at the ready, they rushed the barrels. But it was only Bill Chadwell struggling to get to his feet. The holder was grasping his wounded head and trying to explain what had happened to him and to the precious charges in his care.

"Get him inside!" rasped Jesse, catching Chadwell by one arm, as Frank caught the other. Pitts and Clell Miller covered the retreat back into the depot, but no sight or sound of the hidden enemy pursued them.

Within the stationhouse, the telegrapher was making good his departure through the opposite door giving onto the trackside loading dock. Jesse stretched him coolly with one crack of his revolver barrel. Cyril Peebles fell with a thud to the rough planks of the floor. His body blocked the townside door. Clell Miller kicked and rolled his unconscious form out of the way, slammed shut the street door and barred it from the inside with a propped chair.

Pantingly, the gang crouched, eyeing one another.

This could be the big trouble, or it could be only a matter of searching out the town to locate their stolen mounts and retrieve them from the sap-headed farmers who had made off with them.

Jesse saw the signs of fear beginning to shadow the faces of his fellows, and moved to halt its spread. Panic was the surest enemy of the trapped.

"Now, let's stand easy," he ordered. "All we got to do is figure out what's the most likely thing these rubes have done with our horses, then go and fetch them back. Frank, what you say?"

Frank, who had been peering out one of the windows, did not answer with words but with action. Leaping to Peebles's desk, he seized up the station lamp and blew it out. As its acrid smoke coiled through the darkness of the depot, he said, "It ain't what I *say*, Jess, it's what I *see*." He paused, and the men moved in behind Jesse, but looked to him. "Them farmers not only took our damn horses, they've took up ambush posts all about out there to make the horse-lift stick. I can see them all around the depot. We ain't just set afoot, Jess, we're cut off!"

Clell Miller growled a curse. His comrade Charlie Pitts told him to "hesh up and look to Jess."

Jesse, meanwhile, sprang to the window Frank had abandoned. He held himself flat to the wall, craning head to peer out into the stillness. He seemed reassured. Slipping to the other side of the window, he repeated the performance in the opposite direction, the bloodshot blue eyes blinking rapidly. In a moment he was back.

"I don't see nothing out yonder." He frowned. "You certain sure you wasn't shagging wind shadows, Buck?"

"No mistake," Frank replied. "I seen them moving into place. They're just a-laying low and waiting now."

Jesse shook his head like a dog with a wrong-sized bone. The men scowled, demanding some action of their young leader with their very silence. Jesse threw one more glance out the window, wheeled on Frank.

"We got to get them horses back," he said in that tightly worded way of his which permitted no discussion. "Come on, all of you."

The men looked to their weapons. Carbines were levered, Colt cylinders spun. Levi's were hitched up, dry lips licked, Stetson hats set down hard on shaggy heads. They moved as one toward the door, following Jesse. The latter pulled the chair away, swung the plank door creakingly open, nodded tensely. "All right, here we go."

Jesse went first, Frank next, the others flanking him.

Three steps onto the platform and they were met with a blast of gunfire that withered their number like flame, drove them staggering back into the fortress of the depot.

Frank had been right; they were cornered.

Gunfire from the surrounding citizens of Hatpin continued sporadically. Its ricocheting lead whined through the stationhouse. The gang, holding its fire, watched the station clock tick away the minutes, and possibly their lives with them. Clell Miller had one arm in torn bandage and sling. A blood-soaked rag bound up the head of Charlie Pitts. Whatever of disdain any of the Missourians may have felt for the

Hatpin farmers was now long extinct. There was no question remaining: they were in final trouble.

"Near ten P.M.," muttered Jesse, again checking the station clock. "Number 1608 is just about pulling out."

"I wisht we was on it," averred Bill Chadwell honestly.

"I wisht *you* was on it," Charlie Pitts told him pointedly. "In a damn pine box."

"Yeah," sided Clell Miller. "Next time I need a horse helt, I'll hire me a hitching post."

"That's enough of that," Jesse ordered quietly. "Bickering amongst ourselves ain't going to get us out of Hatpin."

At his guard post by the front window, Frank James, the educated outlaw, quoted softly. " 'A horse, a horse, my kingdom for a horse.' That's from *Richard the Third*. Feller named Bill Shakespeare writ it."

"Ain't that just grand?" sneered the wounded Charlie Pitts. "Quote me something I can saddle and straddle in Hatpin. Never mind old Bill What's-his-name."

"Yeah, nor old Richard, neither," agreed his friend Clell. "You got any idees yet, Jess?"

The leader only scowled and blinked the harder.

Frank James snapped a shot at a shadow in Main Street, ducked as an answering shot nearly beheaded him. "You'll think of something, Dingus," he said in simple faith. "You always do."

As he spoke, the receiving key of the telegrapher's instrument began to chatter with an incoming message.

Jesse leaped to the side of the telegrapher, whom they had bound in his swivel chair. Cutting the man free, he spun him around to face the desk. "Take it down, friend," he grated. "Get it precisely as it comes over. Every dot and dash of it. Change one click of that key, and your wife's a widow."

The white-faced hostage nodded, began taking down the message: . . . REGARDING YOUR EARLIER INQUIRY FOR HELP IN APPREHENDING JAMES GANG SAID TO BE IN HATPIN, CAN VERIFY YOUR INFORMATION REGARDING MOUNTED POSSE READY HERE, AND AVAILABILITY YOUR NEEDS HAT-

PIN. PLEASE GIVE YOUR SITUATION NOW. CONFIRM GANG'S
IDENTITY, URGENT, TIME EVERYTHING. J. W. WHICHER,
CHIEF DETECTIVE M&W RR, KC MO DIV.

When these words appeared, read aloud by Frank James
from the telegrapher's pad, Jesse's eyes took fire. His dark
face was literally alight when the message had ended. His
men sensed his deep excitement, all watching him.

"Buck," he said to Frank. "Are you remembering what I
am? About 'Whicher's Posse'? That inside report we got
from our spy at the M&W? The one about the special James
Gang Posse gathered together in Kansas City by old
Whicher? The ready-mounted bunch?"

Frank's gray eyes widened.

"You meaning that stretcher we was told about the railroad fixing up a baggage car into a horse car and keeping it
all set to roll? To hook on to any train? Get to the scene of
any robbery quick as a sheep dog on a coyote?"

"That's the one; named special in our honor."

"But we don't know nothing for real about that posse,
Jess." Frank was frowning now. "We ain't never seen it.
Far as we know, it's just a story."

Jesse eyed them all.

"Supposing it *ain't* just a story," he said softly, but with
clear implication, and the light came on belatedly for Frank
and the others. All of them gaped at their leader.

"Ding! You ain't actually meaning to find out?"

It was brother Frank. Neither he nor the others, even
thinking they knew Jesse, could have imagined such a daring outlaw gamble. No, only Jesse James could have
thought of it. Who else could have figured out *this* possible
escape from the deadly trap of aroused citizenry in Hatpin,
Kansas? But Jesse *had* thought of it, and Jesse *did* mean to
give it his best try.

For the last time his Navy Colt swung to cover Cyril Peebles.

"Mister." He blinked. "Take a message: TO J. W.

WHICHER, CHIEF DETECTIVE M&W RR, KANSAS CITY, MISSOURI . . .''

In the home office of the Missouri & Western, the night operator took down the message with a yawn. Suddenly his eyes bugged. Tearing loose the message sheet, he sprinted across the hallway into the office of J. W. Whicher, chief of railroad detectives. The latter took the message sheet: JESSE JAMES HERE HATPIN NOW . . . GANG SET TO BOARD TRAIN 1608 WITH DENVER UNSIGNED NOTE SHIPMENT . . . MIDNIGHT HATPIN TIME . . . ACKNOWLEDGE YOUR RESPONSE, URGENT.

Chief Whicher gave a strangled cry, leaped up from his desk. He was a man on the verge of a purple stroke.

"Any answer, Mr. Whicher?" asked the telegrapher.

Whicher did not reply. He ran out of his office, down the hallway, and out into the switch yard, waving the message sheet and shouting desperately, "Hold Sixteen-Ought-Eight!" Then, changing directions: "Shunt the posse-car, shunt the posse-car!"

The switch yard became instant bedlam. Somehow, out of the confusion, order emerged. The special express car fitted out to hold saddled horses stood upon its siding already hooked to a caboose similarly of special fitting to accommodate the riders. Its side ramp door was now let down and the horses loaded with precision into its narrow confines. A group of very hard-looking possemen showed up, trotting on the double. Lanterns were awave throughout the yard, and trainmen shouted everywhere. Train number 1608, halted in time, was backing onto the posse-car siding. It hooked onto the horse car and caboose with a banging jolt, as the last of the mounts were run up the ramp. The ramp was drawn up, the door slid shut. J. W. Whicher puffed into view.

Seizing a lantern from a switchman, Whicher mounted the caboose steps, waved the lantern frantically ahead to the brakeman. Number 1608's whistle blasted shrilly. Sand screeched on steel as the drivers of 1608 bit into the rails. Horse car and caboose started to roll.

The Jesse James Special was under way.

In Hatpin, midnight neared. Jesse and his men were still pinned down in the depot by citizen sniper fire. But all were busy, and there was no grumbling now. In the bandit life, bullets were a part of the natural environment. Bad luck hit everyone alike, even Jesse Woodson James. It was the way a man responded to these chancy breaks which marked him what he was, or ever hoped to become, in the minds of his fellows.

And Jesse was responding with all his cunning.

He was at the moment drawing a can of coal oil from the drum in the depot. Frank was hefting a sledgehammer, getting ready for his part. Clell and Charlie Pitts were slicing open sacks of wheat, spilling the grain out upon the station floor. Bill Chadwell was on lookout at the windows, firing first out of the Main Street side, then running to blast at the other farmers hidden across the tracks.

Far down the track, just then a whistle screeched.

Number 1608!

Frank handed Jesse the sledgehammer. With a glance at the wall clock, then showing a minute till midnight, he grinned and said, "Right on time; good luck, Ding."

His younger brother picked up the can of coal oil and snuck out of the station by way of the small swinging door which serviced the depot's woodbox from the outside. Old guerrilla fighter that he was, he managed to slip through the citizen lines and on down the track toward the train's whistling. A short distance beyond the station he found the stack of creosoted cross-ties that he had prayed he remembered being there. Piling these on the tracks, sweating and grunting at the labor, he doused them with the coal oil, just as number 1608 rounded the near bend east of the Hatpin water stop. Jesse scraped the match on his haunch, tossed it into the coal-oiled timbers. They burst into smoky flame, and number 1608's engineer fed the sand to the rails and clamped on his brakes. Number 1608 screeched to a halt, sat steaming and chuffing.

Up into its cab swung the bearded desperado, with the sledgehammer in one hand, a Navy Colt in the other.

"Get down, get down!" he shouted. "It's Jesse James!"

With the dread name, he fired over the heads of fireman and engineer, both of whom went to the floor of the cab and remained there praying. Jesse swarmed up on the coal car, and from there to the rounded tops of the passenger coaches, to race down them toward horse car and posse caboose. As he approached, the loading ramp of the horse car came open and down to the ground with a great slam. Out galloped the possemen, ready-mounted and hell-bent to ride. With a company yell signaling doom to the James gang at last, all spurred their animals uptrack toward the halted locomotive.

Laughing aloud, Jesse dropped down between cars and with the sledgehammer began to drive out the coupling pin between caboose and horse car.

The excitement of it fired him through and through. By God, Jesse had a plan! He always had a plan! Whicher, the Pinkertons, the private bank dicks—none of them could think along with Dingus James. Just let them try!

At the head of the train the special posse thundered by, firing into the night, and at nothing. The engineer yelled down from the cab that it "was so" Jesse James, and he had dashed off with his entire gang "of near a dozen desperate murderers" into the open prairie off to the north.

Away went the posse, cursing and firing.

At the depot, the Hatpin citizens, hearing this wild bursting of gunfire, broke their ambush to run down the tracks and join the kill. Watching them abandon their stations about the depot, Frank James said dryly, "All right, boys. Fetch along the coal oil and the gunnysacks."

Once free of the stationhouse, he led the others westward

along the tracks, in the opposite direction of Jesse's halting of number 1608. "Keep a-coming, keep a-coming," he urged his panting fellows. "Who's got the matches?"

Back down the line, in the glare of 1608's headlamp, the posse had returned from the prairie, to mill in disgust under the beginning jeers of the Hatpin men.

Big-city lawmen, humpfh!

Kansas City railroad detectives, hah!

But then they remembered, suddenly, their own deserted posts about the stationhouse. Too late, they stumbled back to the depot. It was as dark and empty as the outer night.

It was now the Kansas City posse's turn to curse the local vigilantes and tell them they were full of jayhawk corn and that heads would roll for this false alarm. A red-faced J. W. Whicher vowed personally to see to it that the track was ripped out and relaid wide around Hatpin, Kansas.

Returning glumly down along the stalled train, they reloaded the sweat-caked horses, and number 1608 shortly pulled on out for Denver. In the caboose, short-tempered possemen swore a vengeance upon whoever could be nailed for the fiasco they had just performed. But even as they took oaths, one of them looked out the caboose and yelled, "What the hell! We ain't moving. Yonder goes the train with our horse car!"

The startled lawmen rushed as one out of the motionless caboose. All of them remembered the jeering figure waving to them with the sledgehammer from the disappearing roof of their famed horse car, just then sweeping out of sight around the Hatpin depot bend.

It was Jesse Woodson James.

Number 1608, all innocent of the detached posse caboose, gained speed quickly. Hatpin and its feeble lights were soon a pinpoint on the black prairie. Hearts grew lighter.

"Well, anyways," the engineer consoled his recovering

fireman, "we still got the Denver banknotes aboard and safe."

He was entirely correct, justifiably gratified.

For about four minutes and three-quarters of a mile.

Then a second pile of oil-soaked cross-ties was blazing in the right-of-way, and another James brother was leaping to the locomotive's cab as the engineer again poured sand to steel and brought his train to another groaning halt in the Kansas night.

"Hello, there, neighbors." Frank James nodded to fireman and engineer. "Down on the floorplate, and think about your sins. We shan't be long."

The two went again to the floor of the cab, and Frank left them there to climb the coal car and supervise from its black cargo the loading into the Kansas wheat sacks, by Chadwell, Pitts, and Miller, of the total cargo of unsigned Denver banknotes found in the express car next behind.

With this task in progress, the loading ramp of the horse car at train's rear banged down once more, and Jesse came prancing down its cleated path riding J. W. Whicher's famed white Kentucky racehorse. Behind him, on a long lead rope, came the others of the posse's prized horses. He was no more than just up to the express car with the mounts when the door slid open, and his men, complete with stuffed wheat sacks, leaped out to saddle up on the horses of the Kansas City posse. They had to wait but a second only for Frank James to scramble down from the coal car and get safely aboard his mount, being held for him by brother, Jesse Woodson; then they were ready to ride out into history.

But the two brothers, with a true sense of that history, held in their mounts one last pinch of time.

"Well, Jess," said Frank, sober as a hanging judge, "you sure thought of something this time! Mail-order horse thieving! By jings, that's a buster, even for old Dingus!"

Jesse and his hard-faced men looked at one another.

Then all of them, with brother Frank, threw back long-locked heads and laughed crazily as loons on a sunset lake.

Then a common *"Heee-yahhHHH!"* shattered the night.

The wild Missouri guerrilla yell burst from all of them, and at the same time. But there was in it a note of danger shared and defeated, a tribute singularly from them to their driven youthful leader, who, in outlaw truth, always thought of something, always had a plan that worked.

With the yell, they spurred off, filling the night and the silent streets of Hatpin, Kansas, with overhead gunfire and the thunder of the hooves of the splendid remount horses shipped, rush order, to them through courtesy of J. W. Whicher and the main office of the Missouri & Western Railroad.

When they had gone, the legend of the Robin Hood of the Little Blue had grown another folklore larger, and $35,000 richer, for the simple want of a horse.

*In a career spanning nearly half a century, Wayne D. Over-
holser has published exactly one hundred Western novels
and several hundred short stories. Two of his novels,*
Lawman *(1953, under the pseudonym of Lee Leighton) and*
The Violent Land *(1954), were Western Writers of America
Spur Award winners. His first collection,* The Best Western
Stories of Wayne D. Overholser, *was published in 1984;
"Steel to the West," which is concerned with the coming of
the Union Pacific to Cheyenne, is one of the fine tales in-
cluded in that volume.*

Steel to the West

Wayne D. Overholser

My name is Jim Glenn. I had come to Cheyenne months
ago—when it was no more than a collection of tents and
shacks—knowing the Union Pacific would soon reach it. I
believed in the future of Cheyenne, so I invested everything
I had in town lots and was building on one of them.

I had heard that steel would reach Cheyenne on Novem-
ber 13, 1867. After breakfast that morning I told my girl
Cherry Owens and my preacher friend Frank Rush that it
was a historic occasion and we'd better be down there somewhere along the grade and watch the spectacle. That was exactly what we did. Frank's wife Nancy came along.

Cherry was running a restaurant at the time and had all the
business she could handle, so she was reluctant to leave, but
I told her every man and his dog would be standing somewhere beside the grade watching the rails being laid and she

might just as well enjoy the show. Besides, she wouldn't have any business if she stayed in her restaurant all day. When we arrived, we found that I was right. Every man and his dog was there, particularly the dogs.

We weren't disappointed. Laying the rails was the most interesting show I had ever seen, and the others agreed. The surveyors, bridge builders, and graders were all working miles west of Cheyenne. There had been some Indian trouble, even though soldiers out of Fort D. A. Russell near Cheyenne were constantly patrolling the route the railroad would take.

Most of the men employed by the Union Pacific were Civil War veterans who worked with their guns close at hand, but still we were constantly hearing of Indian trouble—particularly with the surveyors who had to work far out ahead of everyone else. They were the most likely to get killed, and many of them were.

The Casement brothers, General Jack and Dan, were responsible for laying the track, and much of the grading, too. Jack Casement had been a general during the war and had put together a well-organized, disciplined group of men. Most of them were Irish, a tough, brawling, hard-working bunch who would have been hard for anyone else to manage, but the Casements handled them well.

As we stood in the crowd and watched the rails being laid, I was amazed at the proficiency and speed with which the job was done. A light car pulled by one horse came up to the end of steel, the car loaded with rails. Two men grabbed the end of a rail. Other men took hold of the rail by twos, and when it was clear of the car, all of them went forward on the run.

At exactly the right second someone yelled a command to drop the rail. They did, being careful to put it into place right side up. Another gang of men was doing exactly the same thing on the other side of the track. I held my watch on them several times and noted that it took about thirty seconds per rail.

The instant the car was empty it was tipped to one side while the next loaded one moved up, then the empty car was driven back for another load, the horse galloping as if the devil was right on his tail. The gougers, spikers, and bolters kept close on the heels of the men dropping the rails.

Just a few minutes watching these men gave me an admiration for them I had never felt for a group of laborers before. I had not seen anything like it, and I never saw anything like it afterwards. It was cooperation to a T.

Then the thought came to me that I would make a fortune out of the lots I'd bought and the buildings I was putting up, and I owed it all to these men who were laying the rails and spiking them into place along with the graders and bridge builders and surveyors.

Of course, I really owed something to the Union Pacific Company and General Dodge who headed the operation and the Casement brothers, but the men on top were making good money whereas the Irishmen who did the sweating and ran the danger of getting an Indian bullet in their briskets weren't getting rich.

There was a hell of a lot of banging as the end of the steel moved past us. I did some quick calculating as I watched: Three strokes to the spike. I counted ten spikes to the rail. Somewhere I had heard it took four hundred rails for a mile of track. About that time I quit calculating, but one thing was sure. Those sledges were going to swing a lot of times before the line was finished between Omaha and Sacramento.

We walked back to Cherry's restaurant in a kind of daze. The whole operation was incredible. Sherman Hill lay west of Cheyenne, then the desert that offered a different kind of resistance, with the Wasatch mountains on beyond the desert. Of course the Central Pacific with its Chinese labor had a worse kind of terrain to cover, with the Sierra an almost impenetrable wall.

Cherry invited us to dinner. Her hired woman, who had stayed behind, had the meal almost ready by the time we got there. We ate hurriedly, having heard the first train to Cheyenne would arrive that afternoon. The whole town would be down there beside the tracks to welcome it.

It was the day we had been waiting for, but still I had an uneasy feeling in the pit of my stomach every time I thought about an offer I'd turned down recently for my property. A thousand dollars was a lot! I'd paid a fraction of that, so it would have meant one hell of a big profit. I thought we hadn't reached the peak yet, so I'd said no, but I wasn't much of a gambler, and now I wasn't sure whether I'd made a mistake or not.

I'd heard plenty about Julesburg, the end-of-track town to the east of us. It had been on the boom for months. Early in the summer—or maybe it had been late in the spring—there had been only about fifty people in Julesburg. By the end of July it had exploded to about four thousand, with streets of mud or dust—depending on when it had rained last.

The prices the merchants had charged for their goods were outrageous. Apparently it was the grab for money that had made Julesburg the hell hole it had been, but it was the absence of law and order that worried me. I think all the businessmen of Cheyenne felt the way I did and had no intentions of letting the same thing happen here. Still there was the question of what we could do about it.

Julesburg had had more than its share of whore houses, dance halls, gambling places, and saloons. The women, it was said, walked around town with derringers carried on their hips. They would rob a man by putting something in his drink, but he would not be allowed to take proper measures against them after he came to.

One reporter wrote that Julesburg had people who would kill a man for five dollars. I believed it. Dead men had been found in the alley every day, their pockets emptied of what-

ever they had been carrying. The part I could not understand
was the obvious fact that the people living in Julesburg were
indifferent to what was going on.

All of this ran through my mind as I ate. I didn't say much
to Cherry, sitting beside me at the counter, but the thought
began nagging me that neither Cherry nor Nancy Rush
would be safe if we allowed Cheyenne to go the way Julesburg had.

In the long run it was the good women like Nancy and
Cherry who built the towns and brought civilization to the
frontier, not the whores who too often worked hand in glove
with the sneak thieves and murderers who had made Julesburg a literal hell. Now that Cheyenne was the end of track,
Julesburg would cease to exist as a town. I knew exactly
what would happen. The riffraff from Julesburg would
move to Cheyenne.

I knew what most of my friends thought: A vigilance
committee was the only answer. As we hurried back to the
track, I wondered if they were right. A few minutes later
when the train pulled in with the cars banging and the bell
ringing and the whistle shrieking, I decided I'd better think
about it some more. Maybe they were.

A man on the train yelled, "Gentlemen, I give you Julesburg." That wasn't any news to me. While everyone else
was whooping and hollering as the passengers left the train,
I stood there as if paralyzed.

Frank nudged me in the ribs. "What's the matter with
you, Jim?" he asked.

I shook my head and came out of it right away. I managed a weak holler, but my heart wasn't in it. I could see
that the train was carrying the frame shacks and tents that
had made up most of Julesburg, along with the barroom
equipment and gambling devices that had given Julesburg
the reputation of being the most notorious sin city in the
West.

Along with the railroad men, mule skinners, and hunters
who were on the train, there were the whores and the pimps

and professional gamblers and con men. Within a matter of hours the Cheyenne of today would be a city of sin that would match the Julesburg of yesterday. It struck me that this historic occasion was not what I had expected it to be. Certainly I was having second thoughts about it.

Cheyenne had planned a big celebration, with a platform for speakers and big signs that read "The Magic City of the Plain greets the trans-continental railway" and "Old Casement we welcome you" and "Honor to whom honor is due." I wanted no part of it, and I wondered if progress always meant that you had to swallow the bitter with the sweet.

I'd had more than enough. I said, "Cherry, let's get out of here."

She nodded. As we walked back along Ferguson Street, she glanced at me and asked, "What's the matter, Jim?"

"It's funny how it is when you actually see something that you knew was coming," I said. "Cheyenne will be the hell on wheels that Julesburg has been. It scares me. Have you got a gun?"

"Yes," she said. "I knew this was coming and it scares me, too. I bought a pistol just the other day. I'll use it if I have to."

"Good." I said. "If you need any help, get word to me as fast as you can."

She laid a hand on my arm and squeezed it. "Thank you, Jim," she said.

I left her at the restaurant and went on home, more worried and upset than I wanted to admit. We had policemen, and we had a civilian auxiliary police force in which I had very little confidence. I knew damned well that our official law enforcers simply could not handle the number of toughs who had come in on that train. To make it worse, more would come. I had no doubt of that.

Frank Rush stopped in later and said it had been a festive day and wanted to know why I was so glum. I told him, adding, "If you're the kind of preacher who is looking for souls to save, a lot of them came in on the train today. I guess the people who have been in Cheyenne from the day the first settlers arrived aren't angels, but we've been pretty close compared to the riffraff that was on the train."

He frowned and scratched his chin thoughtfully, then he asked, "How do you know the train was carrying that kind?"

"I saw enough of them to know," I said. "All you had to do was to look at them to know what they were. Besides, we saw the stuff they were bringing in from Julesburg. I guess there isn't any way to keep the undesirables out, but we've got to control them once they get here."

He hadn't even thought of it, I guess. He was about like most of the Cheyenne people. He finally nodded and said as if only half convinced, "I guess you're right."

"Has Nancy got a gun?" I asked. When he shook his head, I said sharply, "Damn it, Frank, get her one."

He nodded again and said, "I guess I will."

I didn't think he would. If one of those hardcases ever so much as touched his wife, I'd kill him if Frank didn't, but killing a man after it was too late wouldn't help Nancy.

I had another visitor that day after Frank left, a man who introduced himself as Jess Munro. He came after it was dark and for a moment I didn't know who he was. After he came inside and I saw him in the lamplight, I knew I had seen him around town, but I had never actually met him or talked to him.

He was about thirty, I judged, a dark-faced man with a black mustache and beard and black hair. His eyes were dark brown, his jaw square, the kind of jaw you'd expect to see on a forceful man. He was stocky in build with large hands and muscular shoulders. He'd be a hard man to whip, I told myself.

Munro carried himself with a straight-backed military stiffness that I associated with army men. I suspected he had been an officer during the war, probably on the Union side because his speech gave no hint that he was a Southerner. I had never seen him without a gun on his hip. He had one now, and I wondered about it because he claimed to be a real estate dealer and had an office on Ferguson Street.

He shook hands with me, his grip very strong. He pinned his gaze on my face as if making a judgment about me, then he said, "Some of your friends have told me you're a tough hand. I can believe it because I've seen how you handle yourself in fights. I think you'll do."

"Do for what?"

"You saw what the train brought in this afternoon," he said, ignoring my question. "Not that it had any surprises. The police can't do the job, even with the help of some of us who have been appointed law officers on a standby basis." Then he shrugged, and added, "I guess we would be of help in case of a riot, but that's about all."

I nodded as if I agreed, but I wasn't convinced the standby police would be of any help if the chips were down. Still, I had considered volunteering for police duty, in the hopes that something might be better than nothing.

When I told him I'd been thinking about volunteering, he said, "Good. Then you'll be willing to serve on the vigilance committee we're organizing. Several men, just four as a matter of fact, will serve as chiefs. That's why we want you. You'll have fifteen men under you to carry out any job that the central committee decides on. Will you do it?"

Here it was at last, laid out in the open. I had to make a decision now, one way or the other. I hesitated, looking straight at Jess Munro. I'd had doubts of the Vigilantes for years, but I'd been worrying about the situation here for a long time, too. Something had to be done if Cheyenne was to be saved.

Still I hesitated, saying, "I've always been leery of vigilante rule. They operate outside the law. It can become mob law very easily."

"That's right," he said grimly. "That's why we're seeking men like you to be leaders. We intend to take steps to safeguard against that very thing. I have appointed myself chairman of the committee for the simple reason that I've had some experience with vigilance committees and I know the dangers. Of course I will be subject to removal by a majority of the committee."

He paused, scratching his chin, then added, "Glenn, damn it, we just don't have much time. The toughs will be in control of the town before we know it if we don't do something. We've got to get on the job and do it quick. I'll be surprised if we don't have two or three murders before morning. We've got to organize and stay organized as long as Cheyenne is an end-of-track town."

I realized then I had no choice, doubts or not. I had as much responsibility as any man, maybe more than some because I was aware of what would happen if we let things go. I had to become involved because I knew damned well that the average Cheyenne resident wouldn't, any more than the good men in Julesburg had.

"Fine," he said. "We're meeting in the hall over Miller's store tomorrow night at eight o'clock. Don't mention this to anyone. Just be there."

We shook hands again and he left. I still wasn't sure I had done right, mostly because there was no certainty that Jess Munro wouldn't use the vigilance committee for his own purposes. But it was a chance I had to take. Maybe it would be wrong to participate in the Vigilante movement, but it would be more wrong to sit on my hind end and let Cheyenne go to hell.

We saved Cheyenne so that in time it really did become the Magic City of the Plains. You know, during all the years that followed, as I watched Cheyenne settle down from an end-of-track town to a solid city with schools and churches and women and children, I was never sorry about the decision I made that day when steel came to us from the East.

Flying Switch

H. L. Davis

Railroad track work has changed radically within the last dozen years. But there is one thing that improvements and innovations have failed to change at all, and that is bunkhouse conversation. The subjects are the same, the arguments are the same, and they yank the facts around to make a good knockdown story, with as little regard for the way things actually happened as they ever showed in the days when the Santa Fe ran no farther west than Dodge City, and all the locomotives burned cordwood.

They will all be teaming up to prove, for instance, that any man who works on a railroad track is a born idiot, and that abuse and outrage are his daily dish. If you don't know any of the men they tell about, you will be ready to believe that the railroad company could make the emperor Nero look like the teacher in a kindergarten.

Look at the way they treated old Stub Johnson, the section

boss at Tuskan Siding. Worked him like an old dray horse for years, and then, six months before his retirement pension was due, they began shipping in bullies, yeggs and prize fighters to work on his gang and make his life miserable and his job impossible, so he'd quit. They wanted him to lose his pension; that was their game, and don't you forget it!

Did he lose it? Of course he did! He stood it as long as he could, and then he threw his job in their faces—tole 'em they could take their blamed old pension and go to blazes with it. That was all they wanted out of him. When they got it, they hired him right back again to run the section at Tuskan Siding. He's there yet—he and the two rickety old sagebrushers who work for him and bach with him. No pension, no rest, no entertainment, no nothing. That was the kind of deal they handed Stub Johnson, and they made him like it, too. A man's got to live, hasn't he? That's railroading for you, boy!

It makes a strong case, unless one happens to know about Stub Johnson. The facts about him were considerably less convincing. Long before his retirement pension ever came in sight, he had become famous all along the line for his crankiness and surliness. He had worked on the Tuskan section so long that he imagined he owned it, and nobody, from the president down, could offer him the smallest suggestion about it without being insulted.

Nobody ever called him for it. The president, who offered Stub a nice new bunkhouse in place of the ramshackle old outfit car he was living in, got told to mind his own business and went away to tell it as a joke on himself. It was veterans like that, he urged, who took a real pride in the line, and as far as he was concerned, Stub should live in his section car until it fell in on top of him. There was real sentiment in it, he claimed. No doubt he was right, but he had the advantage of being able to let Stub alone.

Some of his subordinates were less lucky. The worst off was the division engineer, young Fosnot. He was kind-hearted and well-meaning, but, on account of his youthful appearance, Stub had decided that he was a little smart-aleck, and treated him accordingly.

By rights, young Fosnot should have had Stub fired. But he was new to his job, and he hated the idea of acting like a martinet merely to assert his own importance. This was bound to cause trouble, and trouble came when Stub's re-tirement pension was still six months off. There was a spell of zero weather, beginning with a two-foot fall of heavy snow which froze in the cuts and drifted in behind the rotary plow like dry sand. It had to be shoveled out by hand, and young Fosnot, hiring extra shovel men, thought of Stub, who hadn't asked for any, and of Stub's two old section hands, who certainly hadn't looked capable of clearing the cuts on the Tuskan section by themselves. So he decided to send reinforcements to Tuskan, and he picked four of his huskiest applicants for the job. What was equally important, they were all men who looked as if they didn't mind getting their feelings hurt.

"Because it's hard telling what kind of welcome you're likely to get," Fosnot warned them. "He's a hard old wolf, this Johnson, and he's apt to get mad and try to throw you out, whether he needs you to work or not. I want you to stay and work anyhow, no matter what he orders you to do. Do you think you can stand up to him?"

They promised that they could and would. "One of these old sour-bellied cussers, huh?" they scoffed confidently. "Leave him to us, Cap!"

From their looks, it seemed a safe thing to do. Fosnot wrote out their passes to Tuskan Siding, told them when their train left, and turned to other work. It was not until evening that he realized the misplay he had made. The train down the river brought in a note from Stub Johnson. It was written on the back of a material report, in pencil, smudgy and misspelled; but the purport was clear and shocking. Mr. Fosnot had pulled a boner.

"You have sent four men," read the note. "They have not got eny place to sleep. They have took our beds. We have not got eny place to sleep. They have kicked us out. I am resining my job. Very respeckfuly. S. Johnson, Foreman."

Young Fosnot's first impulse was to resign, too. But, outside, it was five below zero, and resigning wouldn't keep Stub Johnson and his two old men from freezing to death. He grabbed the telephone, and called up the railroad yards.

"An empty bunk car to Tuskan Siding, and hold the night freight to take it, heh?" repeated the yardmaster. "There ain't any bunk cars empty, and the night freight's due out right now."

"Empty one, then!" Fosnot implored him. "The men in it? Send 'em to a hotel! Get 'em out or I will! This is life or death, Joe," he urged. "I've stubbed my toe sending some men up the line without any place to sleep, and it's going to play hell if you can't help me crawl out! Stub Johnson has resigned, and—"

No more was needed. The yardmaster didn't even ask for particulars. "I'll get your car," he promised. "And send it up for you, too, if I have to tear up the track to hold the freight. Anything that could make Stub Johnson quit—"

He hung up. Fosnot was unable to stay away, even though he couldn't be of any help. He got to the yard as the freight, with its entire crew leaning out to cuss back at the yardmaster for making them late, took the switch onto the main line, the bunk car bouncing and lurching at the tail of the caboose. Watching beside the yardmaster, Fosnot let out a sigh of relief. The yardmaster turned on him pityingly.

"You'd better save all that till you see how things come out," he advised. "Do you think getting an extra car up there at one in the morning is going to do any good? You ain't over the hump yet, boy!"

* * *

There was one thing on which young Fosnot had figured right. Stub Johnson's two section hands weren't good at working on the track. They were too old to handle a job on nothing but muscle, and they hadn't enough experience in track work to know how to save themselves at it. Stub Johnson hadn't hired them to work, anyhow. What he wanted of them was their company. They were both about his own age, though both looked older on account of the hardships they had gone through, and Stub, who couldn't talk at all, enjoyed listening to men of his own generation who could.

Both, when he found them, were up against it. Old Asa Whitmore had been brought in from a bush homestead in the hills, where a rescue party had found him crippled with rheumatism, and starving in a shack without even a fire in it. Stub hired him, and that fall the two of them found old Skookum Sheldon sitting on the right-of-way fence near the Tuskan water tank, looking uneasy and hollow-flanked. His trouble, he explained, was that he had to climb a freight train to get out of the country, and he didn't know how it was done.

"I been waitin' in hopes I'd see where them hoboes ride," he told them, "but dogged if I could see any hoboes on the trains at all. And now it begins to look like I wasn't goin' to see no more trains. You fellers got any notion when they'll be another one comin' along here?"

He was broke and jobless. Harvest work in the country had been barely enough to feed him. Sometimes he walked between jobs, and sometimes other crop-hands gave him a lift in a flivver. Now the crop-hands were all gone, and it was too far to walk, and, at the moment when the freight-jumping era had vanished, he was having to learn how to jump a freight. But he never did learn, for Stub hired him, and he helped pump the handcar back to Tuskan Siding, where he keeled over because he hadn't had anything to eat for twenty-four hours.

Asa and old Sheldon became Stub's men. They would have gone to the gallows for him, and the trio got along so perfectly together that they didn't even quarrel about the housekeeping chores. They kept the rickety old bunk car as slick and shiny as the inside of a new gun barrel.

Young Fosnot's four hard-crusted young bullies got off the train while Stub and Asa and old Sheldon were out working. There was nowhere to get out of the cold except the bunk car, and they kicked the lock off the door, went in, and made themselves at home. They built a fire in the stove, so hot it threatened to melt the stovepipe; and they helped themselves to the grocery supply, also to a quart bottle of whiskey which old Sheldon had planted under his bunk against his birthday. By the time Stub and his two men got back from work, the tidy section car had been turned into a regular boar's nest, with the four despoilers, still a little cocky from old Sheldon's whiskey, grinning in the center of it.

It was the worst possible kind of introduction. Probably nothing could have staved off a row anyway, but this not only brought it on instantly but squelched any chance of a reconciliation. The young men started to explain who they were, and Stub cut them off.

"It don't make no difference who you are," he said. "Git up and git out! Be damn quick about it, too."

The four invaders didn't move. They laughed, and kept on laughing because old Sheldon discovered his emptied bottle in the corner. It was all a big joke. They had Stub and his men foul. They proceeded to make that clear.

"Suppose we don't want to move?" one of them inquired. "Suppose we take it into our heads to make you move? Hell, Grandpa, we ain't worried about where we're goin' to sleep! It's you! Do you think you'll make out all right if we let you sleep on the floor?"

Stub at last realized what he was up against, so he wrote out his note of resignation which, sent in on the evening passenger train, raised such a racket in the yards at the Junction, lost young Fosnot a night's sleep, and got a gang of twelve Mexicans the privilege of living in the senatorial suite at the Junction's new fireproof brick hotel for a week because their bunk car had been taken out from under them and sent to Tuskan in the night.

Hooping the note onto the passenger was a diversion. After that, there followed a long spell of monotonous waiting. The old men sat in a corner while the cold crept up through their feet to their bodies. The four intruders didn't have it so easy, either. They had the blankets, but they couldn't sleep for fear Stub's men might gang up on them while they were helpless. Finally one of them—a huge-shouldered man with a broad white scar down the middle of his skull—got up and pitched his stack of blankets back into the bunk.

"Be damned to this, anyhow!" he pronounced. "Come on out of that corner and git into bed, you old guys! I don't want your cock-eyed blankets!"

A couple of the other men sat up and bundled their covers, too, looking ashamed of themselves. Then Stub Johnson spoke.

"Set down here!" he ordered his men. "You don't touch them blankets till these thieves git out of this car!"

Then something happened. The freight train, bringing the extra bunk car and running late on account of it, attempted to sidetrack it by a flying switch, to save time. The conductor, who was supposed to catch it and brake it down on the siding, missed his hold. It went through the switch like a runaway steer, and hit the section car with a crash that almost caved in the walls.

There was complete darkness in which things happened without anybody knowing it. The impact knocked everybody in the section car half senseless. The one bracket lamp fell off its nail, broke, and, luckily, went out. The stove coasted halfway down the car, pulled loose from the pipe, and belched the whole place full of choking smoke. Everything on the floor slid into corners, and everything on the shelves fell down and broke. The train crew, hearing the crash, concluded that the loose car was stopped, and went away without trying to find out whether it had killed anybody or not.

. What it had done was plenty. When the men in the section car came to, they were moving. The car bumped down the siding, hammered across the ice-clogged switch leads, and, loose on the main line with a three percent grade and nothing holding it, began to travel.

"What's that engine switchin' us around this way for?" demanded one of the invaders, out of the dark.

"You'll know soon enough!" Stub answered. To old Sheldon and Asa, he explained what was up. "There ain't any engine behind us," he told them. "We're loose, and we'll be runnin' like a bat when this grade takes hold of us. Then you'll see 'em start jumpin' off!"

"It'll kill 'em," Old Asa protested. "We're goin' too fast for a jump right now! They'll git killed, Stub!"

"So will we," said Stub Johnson. "We'll be up to a mile a minute when we hit Centerville. That's all right. We'll last long enough to see them fellers killed first. We're old, anyhow, ain't we? Set tight, and don't interfere. Let 'er run!"

The man with the scarred skull was the first to make the discovery, for his side, that they were running away. They took it with disappointing absence of panic. The only one of the four who favored jumping off was a young man in a checked shirt, whose name was Wilcox. He wanted to, but the others wouldn't let him.

"We've got to git that stove out of here before it sets the place afire," announced the man with the scarred skull. "Wilcox, shut up and keep away from the door! Stricklin, you come here and give me a hand on this stove! Open the door, Steve! One, two—"

They pitched the stove out, and as they did so the car felt

the pull of the grade. It slewed and plunged, and the wheels sang like tent cloth being ripped endlessly.

"We got to git this thing stopped, Doss!" yelled the man named Stricklin. "We got to git somebody up to set them brakes!"

"I know it!" said the man with the scarred skull. "Find something to work with, and we'll try to bust a hole in the roof!"

There were ladders outside leading to the roof, but they were in the wrong places—one on each side, and one on the back of the car, but all at the corners. From inside, there was no way of reaching them—unless one knew the car well enough to remember what was under the washable wallpaper. Stub and his men knew, and old Sheldon straightened up and said, "Why, the poor, damned fools!" But Stub pushed him back.

"Be still!" he said. "They think they can run this. You let 'em do it!"

Breaking through the roof didn't work. Doss stood on the table and hammered at the ceiling with a spike-maul handle while Stricklin held it from sliding out from under him. Then Doss gave up and got down. His voice sounded light and queer.

"We can't bust through," he said weakly. "But we got to get onto that roof. Wilcox, come here!"

Doss's plan was for two men to lift Wilcox through the door until he could get a hold on the roof. It was dangerous and desperate. The roof was a solid sheet of ice, the car bucked like a wild steer, and there was nothing that a man could get hold of with anything but his fingernails. Wilcox pronounced the job impossible. But Doss was the one who ran things.

"When you're ready, say 'Lift!' " he instructed. "We'll both heave you together. Get your elbows on top first, and then put your foot on that slat over the door. All ready?"

* * *

Wilcox, standing between them, stood for a moment watching ahead. Suddenly he yelled, "Lift!" They hoisted him, and he flung himself—not for the roof at all, but out at a path of scarlet willow brush, soft with snow. It would have broken his fall, except that, miscalculating the speed of the car, he waited too long, and missed it. His limp body skidded on icy gravel, and pitched over the bank into the rocks as they thundered out of sight. Wilcox had, at last, been caught with a bad hunch, and it had finished him.

"The dirty little crook!" Doss gasped. "I wish I had him back here for two minutes! I'd . . . Steve, you're next!"

Steve, dark-faced, his black eyes shining with excitement, listened while they explained. The only thing he did by way of making ready was to get out a long sheath knife to dig a hold in the ice with when he hit the roof. "Less go, huh?" he said.

They heaved and lifted him—and presently he was up.

But the brakes didn't go on. Full daylight came while they sat and listened. Rocks and snow streaked past at a speed that mixed them in a gray-white blur. Old Sheldon couldn't sit idle any longer. Stub, he knew, was set like a rock to let things smash; but perhaps, if Asa would help argue, the two of them might bring him to relent.

But, from a look at Asa in the light, he saw that to be hopeless. Asa was sick. His cheeks were bright red, his head rocked helplessly with the car, and his lips moved without saying anything. Old Sheldon would have to play his hand alone or not play it at all.

"I'm sorry, Stub," he said. "I just can't stand no more of this. I got to go up and set them brakes!"

Stub didn't move from his seat on the floor. "If you do, we're through," he said. "I mean it, Skook!"

Old Sheldon knew that he did mean it. Stub Johnson had befriended him when nobody else wanted him at all. There was nobody else in the world whom he could tie to, nobody else in the world who cared whether he lived or starved. Now he was throwing Stub over to side with Doss and

Stricklin, about whom he didn't care two whoops. But the job now was to set the brakes, to fight with the men, who wanted to live, against the forces that wanted them to die.

At the rear end of the car, covered with the bright washable wallpaper, was a door. It had been nailed shut, but he burst it open with a couple of kicks, not daring to look at Stub, who had forbidden him to tell Stricklin and Doss that it was there. Through it he could get out on the bumper, and from there to the rear ladder. He crawled through, taking with him the spike-maul handle which Doss had dropped in his seasickness. He would need that to lever the brake wheels with. If he ever got up there. The bumper was iced over. So was the ladder, every rung an icicle. And the car swung and bucked and lurched, almost shaking him off on the curves. He stuck his head back inside, for a plea, that from all the prospects, was likely to be his last.

"She's liable to buck me off, Stub," he said. "If she does, you and Asa remember—"

"Get out of my sight!" said Stub. He didn't even look around. He seemed totally, fiercely alone, not only in the car, but in the whole universe. When, after a long, freezing, pitching, slewing, roaring-wheeled interval, Doss ventured that old Sheldon must have been a good man to lose that way, Stub didn't turn his head.

"Sheldon ain't any man of mine," he said. "Asa, here, is the only man I've got."

Doss looked at him curiously, and then at Asa.

"You ain't got very much, then," he said. "Your man's sick. High fever, by the looks. Out of his head, too—Stricklin," he called, "come over here a minute. This old man's about to die on us!"

Stricklin came, edging along the rocking walls, and leaned over Asa; but, for Stub, one look at his man's glazed eyes too, and he was cleaned out. His stubbornness broke, too late to save anything, but in time for him to realize that he had lost everything. His job, by resigning when he didn't need to; old Sheldon, by not letting him tell Doss about the door when Wilcox went up; Asa, by forbidding him to take his blankets when Doss offered them . . . .

"What's the use workin' with him?" he mumbled, as Doss and Stricklin laid old Asa down and knelt to work on him. "Let him go—we'll all be dead in another half hour anyway."

They paid no attention to him. "He's got pneumonia, I guess," said Stricklin. "See if there's a can of mustard knockin' around anywhere. I'll rub snow on his head. Bring some of them blankets, too, while you're at it. See if you can git his feet warm. We'll set the brakes when we git round to it!"

They had given old Sheldon completely up, but that was wrong, for he had found more work to do than they could have imagined, and he had run into hard luck in doing it. Indeed, he was almost at the point of giving up himself. He was stripped, above the waist, to his undershirt, and half-frozen. One of his ribs was broken, and the pain of every breath almost made him faint. He hung with one hand to the brake post and held on, with the other, to the dark-faced boy who had climbed up to set the brakes with a long-bladed sheath knife to dig a hold in the ice.

Steve, whom they had also given up, was alive, too, though that was about all. It was his knife that had done the damage. Slipping on the lurching roof, he grabbed the blade and caught the edge on his naked wrist. It saved him, but it cut deep; and, having hooked on it, he could neither shift to a safer hold nor change the one he had. At every surge of the car the blade worked against his wrist. He went senseless from loss of blood, and it was so that old Sheldon, topping the roof, found him, frozen in place by his clothes against the ice.

* * *

The first job, old Sheldon decided, must be to get Steve loose, tie up his wrist, and plant him where he wouldn't fall off. Setting the brakes would have made a rescue easier, but he dared not wait that long, for it might also make one unnecessary. Steve was too far gone to be put off for anything. Old Sheldon, feeling like a monkey on a bucking horse, toe-nailed down the pitch and set to work to make a tourniquet for the wounded wrist.

It was in that work that he lost his coat, mackinaw, and shirt. He yanked his outer clothes off to get material for a bandage, and tossed them behind him without noticing that the draft of the car's speed drove the heavy garments out like dead leaves in a gale. He tore a strip out of his shirt with his teeth because his hands were too numb, and turned the rest of that loose on the wind, too. Then, loosening Steve's wrist from the knife, he tied his ligature and twisted it tight with the leather punch of his pocket knife. Not until that was done did he take time to look around him.

The grade still dropped away in front, but it no longer drew at the car wheels. It didn't need to. Their speed was maniacal. It seemed that the car might fly into pieces under it at any second. Ahead, like a floor toward which they were falling, was a flat expanse of snow, patched with yellow—the grain fields around Centerville. If they hit the switching tracks there, at their present speed—

Old Sheldon, with carefully timed jerks, not to lose his balance, loosened Steve's clothes from the ice and then dived for a hold on the center walk and pulled himself and Steve to that safety. At least, it was safe for the moment. That was about all. It was as slick as glass. The motion of the car seemed timed as if trying to throw them off, and the air was full of minute little blades of ice that cut through lips and eyelids like razors. Old Sheldon couldn't stay there, for he had to set the brakes; nor leave Steve there, for there was nothing to hold him from falling off. Tie him on? There was nothing to tie with, nothing to tie to, no time to monkey with tying anyway. Steve would have to come along.

"They probably think I've fell off," old Sheldon reflected. "I ort to, I reckon. Ain't this my lucky day, anyhow, damn it all?"

He set the unconscious boy on the walk in front of him and crawled, pushing him along, to the brake at the front end. Taken together, the brake and Steve made an awkward combination to manage. It was in trying to handle them both that he got his rib broken. He set his spike-maul handle in the spokes of the wheel, holding Steve carefully by keeping a foot planted on either side of him. The brake wheel stood two turns, and then the ratchet slipped. The wheel spun back, and the spike-maul handle spun with it.

Old Sheldon saw it coming, but couldn't dodge without letting go his hold on Steve. He chose not to dodge at all, and the handle hit him over the lung, breaking the rib like a stick. The pain, though it sickened him, did bring him out of his numbness. He caught the spike-maul handle and drove the brake wheel back again—back to the slowing-notch, and the notch beyond, and the next, until the tough ash bent and the wheel refused to turn farther.

"I'm weak," he accused himself fretfully. "Well, that'll have to do for it, the damned egg-suckin' hound!"

His weakness wasn't imaginary. He hadn't had anything to eat for eighteen hours, and no sleep for twenty-four. An old man, too. The cold was inside of him, so strong it almost drove out the pain of his rib.

"I ain't up to a job like this," he mumbled. "Stub told me not to tackle it. I ort to minded him. No kick comin'. . . . Well, let's see how much of it I can stand! Come on here, woppo!"

The rear brake locked down without any accident. When it was set, old Sheldon saw that his fingers looked funny, and didn't act right. Frostbite. . . . "Oh, well," he told himself, "hell with it, anyway! I done my do. Pulled the kid off the roof, and cinched the brakes. And now the kid's dead, and we're still movin'. Hell with all of it! I wouldn't have no place to go if we had got stopped. Stub's fired me. . . ."

He was too numb to realize that the car had slowed, that it was stopping, and that the continuing motion which he felt was himself, falling off the roof, still holding on to Steve's collar. The two of them hit together in the snowbank heaped alongside the track by the Centerville section men when they shoveled out the switch leads, and it was in a bed in the big Centerville section house that old Sheldon came to.

Division Engineer Fosnot was rubbing his frostbitten fingers with snow out of a bucket, and praising him hysterically. Old Sheldon, he insisted, had done a big thing, a thing that very few men would have tackled, and that still fewer could have managed to accomplish. A man who could do what old Sheldon had done was too good to be frittering away his life as a section hand, taking orders from an old sourbelly who hadn't done anything except start rows and make trouble for everybody he could. Meaning, of course, Stub Johnson.

Young Fosnot had caught the early morning passenger after a sleepless night of wondering how many men had frozen to death through his idiocy, and whether the company would turn him over to the grand jury or merely fire him for life. He had intended to go straight to Tuskan, and find out the worst before anybody else did, at least; but the runaway car at Centerville made the rest of his trip unnecessary. His train got there just as the switch engine tied on to pull the broken-windowed old crib off the main track. The men from it were being carried into the section house, where there was a crowd. Young Fosnot, praying for a change in his luck, got off and went over.

It was really far better than he had dared, at any stage of the action, to hope. There were plenty of casualties, of course; and Wilcox, who had picked a bad place to jump off, was dead. But that had been Wilcox's own fault. Strick-

lin and Doss testified to that, and also volunteered that he
had needed killing, anyway. And not only that, but all the
damages to the others could be blamed, not on Fosnot, but
on the train crew's carelessness in making a flying switch in
the dark.

If he had kept his nose out of Stub Johnson's section to
start with, nobody would have got hurt, and nothing would
ever have happened. He owed it to his luck, and to old Sheldon's fighting instinct, that it hadn't been worse. It could
have been ruinous.

If the car had jumped a curve with all the men in it, if it
had gone wild through the Centerville switches, if it had got
past them and come sailing round a curve into the head end
of the morning passenger—blooey! There would have been
real happenings then—pieces in the papers, a coroner's jury,
a rising young division engineer reading the Help Wanted
sections to find an opening where they didn't demand rec-
ommendations. . . . Old Sheldon had got him out of that.

Who had got him into it, then? Nothing had gone wrong
on any of the other sections; nothing ever did go wrong on
them. It was only on Stub Johnson's section that anything
like this could have happened. Well, Fosnot vowed, it
shouldn't happen again.

"Your section boss has quit his job," he told old Sheldon. "Resigned. You probably know, working for him, that
he spends most of his time being hard to get along with. Of
course he resigned because he hoped it would get me in trouble at the main office. I don't care if it does. I've sent his
resignation in, and I'm going to hold him to it! What do you
think about it?"

"It don't mean nothing to me," said old Sheldon.
"Stub's done fired me off his gang and told me he was
through with me. A man like him won't have to worry about
findin' another job. . . . Don't rub that snow on so damned
hard. You ain't raspin' a horse."

Young Fosnot applied the frostbite treatment with a little
less zeal. "A man like you don't have to worry about an-

other job, either," he said. "Not as long as I'm around here, anyway. Johnson's job is open. I've taken all the meanness off him that I'm going to. If you want to boss the Tuskan section in his place, it's yours. Take it and run it to suit yourself. And if you need anything, why—"

"Much obliged," said old Sheldon, not at all effusively. "I don't want to boss any of your sections. I wouldn't know how, for one thing. Stub Johnson always said what he wanted done, and I worked like he told me. I wouldn't want to hire out to anybody else, anyhow. I'll move on, I reckon, as soon as I can git up from here. One thing, I've learnt how to climb them freight cars."

It was plainly up to Fosnot to revise his plans. He hated to think of having to put up with Stub Johnson again. But old Sheldon didn't want anything else, and decency demanded that he should be given what he wanted. Fosnot decided to do the thing like a sport.

"You don't need to move on," he offered. "I didn't know you felt that way about Johnson—as a matter of fact, I didn't know anybody did. Since you do, I'll hire him back and see that he gives you your old job. He probably expects me to do something like that, anyway. What do you say to it?"

"No," old Sheldon replied. "No, I'd ruther you let things alone. Stub fired me and said he was through with me. He had a right to do it, and he's got a right to say who he wants workin' for him. That ain't any of your put-in. If Stub Johnson don't want me to work for him, it's his business. And if I don't want to work for anybody else on your railroad, that's mine! You don't cut no figger in it at all!"

Fosnot had to admit that, the way things looked, he didn't. The devil of it was that he felt he ought to. "Suppose I call Johnson in here?" he suggested. "Maybe, if we talked to him, we could persuade him out of his contrariness. . . ."

"No, we couldn't," old Sheldon denied, almost proudly.

"Stub's said his say, and there ain't nobody alive that can talk him into backin' out on his word. You might as well— Come back here!"

Fosnot opened the door. Stub Johnson sat in a chair just outside. He had been trying to tune up his nerves to come in, and making hard work of it. Reconciliations and apologies were out of his line. Being discovered, he came in, looking grim and rather ashamed of himself, and addressed himself, in bashfulness, to Fosnot.

"That doctor of yours says Asa'll pull out of it," he blurted. "He says them two fellers in the car had him pretty well over the worst of it before we stopped. I guess that doctor knows his business, all right, don't he?"

This was mostly for old Sheldon's benefit, to let him know that Asa was doing all right. What Stub forgot was that old Sheldon had heard nothing about Asa being sick. Fosnot explained about Asa's pneumonia. Then, turning on Stub, he brought the talk down to cases.

"This is a good man you've got here, Johnson," he said. "I've been trying to persuade him to take your job, and he won't do it. Says he'll either work for you, or he'll quit the railroad. It's a kind of a fix, because you've quit; and it won't do any good to hire you back, because you've fired him and he insists on staying fired."

"I didn't fire him!" said Stub Johnson. "You don't fire a man without writin' out his time, don't the old fool know that? And I didn't write him out nothin'. These men of mine ain't the kind that needs to be fired! I wouldn't have 'em if they was."

He had called old Sheldon his man. That part of it was all right, then. "Well, how about coming back to work for us?" said Fosnot. "I'll arrange to square up for the property that got destroyed in the car and by that gang of yeggs I sent up there. And I'll . . . I'll promise that you won't be sent any more extra help unless you ask for it. Those jungle punks—''

Old Sheldon reared up in bed, forgetting his broken rib. ''You mean them low-down pot-robbers that stole my whiskey?'' he demanded. ''You send 'em back one at a time, and if I don't wring that liquor of mine out of their worthless pelts—''

''Now, Skook,'' protested Stub Johnson. It was the first time in the room that he had addressed old Sheldon directly. ''You got the wrong line on them men, Skook,'' he argued. ''They ain't anything but a little high-spirited. Them two that worked over Asa when he was out of his head is as good men as you'll find anywhere. They—they remind me some of you, Skook.''

That, maybe, is where all the bunkhouse accounts of Stub Johnson started. There were a good many men around the Centerville section house that morning, and none of them ever stopped off at Tuskan Siding to find out whether the softening of his spirit was permanent or not. Young Fosnot stopped off, though, to notify Stub that his retirement pension had gone through in spite of his having resigned, and that, if he wanted it, all he needed to do was to sign a form saying so.

Stub was leveling track by squinting one eye along the rail. Asa and old Sheldon were teamed on the jack bar. Fosnot spoke to them, but they only nodded, watching Stub anxiously as he got up and took the blank out of Fosnot's hand.

They needn't have worried. Stub tore the blank into pieces, and tossed them over the embankment into the brush.

''Don't come packin' any more of them things around there,'' he said. ''I don't have no use for 'em. When I git ready to quit, I'll send you word!''

He lay down on his belly again, and the two old men tied

on to the jack bar proudly, grinning at each other with elation. It wasn't on account of the pension which Stub gave up because he preferred working with them. They were glad of that, of course, but they had expected it of him. The thing they had doubted and felt anxious about was that Stub might have changed, that the runaway might have altered his character. This was definite proof that it hadn't. He was as mean and surly and sour-bellied and ill-mannered as ever. They wanted him to be that way. What they were most afraid of was things changing. Too many things had; and Stub, even in his meanness and cussedness, was the rock to which they had to hold or be destroyed in the fierce current of unknown waters.

Relief made them genial. As Fosnot passed them to get back on his speeder, they spoke cordially, eyeing Stub as if he was something they carried around to show off to strangers.

"Ain't he an old catamount, though?" old Sheldon asked complacently. "He like to bit your head off, didn't he?"

"He's sure on the peck," Asa put in pridefully. "Gad, if I don't believe he's worse'n he ever was!"

Under his own name and such pseudonyms as Gene Thompson, Reese Sullivan, and Hunter Ingram, Giles A. Lutz published more than seventy Western novels between 1954 and 1982. Notable among them are his 1961 Western Writers of America Spur Award winner, The Honyocker, The Long Cold Wind *(1962), and* The Great Railroad War *(1981). "Westward Rails" is one of the last and most accomplished of his more than three hundred short stories and novelettes.*

Westward Rails

Giles A. Lutz

*C*ass Dalton glanced *wistfully* at Neva Moran across the aisle of the emigrant train. He knew he was losing her. It had started a couple of months ago when she first saw Quincy Ridgeway. He wished to God he had never heard the name; he wished Neva hadn't, either. But if it hadn't been Ridgeway, it would have been somebody else. He knew what he had to offer a woman. He had made that analysis a long time ago, and it wasn't pleasant to him.

He shifted uncomfortably on the hard seat. The floor of the car was a huge sounding board, sending each jar and jolt of the uneven roadbed to numb passenger flesh.

An emigrant car was little more than a long, narrow box on wheels, sparsely furnished. Unupholstered benches lined each side of the car, a wood stove at one end, a water closet at the other. Feeble lamps suspended from the ceiling furnished inadequate lighting at night. The sleeping accommodations fit the rest of the car—a board cut out to fit the space between the facing benches with cotton bags leanly stuffed with straw that did little to soften the boards. A passenger furnished his own blankets, or he slept without.

The long string of cars creaked and groaned as the engine picked up speed on its plunge from the summit. The floor of the California desert rushed to meet the train, and each hundred feet of drop intensified the heat. Most of the four days and nights from Omaha to here had been spent in heat: at first the summer heat of the seared prairies, then the blistering reflection of the sun's rays from Utah's salt-encrusted, barren land, followed by the equal aridity of Nevada's high plains with their persistent, irritating alkali dust. The wind's constant stirring kept great clouds of dust in the air, clouds that enveloped a man until his skin itched from it. Each successive crossing of a state seemed to increase the heat, or else a man's weariness had weakened him to it. There had been a brief relief in crossing the crest of the mountains, but that had been short-lived.

Usually one car was allotted to a family, because of the possessions they owned. This car had two families, three if he counted himself as a family. The rest of the car was crammed with household furniture, farm implements, horses, cows, dogs, and cats. Young fruit trees and seed for the first season's planting were jammed in every nook and cranny. The reek of unwashed human bodies was becoming overbearing, and when the smell of hot animal flesh and the rich, ripe aroma of manure rose, a man gagged on it.

His fretting grew with each passing mile. Impatience was a great fault of his, and he fought constantly to contain it. He could add another flaw, a more serious one. Since he had been twelve he had fought to curb his temper. Even now he couldn't say with certainty that the temper was whipped. The first time Cass knew his temper was a serious problem had occurred in a boyish fight with his brother. Jim was four

years older and bigger at the time, and he had hurt Cass
enough to make the hot tears of rage flow. Jim had made a
serious mistake then; he had jeered at Cass, and Cass had
lost all restraint. When his father had broken it up, Cass was
astride Jim, holding him by the ears and banging his head on
the hard ground.

"Are you trying to kill him?" his father had roared.

Cass had looked at the white, unconscious face of his
brother. That was exactly what he had been trying to do. His
father hadn't whipped him, but he had talked to him for long
hours about it. "A temper like that is a frightening thing,
Cass. You're going to be a huge man. A man that size can't
afford the luxury of an insane temper. Do you want to kill
somebody?"

Cass had never forgotten it, and he had backed away from
potential fights until other men looked at him with speculating eyes. But he managed to keep the promise he had made
to his father and to himself.

He shifted his position again and stared at his knuckles in
gloomy meditation. The oversized hands fitted the rest of
his body. He was a huge man, his arms and legs massive.
Those hands could tend sick livestock, or give an ailing
plant additional care. But they would never be able to do
delicate, fine work.

His shifting gave him the briefest of relief. He changed to
the other cheek. How did women stand this trip? He supposed their padding was deeper and better placed. He smiled
sourly at the thought.

He looked across at Neva, and she was smiling. Maybe
she guessed his thoughts. That smile could have been mocking or in sympathy, and he hoped it was the latter.

He crossed the car and sat down beside her. "Rough trip,
Neva." He knew he would never be the master of light talk,
either.

"Yes," she sighed. "I'll be glad when it's over."

He wouldn't be. As long as the trip lasted he would be
thrown in close proximity to her. Her father didn't think

much of him. Neal Moran had the same opinion of him that so many other men had. Despite his size, Cass was a timorous man.

He stole glances at her profile. She was graceful when she was still and graceful when she moved. She was six years younger, and he had always been dumbstruck in her presence. Her startling blue eyes had a fathomless mystery that he would have been willing to explore for the rest of his life. She was only eighteen, but already she was a woman in all ways. For a while he had imagined that she returned his interest, then he had realized that he was only fooling himself.

He knew a deep sorrow when he realized how clumsy and inept he must appear to her.

He wanted to catch her attention, and a brilliant thought occurred to him. "Neva, how do you manage to keep so fresh?"

She made a small grimace. "I'm not. It's the perfume you smell. Women have that advantage over men."

"Maybe we should use it, too," he said, and grinned.

She laughed, then broke it off, and her nose twitched. "There's that awful smell again."

For an instant, he was afraid it was him, then he identified it. That wasn't hard; he had smelled it before: Ben Andrews had tongue in this car again.

She started to rise. "I can't stand that any longer."

He caught her wrist. "I'll do something about it, Neva."

He stood, and the old promise picked at him again. But there was no reason for violence to spring out of this; not if he kept his temper.

He approached the Andrewses at the far end of the car. Ben and Bess Andrews were a fat couple. They had fat people's joviality and weren't too clean. A man kept a high wall between himself and the Andrewses, or they absorbed him.

This train was made up of people of the same ilk; the

shiftless, the hard-luck ones, the beaten people. All of them were running from one piece of land to another, fooling themselves by believing they would find better luck at the end of this ride. It worried Cass to think that he was one of the same breed—but with one small difference. He wasn't leaving any land. When his father had died, the farm had gone to the older brother, and that was as it should be. Cass had received a small cash inheritance. He could have stayed in Ohio, but it would have been as his brother's hired hand. He didn't have enough money to buy another piece of land. He had jumped at the railroad's offer of land in California. There were many things he didn't like about it, but a man couldn't tailor-make everything that came his way. Deep down, he admitted the real reason. Neva's father had wanted California land, and Cass had come along to be as near to her as he could be; at least, until he had permanently lost her.

He stopped before the Andrews couple, balancing himself against the lurching of the car. He didn't want to do this, but a man's right shouldn't be big enough to forgive spoiled tongue. Tongue was either cheap, or Andrews' favorite food. This had happened in Nebraska and again in Nevada. Tongue turned bad in a few hours of heat, and its stink could be unbearable.

Bess Andrews fawned on him, and Cass gave her a pained smile. Andrews stared out the window, and Cass touched him on the shoulder. At the same time, he saw the food box under the bench.

"Have you got tongue in there again?"

"I told him to throw it out last night," Bess Andrews said.

Cass never liked this kind of woman. She would do anything, even turning against her husband, to get attention.

Cass stooped and dragged out the box.

Andrews grabbed Cass's wrist as he straightened. "Here now. That's my property. A man's got a right . . ."

The words faltered before Cass's eyes, and Andrews let go of his wrist. Cass took out the tongue, and this close to his nose the stench was nauseating. "Your right doesn't include spoiled tongue." He pitched it out of the window. "If you want to buy tongue, eat it. Don't try to store it up."

Andrews met Cass's stare. Which way this went depended upon the depth of Andrews' truculence, but then, he didn't know Cass's reputation.

Cass's size overawed him. "All right," he said sullenly.

Cass thought, he doesn't know if he pushes, I'd back up. He nodded to Bess Andrews and moved back to Neva. Could that be approval in her eyes?

"I guess he looked at you, Cass, and decided it was smart to let it go."

"Maybe," he said moodily. He tried never to intimidate another man with his size. "I didn't wave a fist in his face."

"You didn't have to. He was there, too, when the engine went off the track. He saw you help pry it back on."

Cass frowned. Maybe some of the passengers gave him most of the credit for that, but he denied it. "Damn it, Neva, there was twenty of us prying at that engine." The seventeen-ton engine had jumped the track in Nebraska. The derailment wasn't bad enough to warrant calling out the wrecker. A nearby fence had been stripped of posts which they used to lever the engine back onto the track. Cass wasn't waving his part in the incident around.

"What would you have done if he hadn't let you throw the tongue out the window?" Neva asked softly.

He gave her a pained smile. "I dunno, Neva." He wished he knew what thoughts were behind her eyes. Would it have made any difference if he had told her about the fight with Jim? Maybe she wouldn't even be able to understand the promise he had made his father.

He started to say something more to her, but her eyes were fastened on the far end of the car. He turned his head, and that numb sickness hit him again. It always did when he saw Quincy Ridgeway.

The man was tall and lean. He came down the car, balancing effortlessly against its lurching. He paused to exchange a word with the Andrewses, and Cass saw how eagerly they answered him. Oh, the man had charm, all right. Beside him, Cass looked like a huge, misshapen clod. Ridgeway's clothes were good, and he wore them with flair. His blond hair was thick and wavy, and he carried his head high. Either for people to see his hair, or to show off the clean cut of his chin, Cass thought sourly. How many times had he wanted to wipe off that smirk on Ridgeway's face! He had never given in to his wish, but it hadn't done him any good; he had lost Neva.

Ridgeway worked for the railroad, though Cass didn't exactly know what his job was. Maybe he was on this train to herd the passengers to California, or maybe he had taken it solely because of Neva.

Ridgeway stopped before them. "Neva, I had hoped to find you alone."

He hadn't spoken or even nodded to Cass, and it put a dull flush in Cass's face. If he could only break the promise he had made to his father, for only the few seconds it would take to cut Ridgeway down!

"Cass was just leaving," Neva said brightly.

Cass was sure that was contempt in her eyes. "Why yes, I was," he mumbled. He got up and didn't look back until he reached the end of the car. They were in animated conversation, and he had never seen her eyes sparkle more.

There it is, he thought dully, and stepped into the vestibule between the cars. He was a damned fool to have ever thought of coming to California. He had been a glutton for punishment, but he would correct that. He would catch the next train back.

The train was pulling to a stop, and Cass indifferently

looked out. This was a sorry excuse for a town. A sad, small building that might be called a station and a water tank were beside the rails. Behind them was a dreary-looking house, stripped of paint by the sand-laden winds. The train had stopped to take on water, and Cass had seen these jerkwater towns before. Up ahead, the water spout was being put in place, then somebody would jerk on a rope, releasing the water. The train would be here only long enough to fill its boilers.

"Excuse me." There was impatience in the voice.

Cass had heard this man called Waverly. He had a furtive expression on his ferret face that only heightened the air of sharpness about him. Cass had seen him in several card games, and yesterday Neal Moran had been involved in one. He had wanted to warn Neva's father that Waverly was a professional gambler, but he had held it.

"Sure," he said, and stepped aside. He wondered idly what Waverly wanted to get off here for. He watched Waverly until he disappeared into the depot, then moved on into the next car. He had no aim; he only wanted to put distance between him and the couple behind him.

By the time he had walked through the next two cars, the train was moving again. He saw Neal Moran in the next car. At first he thought that Moran was playing solitaire. He had a deck of cards before him on a makeshift table. Then he realized that Moran was waiting for somebody. Moran's frown increased as he looked beyond Cass to the door of the car.

Moran was a small man with a quick, explosive temper. It was odd to look at him and think that Neva was his daughter. Surely she had gotten her beauty from her mother, and Cass wished her mother hadn't died before he had known her. An old thought came back into his head. Would Neva's mother have accepted him with more approval than Moran showed?

He stopped before Moran and asked, "Are you waiting for somebody, Neal?"

Moran gave him a contemptuous flick of his eyes. "Any of your business?"

"Why, no," Cass said, and swallowed hard. He knew Moran's opinion of him. Moran had seen Cass back away from incipient trouble. That wasn't Moran's way at all. He bragged he had never taken a backward step regardless of the size or odds he faced. How many times had Cass heard him say that if a man wouldn't fight, he wasn't worth his salt?

Cass had no desire to make things easier for Moran. "If you're looking for Waverly, he got off at the last stop."

The agitation in Moran's face puzzled him for a moment, then he put it all together. Moran was an inveterate gambler, and Neva was always scolding him for it. Oh, damn, Cass thought. He'd gotten tied up with Waverly.

Moran's eyes turned wild. "You're crazy. He said he'd be back."

Cass knew distress for Neva; none for Moran. "He won't."

Moran read the truth in Cass's face. Profanity dripped from his lips, despite the fact that women were within earshot. He broke off and muttered, "He promised to come back and let me get even. My string of bad luck was beginning to wear out. Why would he want to get off?"

Cass didn't feel like sparing Moran. "How much are you behind?"

"Two hundred dollars," Moran said unwillingly.

"That's your answer as to why he got off. He'll wait for another train, going in either direction. He won't care. That's his business—riding these trains until he finds another pigeon like you."

Moran stared at him with rage-widened eyes. "I'll prove he's still on this train."

He jumped to his feet and rushed down the car, and Cass reluctantly followed him. He had to calm him down before Neva heard about this.

He followed Moran through two cars, and Moran's stubbornness was showing. He wouldn't believe Cass until he searched every car.

The conductor blocked his way in the next car. The brakeman was behind him, a burly man with a massive head set on a short neck. His face was red and coarse-featured, and his eyes held a hungry shine. The shine said he remembered the derailed engine and Cass's display of strength. Physical prowess meant everything to this man. He wouldn't be happy until he tested his own against Cass's.

The conductor scowled at Moran. "What are you storming through the cars for?"

"Where's Waverly?" Moran shouted.

"You won't find him." Both the conductor and the brakeman were enjoying Moran's rage. "He got off at the last stop."

It left Moran speechless, but Cass had something to say. "Did you give him protection while he worked the train? How much was your split?" The sharpening of the conductor's eyes told Cass how close he had hit to the truth.

The brakie's words confirmed it. "Mister, you've got a fat mouth."

The conductor flung out an arm. "Easy, Mike." His eyes never left Cass's face. "If you think you have a complaint, make it at the division office in Sacramento. You'll have enough time. We change engines there." He shoved brusquely past Cass. "Come on, Mike," he said over his shoulder.

Moran trembled with rage. "By God, I'll make that complaint," he shouted after him. "Don't think I won't." His face was pleading as he turned toward Cass. "Cass, do you think the railroad had a hand in this?"

This was the first time Moran had ever asked his opinion on anything. Cass nodded. "At least the conductor, and maybe the brakeman. But I'm accusing the railroad of a lot more than that."

Moran's eyes rounded. He was listening for the first time.

"You think the railroad could be planning to cheat us out of our land?"

"There's something damned funny about it. We paid no money for that land. We're planning on moving onto it before patents are even issued. The railroad says its promise that the land is ours is all we need. It claims it'll fix a price later. What about the improvements we make on that land? Will our improvements jack up the price when we finally go to settle up? I wouldn't put it past them. Look how the railroad handles us; like animals. It takes our fares and gives us nothing in writing. Letting Waverly operate is only a small indication of what the railroad thinks of us."

Moran's eyes were dazed. He had never let Cass point out these things before, and they came too fast for him. "I can do somethin_ bout Waverly. Cass, will you come with me when I make my complaint? You're a witness. You saw everything."

Cass wanted to refuse him, but this was Neva's father. "All right, Neal. But I wouldn't let Neva know anything of this."

"Lord, no," Moran said fervently.

Cass stayed by himself the remainder of the trip to Sacramento. He was an open man, and he was afraid his face would mirror his thoughts. Neva had a way of dragging the truth out of him. If it all came out, he would be caught in the middle between her and Neal.

Moran was the first off the train when it stopped before the wooden station at the foot of K Street. Cass's steps dragged as he followed him.

A ticket counter filled one end of the room. A potbellied stove was in the center of the room, and the walls were lined with hard, uninviting-looking benches. A stoop-shouldered man with a sour face was behind a counter. He wore a green eyeshade and black sleeve protectors. His face turned flinty as though he sensed trouble in Moran and Cass.

"Ask for somebody bigger than him," Cass said in a low voice.

Moran nodded, and his jaw jutted. "No damned clerk is going to block me."

Cass felt a premonition of trouble. He sighed. He guessed he had felt it ever since this started.

"I've got a complaint," Moran said to the clerk. "I want to see the head man."

The clerk sniffed. "Fill out this form."

Moran's eyes ran over the paper. "What happens to it after I fill it out?"

"That ain't your business, mister. Don't bother me anymore."

He started to turn away, and Moran reached across the counter and grabbed him. He hauled him up against the counter, ripping the man's shirt in the process.

"Don't turn your back on me," Moran said hotly. "What did you intend to do with it? Throw it in a wastebasket? I told you to call the head man."

The clerk gulped. The big man was with Moran, and he appraised Cass's size. But suddenly his frightened look disappeared. "Take your hands off me."

The clerk had seen something to change his attitude, and Cass turned. The brakie, the conductor, and Ridgeway were coming through the doorway. The station was filled with passengers, and it wasn't the place Cass would have picked for a fight. He was only glad that Neva wasn't here.

He read the eagerness in Mike's eyes right. The man only wanted the smallest springboard to get into this.

Ridgeway's eyes swept over Moran and Cass, and he asked the clerk, "What's the trouble, Jason?"

"They came in looking for trouble, Mr. Ridgeway. They said something about a complaint, then refused to go through the ordinary channels. This one"—he indicated Moran—"ripped my shirt. The other one was ready to back him up."

"There must be some misunderstanding, Neal," Ridgeway said easily. "Tell me about it."

"I will not," Moran said stubbornly. "I'm going to talk to somebody bigger than you."

Ridgeway's face flushed. "This is no place to start a row," he said curtly. "If you'll walk outside with me—"

"I will not," Moran said hotly.

Mike stepped forward, and his eyes had a burning eagerness. "I'll take him out for you, Mr. Ridgeway."

He grabbed Moran's arm and yanked on it.

Cass blew out a long breath. I'm sorry, Paw, he thought. "Let go of him," he said softly.

"Why, you damned fool," Mike swore. He let go of Moran's arm and swung at Cass.

Cass ducked, and the fist grazed his ear. It must have torn some skin, for he felt a stinging there. He wrapped both arms around the man, and his power showed in the reddish purpling of Mike's face.

He started walking him toward the door, and Ridgeway's cheekbones sharpened under the honing of anger. "Take your hands off him. Jason, Wynn, help me with this."

Cass looked at him. "Keep them out of this," he warned.

Ridgeway swung a blow that Cass couldn't duck, for his hands were filled with the struggling brakie. It landed flush on the side of his face and filled his head with a roaring and watered his eyes.

"Let's take all of them, Cass," Moran said with delight.

It might be what Moran wanted, but it wasn't Cass's choosing. But no man hit him full in the face like that. I tried, Paw, he thought. He shoved Mike from him with enough force to send him spinning across the room. A bench hit him at the back of the knees, and he fell over it.

Cass looked around to locate Moran, and Moran wasn't going to be in this fight long. Jason clubbed him with something he picked off the counter, and Morgan slowly sagged, a stupid look on his face.

Cass bellowed, picked up the clerk, and hurled him half-way across the room. Benches piled up under Jason, and his weight split and broke one of them.

A woman screamed, and people scurried toward the door, trying to get out of this madhouse.

Cass had momentarily forgotten about Mike, and the man was on his feet and took Cass from the rear. At the same time, Ridgeway hit him from the side.

That put renewed vigor in the pounding of the drums in Cass's head. The combined blows were enough to put him down, and Mike aimed a kick at his head. The boot sole scraped along Cass's cheek, tearing skin and drawing blood. He had not even the memory of a promise holding him now; he only wanted to hurt the men who had hurt him.

He clambered to his feet and dove into Mike, his shoulder hitting him in the stomach. The impact tore a great puff of air from Mike. Cass drove him to the floor and scrambled to a sitting position atop him. He took another blow from Ridgeway and paid no attention to it. He wouldn't until he took care of Mike. He slammed a fist into his face, then another. He started to hit him the third time and realized it wasn't necessary. Mike was unconscious.

Cass heaved himself to his feet, and Ridgeway hit him again before Cass made it. He felt something wet and sticky stealing down his face and supposed it was blood. He advanced toward Ridgeway and the conductor, his hands balled.

Ridgeway and the conductor retreated before him, and there was obvious alarm in Ridgeway's eyes. Evidently those two didn't think two-to-one odds were enough. Cass was sorry Neva had her eyes on Ridgeway, but Ridgeway had asked for what he had coming.

Three more men poured through the door, and by the authoritative way Ridgeway pointed at him, he would guess they were railroad men. That made it tougher, but even that couldn't stop him. Five men fanned out as they cautiously advanced on him. Cass picked up a bench and swung it like a flail. He should be allowed that to equalize the odds a little. One of his swings knocked down the stove, and it made a satisfying clatter.

He saw the consternation spread across their faces and said mockingly, "Come on. Isn't this what you wanted?"

He didn't see the man wearing a badge slip through the rear door. He didn't see the gun barrel rise and descend. He only felt a crashing weight against his head, and for an instant, he couldn't see against the blinding red wave. Then blackness swept quickly in behind the red, and his legs would no longer support him.

Justice moved swiftly in this town. The marshal came for Cass and Moran before Cass had fully gotten his normal head back.

Cass speculatively eyed him. "You the one who hit me?" At the marshal's nod he said, "You don't take much chance, do you?"

"I never do with somebody your size," the marshal said dryly. "The judge wants to see you two."

Moran's head must have ached, too, for a groan escaped him as he stood. "Neva will sure know about it," he said.

That couldn't be avoided. Cass had ought to be mad at him; Moran had dragged him into this. You weren't too hard to drag, he told himself. Maybe he had hoped to earn some credit in Moran's eyes that would be transferred to Neva. But none of it mattered now. He was going back just as soon as he could grab the next train east.

The courtroom was filled with curious spectators, and the lawyer for the railroad wouldn't let Cass talk. The judge listened to the lawyer, then put his angry eyes on Cass and Moran. "You people have to learn that you can't come out here and assault people and destroy property."

Cass took a slow breath. "You listen to only the railroad's side, Judge?"

The judge's face purpled. "That will cost you one hundred dollars fine and one hundred dollars for the damage."

Cass caught Moran's arm and checked his outburst. He imagined that his own had already cost them.

"We'll pay, Neal," he said.

It hurt to dig into his pockets for that sum. Moran breathed hard as he laid his money beside Cass's.

Cass turned toward the door, and Neva stood there. Moran had no more reason to worry about her knowing. She had heard it all.

"Oh, Jesus," Moran moaned. "What will I say to her?"

"Just what happened," Cass said.

He took her arm and pulled her outside. He thought she had the same weighing expression that the judge had, but he couldn't understand her eyes. If that was mirth in them, it didn't fit at all.

"Neva," he said awkwardly. He had advised Moran to tell her right out what had happened, but he found that hard to do.

"I'll tell her, Cass," Moran said. He looked at his daughter and gulped. "I got in with a card sharp on the train, and he fleeced me. Cass accused the conductor of being in cahoots with the gambler, and by the conductor's look Cass was right. The conductor brushed us off by telling me to fill out a complaint when we got to Sacramento. I tried to . . ." He made a helpless gesture and stopped.

"Yes," she said. There was no giving in the word, and Cass took it up.

"I was forced into . . ."

"Forced into what?"

Cass groaned inwardly. She was completely unforgiving. "The fight, I guess."

"I started it, Neva," Moran said quickly.

"And you dragged Cass into it."

"I guess I did," Moran muttered.

"He didn't," Cass protested. "Neal didn't have much chance against that many. I had to protect him, didn't I?"

Why was he trying to make her understand? He wasn't going to be around her much longer. "If it's any consolation to you," he said bitterly, "I didn't get much of a chance at your Ridgeway. He kept backing up."

Moran's eyes gleamed with a happy memory. "I didn't see it all. But I was told he was doing all right until that marshal clobbered him from behind."

"It looks as though both of you were wrong," Neva said acidly.

Cass stared at her in astonishment. Now he was the one who didn't understand at all.

"You were wrong, Father, when you said Cass wouldn't fight. You told me he wasn't the man to protect a woman, if she needed it."

Moran flushed. "I didn't know what I was talking about."

She whirled to face Cass. "And you were wrong, too. Quincy was never 'my man,' as you called him."

"But I thought . . . I—"

Neva nodded vigorously. "That's what I wanted you to think, Cass. Though I was beginning to believe that Father might be right. Quincy was a boring man. He thought he was doing me a favor to pay attention to me."

Hope dawned in Cass's eyes. "You mean . . . You . . ." He still couldn't get an entire sentence out.

She met his eyes squarely. "That depends on you. Though I'm not forgiving you for getting in that disgraceful brawl." She turned to her father. "Nor you, for gambling and starting it."

Cass held out his arms. "Neva," he said.

Her face turned a rosy red, but she came into his arms. "You've always been such a thick-headed man, Cass."

He held her close for a long moment, and some of the assurance was flowing back. "You gave me every reason to think like that."

She pulled back enough so that she could see his face, and now he was sure there was laughter in her eyes. "If jealousy doesn't bring out what's in a man, nothing will. Do you still want to leave?"

"We can't let him go," Moran said, and his words were

positive. "What if we run into more trouble? We need him around."

"He hasn't answered yet," Neva said, and the challenge was big in her eyes.

He pulled her back against him, and his laugh was joyous. "What do you think?"

Jeffrey M. Wallmann has published numerous Western novels and short stories over the past fifteen years, among them a pair of recent comedy adventures featuring a gang of aging desperadoes, Return to Canta Lupe *and* The Celluloid Kid, *in collaboration with Thomas L. Jeier. "The Phantom Train Robbers," a Western tall tale, is in the same wryly amusing vein.*

The Phantom Train Robbers

Jeffrey M. Wallmann

*E*ver since it happened, back in the spring of '87, the residents of Altingham always liked to consider they had an unsolved mystery on their hands. Altingham, a fly-speck on the map, where, before radio and television, entertainment was mostly sitting around the clapboard depot watching the daily train go by. So you really can't blame the locals for having gotten into a flap of stories when old No. 732 came busting through the town.

It came like a screaming devil, without baggage-and-mail car, without its couple of coaches; just that ancient 4-4-0 American locomotive and tender, belching smoke and cinder. It thundered open-throttle down the tracks which bisected Front Street, missed the curve at its end, and sailed through Hoskin's Emporium. Slaughtered an unsuspecting cow out back, but luckily nobody was injured—unless you count Butch Mulligan, who broke his arm diving into a horse trough.

That night, the rest of the train was located far on the other side of Pearl River. The mail clerk had been shot dead, one of the passengers had been wounded, and everybody had been picked clean of their money and valuables.

Eighteen thousand dollars had been stolen from the safe in the baggage-and-mail car. Some of the story got pieced together then. It seems that a couple of masked men captured the train as it was stopped for water, then escaped in the locomotive after uncoupling the cars.

A posse was immediately formed, and word was telegraphed to neighboring towns. When two horses were found tethered near the tracks on the Altingham side of the Pearl River flats, the sheriff figured he had the robbers and murderers for sure. The animals were obviously part of the escape plan, and since they were still there, that had to mean the men were on foot.

The two thieves never showed up, despite the searches.

Still, capture seemed certain. The eighteen thousand dollars happened to be a special shipment in which the bills were consecutively ordered. Soon as any of the money was spent, it could be traced, and to this day, in some of the backwood banks fortunate to have weathered the Depression, you can find yellowed, flaking circulars with the list of missing serial numbers.

Yet not a trace of the money was ever recovered. The masked outlaws made such a perfect getaway that it was hard to believe they were human. Even after the construction of a new bridge over the Pearl, lots of folks ignored the facts and continued to talk of swamp ghosts and will-o'-the-wisps. Not that they believed in those things; it was merely more fun that way, with an unsolved mystery to pass the time jawing about.

But the truth of the matter ran something like this:

The winter of '87 had been a boggler, and Pearl River had flooded the flats worse than usual. The railroad bed ran across the flats on a sort of stone and dirt levee, and in a few places the water had actually lapped over the top. But by late March, the Pearl had pretty well receded to its banks, the dogwood was out, and clover, columbine, and scarlet gilia were flowering wherever it wasn't too muddy.

In the granite hills to the east, two men in their twenties were sitting on a stack of ties beside the tracks. The moss-covered water tank nearby was dripping lazily, the drone of flies was thick, and both men seemed to be nodding, half asleep. Most motion came from the younger one, Roy McBain, who chewed on a dandelion stem.

Roy McBain had thick, dark curly hair and a likable face, but he was one mean bastard at heart. Tad Kluette, on the other hand, always wore a filthy black felt slouch hat to hide his premature baldness, and he looked far nastier than he actually was. You had the feeling facing him that he'd do exactly what he was threatening. You wouldn't often be wrong, either.

The warm afternoon air was split by the echoing shrillness of a train whistle. Kluette jerked upright, turning in the direction of the sound. "She's coming," he said tightly. "732's coming."

"She's going to stop, too," McBain added, spitting out the stem. "One whistle means 'down brakes.' "

Both men moved to hunker behind the ties, slipping bandannas up over their noses and drawing their Colts. Some moments passed, and then the train came into view, the old locomotive panting from climbing Sweeney's Grade. Steam hissed from the cylinders and sparks ground from the locking brake shoes as the ponderous engine slowly halted beneath the pipe of the water tank.

The robbers waited for the boilers to be filled. Then they stepped out, Colts cocked. Kluette headed for the last of the day coaches, while McBain covered the engine and mail car.

Two men against the engineer, fireman, switchman, conductor, brakeman, and almost a dozen passengers, not to mention the mail clerk holed up in his car. But McBain and Kluette were pros, the element of surprise was on their side, and the others weren't killers, much less fighters.

After one man tried to draw a derringer and got winged for his trouble by Kluette, the threat of reprisal in case of trouble was believed, and the robbery went without a hitch.

The clerk, after he'd unlocked the safe, was herded with the rest of the crew and passengers alongside the ties, where they could be watched as a group. McBain, on board the locomotive, had the engineer show him the rudiments of running it, and then, kicking the engineer off, he called out to Kluette.

"Okay. All the sacks here?"

"Yeah," Kluette answered. "All in the cab. Looks like we lucked into a real haul, don't it?"

"Come on, then. Steam's up, and all that's left is to uncouple the cars. I'll cover them while you do that."

Kluette jumped up on the rear platform of the tender. He dropped to his knees and began digging at the pin-coupler which joined the mail-and-baggage car. McBain, careless with a sense of success, turned his head to glance at the gauges.

That was a mistake, for the mail clerk drew a Colt 'Lightning' .38 hideout pistol from his pocket and began firing. There was a whole lot of screaming and falling for cover, but the clerk, too full of his own bravado to aim straight, stood his ground and peppered the tender around Kluette with two of his six shots.

"What the hell?" Kluette bellowed, a bullet humming past his boot. He clawed for his revolver, hearing his partner curse vehemently from the cab and then the roar of McBain's Frontier.

"Get that pin out, Kluette!" McBain yelled over the smoke and fire. "I'll take care of the squirrel!"

The clerk began answering McBain with shots, and a couple of lead pellets spanged through the cab, ricochetting off the steel-plated sides. McBain ducked and danced, afraid more of the ricochets drilling him than of the clerk's aim. He fired back haphazardly.

Kluette worked on the pin frantically, knowing he was without cover where he crouched, and finally managed to free the couplers. He pivoted and rolled across the coal into the cab as the clerk's fifth shot plucked at the crown of his hat.

"What took you so long?" McBain snapped.

"Never mind," Kluette snarled back. "I thought you were to shoot that fool, Dead-eye. You goin' blind on me?"

"He's been blessed, I swan," McBain retorted, and shot again. "Release the brakes and pull the throttle open. Yeah, and then notch up the reverse bar."

Kluette moved to the controls, and the locomotive began to edge forward, chuffing loudly, wheels spinning with the sudden surge of steam. He kicked a sack of loot aside and leaned into the throttle; the engine shuddered and pulled farther away from the string of cars.

The clerk snapped off his final shot, and with the luck of innocents, his aim was true. The bullet burrowed into the control hinge of the throttle not more than two inches from Kluette's hand. Kluette sprang backward with a howl of surprise.

McBain braced himself against the lurching cab and fired at the clerk, who was dumbly standing there, trying to reload. He saw the clerk drop the revolver and clutch his midsection, toppling forward like a folded bag of feed. "Got him!" McBain cried, and turned to his partner, who'd begun to stoke.

Kluette glared at McBain as he threw another shovel-load of coal into the firebox. "Looks like I got to do all the work."

"But—" McBain frowned, looking around confusedly. The engine was roaring full-tilt now, and the rails were flowing, the countryside becoming a mere blur of greens and browns. "But why aren't you at the throttle?"

"Why? She's moving, ain't she? Here, you shovel awhile."

"No, I mean that there throttle's a dead-man control. You let loose of it, and the train's supposed to stop."

"Well, it ain't. We're going faster all the time!"

McBain brushed past Kluette and inspected the lever. "Oh, Lord," he groaned, "that fool clerk did it to us good. His bullet jammed it open, and it can't be pulled back. We're on a runaway!"

Kluette leaned on the shovel handle, his face green. "Do something else, then! The engine driver told you all about it!"

"Not that much! I start tinkering and likely as not, I blow us up!" McBain looked out through the windscreen, swallowing thickly. They were speeding erratically down the long grade which led to Pearl River, and the wind howled past his ears. "We're going to have to jump," he said, turning back. "We're going to have to jump!"

"At this rate? We'll be mashed! We must be doing thirty!"

"Twenty-five at least," McBain said sickly. "Got no choice, far as I can tell. We'll have to chance it."

"Not here, not against the trees, we don't. What about the flats?" Kluette was trying to keep his footing like a sailor on a storm-tossed ship's deck. "Ground ain't got so many rocks there, either. We can roll some!"

"But we'll miss the horses!"

"Blast the horses! The land's worse there than it is here!"

"Yeah, you're right," McBain agreed ruefully. "We'll hit the flats and run for 'em. Help me move the sacks; we'll get them ready to take soon's we cross the bridge!"

Straining, lurching, cursing their fate, the two gunmen hauled their take, which they'd stored in U.S. mail bags, to the back of the cab. McBain peered out again and saw the beginning of the bridge dead ahead. "Hold on!" he called over his shoulder.

The engine shivered even more violently as it struck the shaky structure of the spidery wood supports. The hollow sound of its wheels was like a mocking laugh through them, and both men avoided looking down at the sluggish water meandering below. Then came the mucky banks, and without a word, McBain and Kluette stepped to the side guard, each with sacks in hand. The engine swept onto the firmer levee, spewing smoke from its overheating boiler fires. One of the gauge needles moved over to the red, and there was the ominous sound of escaping steam somewhere.

"Now or never!" McBain yelled, jumping clear.

"See you in hell!" Kluette called, and then he leaped.

McBain hit the edge of the levee with his knees, pitched forward, and tumbled down the slant to the flats. Kluette had thrown himself harder, and he landed in the gumbo straight-on. Dazed, Kluette removed his mud-spattered bandanna and threw it from him so he could breathe. Something felt wrong to him; he knew something was wrong. But for an instant he couldn't tell exactly what. He groped for his felt hat, and then heard McBain cry out to him.

"Tad! Tad! I can't move!"

Still dizzy, Kluette said, "What's the matter? Leg broken?"

"No! No! I'm stuck in this mud! And I—I'm sinking!"

Kluette looked at his partner with startled eyes. McBain was up to his legs in the thick, swamplike mud, struggling futilely to lift himself free. There was stark terror in the younger man's expression as he swung his arms and jerked from side to side. Kluette leaned forward to help—and then found that he, too, was imprisoned. Now, with his senses returning, he experienced the dreaded sensation of slowly descending. "No," he choked. *"No!"*

"Tad! Help me! Help me!"

"I can't, Roy! We jumped too close to the river edge, and the floods, they—" He glanced down as the dark brown mud oozed around his belt buckle. "The ground hasn't dried enough—"

"Tad! For God's sake, what are we in?"

"Don't you know? Can't you tell?" Already Kluette could see the mud around McBain's stomach, and his own belly was cold and clammy from the seepage. "It happens after floods in flats like this. It's like quicksand, only worse! It's quickmud, Roy, *quickmud*!"

In less than half an hour, there was no trace of either man. They hadn't exactly made a getaway, but, then, you might say they'd pulled the perfect disappearance.

Nearly three decades later, the Southern Pacific replaced the old bridge across the Pearl with one made of steel. They drained the marshy delta, and their work crew ripped open the earth for new pilings. Bones came up like white roots, and a few of the old hands remembered back to the spring of '87. But most, not being scientists, figured they were only parts of stray animals, and those that didn't—

Well, that would have been the end to a good story, right?

Hell on the High Iron

John Jakes

The land had a familiar rolling quality about it. Rome
rode westward in the early dawn, a big, stocky man in his
early thirties. He followed the movements of his horse easily, his clear gray eyes sweeping over the vast prairies.
Those eyes suggested a quick mind, and his whole bearing
said that he knew his mind could often help him just as much
as the pistol strapped to his right hip.

It was a sort of homecoming. He followed the tracks, two
bands of iron stretching ahead of him. The business was
well taken care of, the morning air had a cool crispness, and
he was in high spirits. The sun glinting from the rails
seemed to symbolize the future, alive with pleasant prospects.

His mood changed abruptly around noon when he rode
into the end-of-track of the Kansas & Western. The place
had an air of idleness. Here and there, groups of section

hands sat near piles of ties, drinking coffee and playing cards. He heard no clang of hammers on spikes, no curses of men sweating under the sun. Work had stopped. The rails no longer crept inevitably toward the Rockies.

As troubleshooter it would be his job to iron out whatever was slowing up the work. His mind moved rapidly over the possible causes as he dismounted and tied his horse to the platform rail of the office car. He took the steps two at a time and slammed the door behind him.

Ben Hamilton, the wiry, white-haired head of the Kansas & Western, sat behind his desk, staring at Rome over the top of a coffeepot. His eyes were red with sleeplessness. Rome waited for him to speak, sensing defeat in the slump of Hamilton's shoulders.

At last the older man sighed. He switched his gaze to the coffeepot and poured himself another cup. "Hello, Mark. You want some coffee? It's cold . . ."

"No, thanks," Rome answered. He swung his leg across a chair before the desk, resting his arms on the back.

"You don't look very good, Ben."

Hamilton laughed in a cracked tone and gulped some of the coffee. "I guess not, Mark. How's things in Saint Louis?"

Rome gestured. "All cleared up. The hitch was coming from back East. We'll be getting rails and spikes to spare in a couple of days."

"Don't know as it'll do us much good," Hamilton commented sourly.

"Ben, you might as well spill it. It's my job."

The older man sighed again. "All right, dammit. It's simple enough. We're stopped. Turns out we don't have the right of way we need through three of the spreads. The owners refuse to sell. So we can't meet our contract. It'll mean an extra week if we decide that we will bypass Warknife."

Rome sat up abruptly. "Warknife!" He hadn't realized they were that close.

"Yeah. You know the town?"

Rome nodded. "I was born there. Lived there until I was eighteen, before I went East."

"Fine." Hamilton's tone was sarcastic. "You must have a lot of friends there. One hell of a lot of good that'll do us."

Friends. The word stung Rome. More than friends. Cathy Thompson. He remembered her, painfully. Remembered how much he'd been in love with her, how many times they had ridden together, hunted together—and laughed at the antics of the young calves together.

Rome knew then it wouldn't work. The cattle were in her blood. They were her life and her heritage. She could only see cattlemen, and no one else. For him there had been another call, from the East, from the world where the iron horse was beginning to move and bellow as it cut the continent in half. Since that morning, years ago, when he saw locomotives standing on the wharf of Saint Louis, the railroad had captured him.

Sitting before Hamilton in the shadowy car as the older man stared at him, Rome thought about each of the two dreams. The iron horse. He had caught that excitement as a small boy and never lost it. Then came Cathy, when he was older. The two couldn't live side by side, not then. The smokestack, the churning pistons, the wheels westward, the whistle-scream . . . the railroad won. He left Warknife and Cathy and went East.

Now he was here again. One dream had been fulfilled, but the other still left its empty ache within him.

"Why all the trouble?" he asked at last. "I thought our buyers had the land contracts sewn up a year ago."

"So did we," Hamilton exclaimed. "Why, dammit, we were set to lay track all the way to the mountains, picking up the contracts as we went along!"

"Didn't the buyers get anything on paper?"

Hamilton shook his head. "They should have. That was where we slipped."

"Everybody slips once in a while," Rome told him. "We've got to correct the slip, that's all."

"Look!" Hamilton exclaimed. Rome realized that the man's nerves were frayed. "We've been trying for the last four days. Somebody's stirred up the three ranchers—most of the town, in fact—and they're dead set against the railroad coming through. Or at least that's the way it stacks up."

"Any particular reason?"

"God knows. A lot of hogwash about too much too quick. I've got a pretty good idea who's behind it. An hombre named Bruce Gashlin. He's got his main office in Warknife." Hamilton paused. "Central Kansas Overland Company."

"Stages, eh?"

"Yeah; and we can't fight 'em, not legally at least. It's all in folks' minds, the way it appears to me. Progress is comin' too fast. The coaches have worked for them well enough for a long time, so why change? A little fast talking here and there, and we're blocked."

"You had any trouble?"

"Not much. Couple of boys got in an argument at the Emporia and got cut up a little, but that's all. But I think this Gashlin has it in him to make serious trouble for us if he wants. He has one boy working for him named Yancey who looks like a real killer."

Rome picked a cigar out of the inlaid box on the top of the desk. He struck a match to it and inhaled the strong smoke. "I've got a pretty good idea of what you want me to do."

"Thought you would."

"I'd like to know the names of the ranchers with the land we need for the right-of-way."

Hamilton pulled out one of the desk drawers, shuffled through a sheaf of papers, and drew one out, laying it on the desk before him. He scanned it a moment. "Harry Drew, Giles McMaster, and Job Thompson."

Once again the knife of memory and regret twisted. Job Thompson . . . Cathy's father, big and powerful and rock-faced, with his voice like velvet thunder. When the children of the Warknife Congregation Sunday School had thought of God, they thought of Job Thompson's voice.

And Cathy . . . The prospect of seeing her again worried Rome. By now she must be married. Any number of younger ranchers with small spreads near Warknife would have found her a fine wife. And a beautiful one at that.

Rome eased himself to his feet and looked straight at Hamilton, trying not to show his tangled emotions. "I'll ride in and see what I can do."

"You're a good talker, a damned good talker. Maybe you can get 'em to change their minds."

"I'll try."

Hamilton jabbed a warning finger at him. "Let me tell you something, Mark. I know you're never anxious to use that gun of yours, but I've met this Gashlin, and, believe me, he's somebody to watch out for. He hates us. And Yancey's nothing but a paid killer. Gashlin's got a bunch of them working for him, but this Yancey's the worst. He hung around Dodge City for a long time, I hear."

"I'll watch out," Rome promised. With a brief farewell wave, he left the office car and swung up into his saddle, moving at a brisk trot out through the end-of-track camp. It still lay quiet under the burning yellow of the noon sun. The sound of a harmonica lifted mournfully from somewhere beyond the cook car.

Outside the camp, Rome kicked his mount to a gallop. Warknife lay less than a half mile away. He felt ashamed that he had forgotten so much of the territory in the years he'd been gone.

Warknife itself hadn't changed greatly. The board fronts were still there, some with new coats of paint, some worn even more from the weather than he remembered. He rode slowly through the main street, noticing the new druggist's shop, the new name posted over the livery stable. A hundred boyhood incidents flooded back: memories of warm summer evenings near the stable, of the excitement of the first rolled cigarette, the first church meeting. His father, his mother . . . They were vague figures; sad-faced people broken by years of work in the general-store business. A man named Hopeman now owned the store, he saw.

No one recognized him. He rode slowly through the main street. People bustled on the sidewalks doing after-dinner shopping. Cattlemen were in the saddle on various errands. The loungers on the front porch of the Emporia Saloon paid no attention to him. He spied the Reverend Paxton, who peered at him from the sidewalk for a minute. Rome stared back impassively. Paxton's eyes took in the gun on his hip, the rawboned body, the determined face. No expression of recognition appeared. Rome felt a little lonely then.

The Circle JT lay three miles on the other side of War-knife to the northwest. Rome caught his breath angrily as he saw that the land would make a perfect right-of-way. Except for a deep cut in the midst of a stretch of uncleared timber that would have to be bridged, construction would be relatively easy.

The yard of the ranch house was empty. Most of the hands, including Thompson himself, would be out on the range. Rome tied his horse and walked across the porch, conscious of the loud sound of his boots. He knocked.

Mrs. Thompson, a stout woman with a retiring manner, came to the door. She stared at him with the gaze she must have reserved for strangers, Rome thought. She made no attempt to recognize him. They had all forgotten . . . .

"Yes, sir, good afternoon," she said, "what can—?" She caught her breath abruptly. "Why, my goodness! Is it . . . Mark Rome? Is it?"

Rome grinned. "Yes, ma'am, it is."

Mrs. Thompson opened the front screen quickly. "My heavens, boy, come in!" She ushered him into the parlor, a musky place smelling of handmade lavender sachets and adorned with the customary motto, *God Bless Our Home,* on the wall. "Sit down, Mark," she said affably. "I'll call Cathy." She raised her voice. "Cathy? Cathy, come see who's here."

Rome turned his hat in his hands. In a moment Cathy appeared from the kitchen. She stared at him, a slender woman with brown hair, frank brown eyes, and a faintly sensual mouth set in an oval face. She was still very good to look at, he thought.

"Mark Rome!" she said, smiling, and Rome felt the inner glow of warmth that always came from seeing that smile. She shook his hand with just a hint of pressure. He saw that she wore no wedding ring.

"When did you come back to Warknife?" she asked.

"Only today. I've been in Saint Louis doing some work for the railroad."

"Railroad?" Mrs. Thompson stiffened perceptibly.

"Yes, ma'am, the Kansas & Western."

Cathy laughed in a forced way. "It always was the railroad, wasn't it, Mark?"

"Yes, I guess it was. I came to see about the trouble over the right-of-way." The moment was broken. The wall had been erected; they were strangers again.

"Dad isn't going to sell," Cathy said evenly. "Bruce Gashlin's stages work well enough. You know that."

"I'd like to talk with Job, if I could," Mark said.

"You'll have to wait for him," Mrs. Thompson told him. "He'll be in about the middle of the afternoon. If you'll excuse me, I'm putting up pickles in the kitchen. Sure was nice to see you again." Her smile carried no feeling.

He and Cathy talked for an hour or so, exchanging news of what they had both been doing in the intervening years. Cathy didn't mention anything of marriage, and Rome avoided the subject. Then they talked of the East, where Cathy had never been.

"Everything's too fast there," she declared. "Always trying something crazy before it's proven."

"There are plenty of railroads in operation," Rome said with a trace of sharpness.

"Plenty of stage lines left, too, I'll bet. They'll never be wiped out, no matter what happens. Dad doesn't like the East. He's been there." The wall between them was growing by the minute.

At about three, Job Thompson rode in, older of course, but his voice still had the quality of majesty. Rome exchanged a brief hello and stated his business.

Thompson thought for a moment. "All right, son. We'll see. We'll call a meeting at the church, and you and Bruce Gashlin can talk it out in front of everybody. I'll make sure Drew and McMaster are there. You haven't got a chance, but we'll give you an opportunity to tell folks in town what you think—so you can see how damned wrong you are. How's tonight?" he finished curtly.

"Tonight'll be fine."

He found himself disliking Job Thompson and respecting him at the same time.

"Make it eight o'clock," the rancher told him.

With an even briefer good-bye than he gave to Thompson, Rome left Cathy and the house and rode out of the Circle JT. Lead-colored clouds were lowering in the north. Even the sky acted unfriendly.

Well, he might be able to get something across at the meeting. He hoped so.

But he did realize that he and Ben Hamilton were entirely alone, strangers in a strange land. The iron horse had become an enemy to a way of life. People were slow to change. Sometimes they never did. And he was losing his contact with the one woman he had ever cared about. Not that there had been much chance of starting things over, though. . . .

As he rode slowly back toward Warknife, his eyes roamed the grasslands. The stalks were dry and brown, sun-parched and tinder-brittle. The gray clouds might bring rain, but until they did the grass was dangerous, like the situation in Warknife. Explosive. There was potential trouble in a man called Gashlin, and another called Yancey from Dodge City. . . .

For once he was thankful for the pistol on his hip.

He tied his horse in front of the Emporia, walked across the porch and in, conscious of the indifference of the loungers. It wouldn't be long, though. Job Thompson had ridden out of the Circle JT behind him. Rome had watched from a distant rise. The word would spread fast.

Feeling the hunger in his belly, he made his way through the gaming tables, past the bar and up the stairs to the mezzanine. It wouldn't look good to be seen downing straight whiskeys when he was to present his point of view at the church that evening.

A tired waiter with a pasted-down mustache sauntered over and took his order for a steak, fried potatoes, and beer. Tired, Rome leaned elbows on the table and fixed himself a cigarette. He was just putting a match to it when someone at his elbow said, "May I sit down, Mr. Rome?"

Rome glanced up, blowing out the match. The stranger was tall, of medium build, and finely dressed with a checked waistcoat. He was about Rome's age, hard-faced and ruddy, with sharp, cold blue eyes. He smiled at Rome, his lips curling faintly as if the whole world was a freakish spectacle that he could control at will. Rome catalogued him as an opportunist.

"Sure, sit down. You seem to know my name. I can't say the same."

"Gashlin, Bruce Gashlin."

News had traveled faster than he'd expected. His eyes moved briefly to the head of the mezzanine stairs. A young kid in dirty denims and sweat-stained shirt was watching him, grinning idiotically. Above the grin were eyes like stone chips. A youngster, Rome thought, taking in the well-worn holsters and pistol butts. That would be Yancey.

Gashlin fixed himself a cigarette with careless precision. "Guess you and I are going to be on opposite sides of the fence tonight," he said as if it didn't really matter.

"I'm going to tell them I think the railroad should come through, and why, if that's what you mean."

"Your buyers didn't have much luck pushing that story."

"That's when I go to work, Mr. Gashlin, when the buyers don't have much luck."

Gashlin nodded. "You know what my business is."

Rome laughed. "Yes, I know."

"I'm not going to give you any line about too much progress. That's for the people I deal with." He waved a hand at the crowded, noisy bar below with its lush nude mural, its rows of bottles. "Frankly, I've got a business to run. My business is essentially the same as that of the Kansas & Western—passengers and freight. It's a good business, and I've worked hard to build it—cutting corners sometimes, I'll admit. I don't want to lose it."

Before Rome could reply, the waiter appeared with the food. When he left, Rome stuck his fork into the steak. "I could figure most of that for myself."

Gashlin shrugged. "Just wanted to let you know what you're up against. I'm not planning to lose the Central Kansas Overland."

Rome stared at him. Gashlin kept his eyes narrowed, not avoiding the scrutiny. "If you can't keep it honestly," Rome asked quietly, "then you'll do it some other way?"

Gashlin nodded. "I reckon so."

"I guess we don't have much more to say." Rome ate a piece of steak and swallowed some cold beer.

Gashlin made no attempt to move. "Now that the formalities are over, I can get down to business. When I heard what Job Thompson planned for tonight, naturally I didn't like it. I'm willing to offer you a thousand dollars to not appear at the church."

"You're wasting your time."

"Twelve hundred is my top offer. It's a lot, but it's worth it to me."

Rome pushed his plate away from him in irritation. "Look, Mr. Gashlin, get something straight. I want to see the railroad come through. It isn't a matter of my business succeeding or failing. I think the railroad will be an improvement. I don't own any stock in the company, and I wouldn't be more than ordinarily sore if they fired me next week, so long as they laid their track when and where they're supposed to. You understand?"

Gashlin stood up abruptly, gesturing with one hand. "Afraid I do, Rome." The youngster sauntered up to the table and stood behind his employer, pushing at the brim of the hat sitting crookedly on his head. "Mr. Yancey, this is Mr. Rome. You might be seeing a lot of each other."

Yancey said nothing. He merely looked at Rome, grinning his foolish smile. But his eyes were angry and hard. Rome shivered inwardly. Yancey was the kind of gun-crazy kid who killed for the sport of it. He would be a good helper for a man like Gashlin.

Anger at Gashlin, the proposed bribe, the whole situation stacked up against the railroad in Warknife suddenly burst to the surface. He jerked a thumb at Yancey.

"Does your hired gunslinger say anything?"

"Once in a while," Gashlin replied. "He's quiet most of the time, except when he's sore."

"Then tell him I'll be watching for him. When he thinks he's old enough to face men, I'll be ready."

Yancey's grin widened even more. Rome knew that the youngster wanted to jerk out his gun and kill him right there. His stomach went cold. He kept his hands rigid on the knife and fork, watching Yancey's fingers moving nervously.

Yancey spoke abruptly, his voice a whine. "It'll be soon, Mr. Rome. Real soon."

"Get the hell out of here, both of you," Rome said.

Gashlin didn't say anything. He moved among the tables, down into the bar and outside, Yancey following behind.

Rome ate the rest of his meal hastily and pushed back his chair. The clock over the bar said twenty to six.

He bought some cigars and sat on the front porch of the Emporia for two hours, listening to the talk around him. There were three main topics of discussion. The first two were almost tied in importance. One was what would be said at the debate at the church, the other was the prospect of rain for the already tinder-dry grasslands. The clouds still hovered, ominously darker as night came on. But they gave no rain.

Rome couldn't tell whether the opinions of the loungers were meaningful since they didn't represent the town's influential element. But the saloon crowd knew what others were talking about.

The third subject was the railroad in general. Most of the loungers thought it might be a pretty good thing. Maybe most of the people would be on his side after all, except McMaster and Drew and, of course, Job Thompson.

At quarter to eight, when the lamps were beginning to glow butter-yellow against the twilight dark, Rome made his way to the church. It was already packed to overflowing. He walked stiffly down the center aisle, looking straight ahead, conscious of the eyes on his back.

Gashlin and Yancey sat in the first pew. Rome sat in the one opposite them. Exactly on the hour, Job Thompson walked up to the platform and told the people why the meeting had been called. He and Drew and McMaster controlled the unsold portion of the right-of-way, and he wanted opinions on the subject of the railroad. His voice rolled out, sonorously rich and powerful, capable of swaying them. But his presentation was fair.

"Our first speaker, representing the railroad, will be one of Warknife's former residents, Mark Rome."

Mark made his way forward amid the whispers of the audience. Many of them, when he turned to face them, peered like bright-eyed birds. Job Thompson, his wife, and Cathy sat stern-faced in the second pew behind Gashlin and Yancey. Behind them in turn were two more families. The Drews and the McMasters, Rome supposed.

He didn't like being first. Gashlin had a better chance for an effective climax. But he would do the best he could. He cleared his throat and began to speak, clearly and with all the sincerity of his convictions.

He told them of the railroad providing faster travel in more comfortable circumstances. He told them of the reduced fares possible on the Kansas & Western because of the larger turnover of freight and passengers. He told them the railroads would eventually link the oceans, whether Warknife liked it or not. That part had to be worded carefully, politely.

And then he told them of the direct shipping of cattle. No more drives to railheads. No more hiring extra hands to make the long and dangerous cross-country journey. Direct shipping. *Direct shipping.* He hammered it home with quiet, forceful tones, then sat down as a ripple of enthusiasm stirred the audience. One rough-garbed cowman started to clap but stopped with a nervous cough.

Thompson showed his partisanship when he introduced Bruce Gashlin more favorably, more glowingly. As the stage-line owner rose to speak, he smiled in an innocently boyish manner, working for audience support. Rome thought, He'll get it, too. He's a showman.

Gashlin's speech was brief. "Friends, you know me, Bruce Gashlin. I run the Central Kansas Overland Company. I don't like the railroads, and you know that, too. They won't last. Things like this, fly-by-night schemes, don't last long. The Central Kansas Overland has done all right working for you, transporting your goods, and I think you appreciate the fact. As for direct cattle shipping, it would mean the ruin of the industry. The drives are one of the most important parts of that industry, and, without them, men who make their living from the range, ordinary hands like many of you once were, would be out of work a good part of the time."

He cleared his throat and smiled at them again. Then he made a pretense of pondering, and frowned. "I don't like to say things like I'm going to say now, but I must. It may help you think this thing through. I can't tell you about the operating methods of the Kansas & Western, but I do know they're afraid of us. A couple of hours ago, Mr. Rome down there talked to me in the Emporia Saloon."

His voice rose. "Mr. Rome offered me five hundred dollars of Kansas & Western money not to appear here tonight. If you want proof, Mr. Yancey was with me."

Rome jumped up, forgetting where he was and started angrily for the platform. "You're a liar!" Hands grabbed at him. "You're a damn liar, Gashlin, and you know—"

The meeting exploded. People pushed out of the pews, milling, shouting. Gashlin moved easily toward a side door, with Yancey following. The youngster's eyes watched the crowd, his hand hovering over his gun.

Job Thompson grabbed Rome's shoulder, thundering accusations. Rome tried to argue back, unsuccessfully. Angry talk, punctuated by denunciations of Rome's language, filled the church. Rome glimpsed a frantic Reverend Paxton standing by the far wall, bewildered by the sacrilege breaking loose.

Rome jerked away from Thompson. He wanted to find Bruce Gashlin, make him admit the lie. He had been warned: every trick available, and a few more Gashlin was probably inventing. He shouldered his way through the crowd. Some of the women struck at him.

He bumped into Cathy Thompson near the door. She stared as if he were a mortal enemy. He took hold of her arm. "Listen a minute, Cathy, I don't want you to think—"

The crowd pushed him away from her, outward, down the steps of the church and onto the plank sidewalk. Job Thompson was following close behind, still shouting questions. The crowd had turned, become a mob manipulated by Gashlin's strategy.

The stage-line owner and his gunman stood at the edge of

the crowd. Rome pushed toward them, fighting his way through. Once he dropped his hand to his hip, making sure his pistol was free.

Job Thompson caught up with him just as Rome reached the other two men. From then on, it happened very quickly, and no one but Rome and Gashlin and Yancey saw what went on. The crowd milled blindly, paying little attention. The four men at the edge of the crowd formed a tight, closed-in band with their gun hands shielded from observation.

Gashlin's eyes widened. Rome felt a quick, terrible sense of the opportunity being instantly seized. Gashlin elbowed Yancey. The youngster reached for his holster.

Rome twisted aside, dodging low and pulling his own gun. He aimed at Yancey's belly as the youngster drew. Just as Rome fired, Gashlin slapped his gun barrel down so that the bullet would plow into the dirt of the street. Yancey's gun roared at the same instant.

The tight group of men stood bunched together. A woman screamed, a high, shrill sound. The noise of the crowd dropped away to silence.

Yancey had already disappeared. Rome whirled, his gun still smoking. Job Thompson was reeling unsteadily, half a foot behind Rome, his eyes closed in pain, his hands clutching the red hole in his belly. Mrs. Thompson and Cathy were pushing through the crowd while Mrs. Thompson screamed hysterically.

Like a great tree, Job Thompson fell forward and smashed face first in the street. A halo of dust rose around his head.

Rome turned to Gashlin, bringing the gun up again, cursing. Gashlin's finger whipped out accusingly.

"Here's your man! I saw him do it. They were arguing— Job didn't even draw. I saw it all."

Rome shoved the gun at Gashlin. A hand jerked it from his fingers. An angry growling rose from him as Gashlin backed cautiously away. The crowd closed in.

Rome whirled once more, realizing what had happened. There was no place to run. They were all around him. The lamp-lit street echoed with their cries for vengeance.

He knew that fighting them was useless. They swarmed around him, raining blows on his face and shoulders. He dodged, to no avail. The angry talk grew louder. Finally one hoarse voice grated above the rest, and Rome knew what was coming.

"Lynch him! *Lynch him!*"

Others repeated the cry. Almost miraculously, the rope appeared. Eager hands darted over it, twisting, coiling, fashioning the death noose. The women crowded on the church steps, watching coldly. Rome had seen two hangings in his time, but now he was caught up in the blood-crazy spell of one. Outside God's house, this mob had become drunk with hatred.

Cathy stood in the middle of the women, stiff and haughty. Rome caught a glimpse of her avenging look. Someone clubbed him on the back of the neck. His knees buckled. Next thing he knew, he was being lifted and set in the saddle. His head spun, full of garish colors and ringing sounds. Then a steady, throbbing pain wiped even his fear away.

Another voice shouted something about the livery stable. Hands seized the reins of the horse. The mob began to move, sluggishly at first, then faster, racing down the street. The horse jerked beneath him; Rome held on tightly to keep from falling. Lamp-lit windows blurred by. Rome couldn't see Gashlin anywhere.

A couple of torches were lit. Rome wondered dully how all this could have happened so fast. But the fury had burned, caught, and spread. Job Thompson had been a respected man.

The trees around the livery stable moved with soft whispers in the shadows. A pungent smell of animals and straw filled the air. A circle of glaring white faces surrounded

Rome. The women had stayed behind—no, he was wrong. Cathy watched from the fringe of the crowd.

Hands pulled him down from the saddle, started to slip the rope around his neck. One of the men with the rope wore a deputy's badge. He wondered what the sheriff was doing. . . .

The thunder of the shotgun roared through the darkness. The leaves stirred with faint hissing as the lead passed through.

The mob stopped.

Like a single organism, its voice died. Frightened eyes peered toward the shadows. The rope fell to the ground. Rome gazed at the figures in the darkness vaguely outlined in the torchlight. He heard a familiar voice.

"Get away from him, all of you."

Ben Hamilton. My God, it *was* Ben! Rome wanted to shout his name aloud.

Hamilton was mounted, a shotgun leveled at the mob. Behind him were other riders, men from the camp, similarly armed. Their gun barrels shone dull blue in the starlight.

"The next blast," Hamilton said, "may get some of you."

The mob stirred, whispering. No one reached for his gun.

"Open a way there," Hamilton ordered. "Mark, are you all right?"

"Yes," Rome called.

"Can you ride out by yourself? Do you need help?"

"I can ride," Rome said quickly.

The men hadn't moved. Hamilton's face, craggy and determined, was dimly visible in the orange glare of the torches. *"Let him through!"*

The shotgun roared again, scattering shot skyward. A pinched-face puncher squealed in fear. The crowd parted.

Rome kicked his horse through the aisle. Hamilton and the railroad men wheeled their mounts and pounded down the dark alley behind the stable. The angry voices lifted again, but they soon faded under the drumming of the hoofs.

The men rode from Warknife to the end-of-track without a word being said. Rome hung on tightly, letting the horse have its head to follow the others. He felt strength slowly returning; he began to think clearly again.

At the camp, Hamilton posted guards all around, then he and Rome went into the office car. Hamilton lit the lamp and pulled the green blinds. His eyes bored into Rome. "This is pretty damned serious, Mark."

"Goddammit, you don't have to tell me that! What I want to know is how you got there. I was almost stretched out. I had the feeling I was going to die. I've never felt like that, so damned sure. It isn't pleasant."

"Two of the boys bought supplies in town this afternoon. They had a drink at the Emporia and heard about the meeting. I was afraid there might be trouble. We rode in just as the meeting was breaking up. We heard the shooting, and it was damned clear that a necktie party was being organized, with you as the guest. I'd like to hear about it."

"There's quite a bit," Rome said shortly.

"Well, make it quick. They'll be out here before long. I've got the men standing by to signal. They won't touch us—they'll be afraid to, because lynchings are illegal. But with you it may be a different story. They're liable to take you anyway."

Rome laughed, sharp and hard. "A price on my head." Rapidly he outlined what had happened since their discussion at noon. When he finished, Hamilton looked even more dismayed.

"God, this looks bad. You didn't try to buy off Gashlin, did you?"

"Ben, don't you know me better?"

"All right, don't get sore. We've got to figure out what to do next. And, on top of that, we still have a contract to meet." He shoved a hand through his white hair, his eyes reflecting the yellow glow of the lamps.

To Rome, the interior of the car with its green blinds and shadowed corners seemed secure and untroubled. The feeling was shattered by the blast of a rifle. Hamilton leaped to his feet, knocking over the chair.

"They're coming, Mark. Get out of here, fast! Ride back when it looks safe, and we'll see what's happened by then."

Rome already had the door open. He jumped off the steps, swung up onto his horse, and booted it hard. From the opposite side of the camp came the noise of a large party of riders. The sound of his horse's hoofs would be muffled by the arrival of the men from Warknife.

He headed away from the camp, to the north, and circled back wide, riding across the dark prairie toward the town. The wind fanning his face was cool and invigorating. He began to organize his thoughts.

He figured Gashlin would be with the Warknife men. Yancey would be undercover, probably holed up in a room at one of the town's boardinghouses. That gave Rome an opportunity.

He didn't exactly know what he was looking for, but he held a hope that he might find something to untangle the web of treachery and death gathering around him. Hamilton and the other railroaders were helpless. He was the free agent—with a price on his head.

The realization struck home with biting force. He rode on beneath the cloud-filled sky, suddenly feeling cut off and alone. The moon came out from under a black veil of cloud, shining down like a bloated pale face. The air had grown very cold.

Warknife lay quiet now, its streets deserted. Rome kept to the back alleys. Most of the lamps in the houses were out, the people in bed. The hoofs of his horse made soft, thudding sounds in the dirt.

He dismounted in back of the main yard of the Central Kansas Overland Company. Coaches loomed against the moon as Rome crept silently among them toward the office building. He saw no guard posted anywhere.

He eased out his pistol, slipping into a patch of shadow. He tried the door. It was locked. Moving to the right, he began a systematic check of the windows. Finally he found one open in the rear.

He crawled over the sill, finding a small storeroom piled with boxes of invoices, shipping forms, and company letterheads. The door to this room was locked. Conscious of the creak of the floorboards, he smashed twice at the lock with his gun butt. Then he listened. He heard nothing but a few faint shouts from the street. Drunks, probably. The lock hung broken. He stepped into the main office.

Across it, behind a gold-lettered door, lay Bruce Gashlin's office. In there, Rome reasoned, might be something to help him expose the man for what he was. Cautiously, he eased the door open and started a methodical rifling of the desk.

One of the bottom drawers was locked. He tugged at the handle, then noticed something and felt a burst of satisfaction. There was no safe in the office. Gashlin would be too sure of himself for that; a locked drawer would suffice.

Rome took a letter opener from the desk and thrust it into the slit at the top of the drawer. He worked the opener back and forth a few moments; cursed when it snapped in two. He found a second one with a heavy ivory handle and finally managed to break the latch and open the drawer.

Three papers lay inside. Rome hesitated, listening again. The drunken shouts again, closer. He crouched under the desk and struck a match, reading the first paper.

Received of Bruce Gashlin 1500 dollars for services.
Signed,
Job Thompson.

The other two, for seven and nine hundred dollars respectively, were signed by Harry Drew and Giles McMaster. Rome blew out the match, working on the significance of what he'd read.

Gashlin had plenty of money. Enough money to pay the ranchers not to sell the right-of-way. Pay them, in effect, to maintain his business. It was more money than the railroad could offer for the small parcels of land. The Kansas & Western was not yet that big a firm; it ran on a tight budget.

Gashlin was the one with capital. Thompson, McMaster, and Drew certainly knew what kind of a man he was. Knew, for instance, that he would buy people off to get what he wanted; that it wasn't strictly a matter of being opposed to progress. The three of them were in on the scheme, while the rest of the townspeople were unaware of it.

"Damn," Rome said under his breath. The church meeting had been a farce, a show staged to keep the townspeople quiet. They could have thrown a lot of weight, but now they were against the railroad. Thompson's wrath at Gashlin's lie concerning the attempt to bribe him must have been an act, and that same anger provided the setting for his murder. Thompson, evidently, was expendable from Gashlin's point of view. But there was one man who might be able to blow things open, if Rome could get to him.

Stuffing the papers into his pocket, he straightened suddenly. One of the drunken voices was coming from the front porch of the office building. A key rattled in the lock. The door swung open.

Rome crouched in the shadows. The watchman's lantern swayed in one hand; a bottle hung slackly from the other. The watchman stumbled against the outer office rail, swearing. Rome started to move toward the storeroom through the open door of Gashlin's office.

The watchman turned, setting down his lantern. "Who in hell . . . Who is it?" he shouted. He reached for his gun.

Rome moved faster than he thought possible. He clubbed the man's gun away and kicked him backward with his knee. He had learned the lessons of running outside the law very quickly.

The watchman staggered, his eyes wild in the smoky light from the lantern. He jerked a knife from his pocket and lumbered at Rome, mumbling, "What the hell are you doing in here?'' Rome tensed himself and swung out, striking the drunken man across the temple with his gun barrel.

The knife clattered to the wooden floor, blade first. A faint whine filled the air as it stuck and quivered. Then the watchman dropped, a splotchy bruise widening on his skin.

He wasn't dead. Rome made sure of that, then blew out the lantern. As he stood in the darkness listening to the watchman's irregular breathing, a new thought twisted the pit of his stomach.

He was now bound to the railroad more closely than ever, though in another way he remained cut off. He was bound to it not merely because he worked for the Kansas & Western—it wasn't that simple. If the railroad went through, Gashlin would be out of business and there was a good chance Rome would be cleared. If the railroad *didn't* go through, he would eventually be a dead man, swinging in a noose.

The thought was ironic. He laughed softly. He had to put the Kansas & Western through. Not with actual rails and ties, not by sweating in the sun, but as an outlaw, with his gun and his mind. It was surely a new way to drive the iron west. . . .

He stopped laughing then. A noose wasn't funny. He remembered how close he had come, how he'd felt death near.

He went out through the storeroom window to the back of the yard, the papers in his coat. His horse waited in the shadow thrown by the coaches, whose angular shapes rose against the swollen white moon.

Yancey. The answer lay with the grinning, death-crazed youngster. At least, Rome thought, the first step lay there. He had to clear himself and thereby clear the railroad. With the moon out and night lying on the town, he had the opportunity. He knew very little about Yancey and yet he knew a great deal. Enough, perhaps, to give him the edge he needed.

He rode leisurely through the shadowed streets. They wouldn't be searching for him at this hour. His horse moved quietly between the rows of houses while he looked to the right and left till he found the object of his search.

The first boardinghouse, run by an Irishman named Harrigan, revealed nothing. The irate and sleepy landlord told him nobody named Yancey lived there. The door slammed in Rome's face. He moved back to the street, mounted, and rode on.

The second boardinghouse stood on a large lot on a dusty street directly to the rear of the Emporia. Rome heard the rhythms of the player piano still dinning into the night along with occasional laughter. He tied his horse at the sagging gate and stepped as quietly as he could onto the squeaking boards of the run-down porch.

He knocked three times before a landlady appeared, carrying a tall lamp. Her hair was put up in papers, her thick face mottled. Her breath reeked of alcohol. Rome felt safe. She was too full of rotgut to recognize him, even if she had been at the church. Judging from her appearance, chances were she hadn't.

"What the hell's the idea of waking a lady at this time of night?" she growled, pulling her wrapper close. The liquor fumes clouded around Rome's head as she spoke.

"I'm looking for a man named Yancey. Does he live here?"

"Sure he does. Cole Yancey. Second floor. First door to the left of the landing."

He moved by, into the hall. She slammed the door and continued to babble drunkenly about being awakened, standing in a pool of lamplight by the newel post. She was still complaining when he turned the corner at the head of the stairs.

He halted at the first door, standing in the gloom, listening. Beyond the thin panel he heard loud snoring. He eased his gun from its holster and shoved the barrel near the lock. Then he rapped on the door.

He kept knocking till the snoring stopped. Yancey mumbled incoherently; footsteps padded to the door. Rome heard the noise of a hammer going back. Even if he was still groggy from sleep, he couldn't get out of the habit. But his reaction would be slow . . . or so Rome hoped.

"Yeah?" Yancey called. "Who is it?"

"Gashlin sent me over," Rome whispered.

"What about?"

"About you and Job Thompson. Now open up." He tried to sound angry and harried at the same time.

Rome's heart slugged out a beat within his chest. The key rattled in the lock. A tiny bit of light appeared as Yancey pulled the door open.

Rome shoved the barrel of his gun against the man's stomach. "Let go of your gun. *Now!*"

Yancey's face lost its look of sleepy idiocy. His eyes flared with the sudden awareness that he was caught. He tried to step back, but Rome jammed the barrel deeper into his flesh, gouging. "Drop it on the floor!"

Yancey giggled and coughed, still not totally awake. He eased the hammer carefully into place. The gun thudded on the carpet, and Rome stepped quickly into the room, shutting the door. Yancey, barefoot, in his underwear, looked like a helpless and frightened boy. He didn't have a gun anymore.

That was what Rome counted on. Without his gun he was nothing; a harmless youngster. Rome scooped up the weapon and thrust it into his belt. Yancey waited submissively, terror in his eyes as he stared at the glinting blue metal in Rome's hand.

"What do you want from me, Rome?" he croaked. "Listen, I only work for Gashlin . . ."

Rome moved to the bed and sat down. A smell of rotting garbage filtered into the bedroom through the open window. The Emporia piano clattered its mechanical melodies.

"I know you work for him, Yancey. That's why I want to know a few other things. You'd better answer my questions. If you don't, I'll kill you. Do you understand?"

Yancey trembled. Rome felt a surge of triumph. He had been right. Yancey was like so many of them, masters of a situation only when armed. The youngster was scared of the cold muzzle eye looking at him. He was seeing the fire of the explosion, seeing the smoke rising before the bullet slammed him. He said, "Ask your questions."

"Did you know you were going to shoot Thompson before the meeting tonight? Was it planned?"

Yancey shook his head doggedly. "No, Mr. Rome." He emphasized the *mister*. "Gashlin give me the nod, and I knew what he meant. I always understand when he gives me the nod. People were packed so tight, nobody could see much. It was easy. I had a few drinks afterward and came back here."

Suddenly a new thought wrote itself across his face. "Say, they were supposed to hang you. I saw 'em start . . ."

Anger filled Rome. He rose, staring. His voice grew loud. "You cheap punk, I'm good and alive, and I've got half a mind to kill you right now. Remember in the Emporia? You said you'd accommodate me soon. Well, here I am."

"Yeah," Yancey mumbled faintly.

"No good without a gun, are you?" Rome couldn't resist the remark.

"No, sir, I ain't."

"You're damned quick with the answers, too." Rome felt angrier by the moment. This crazy kid had put the murder brand on him as casually as he'd taken a drink afterward. Finally, Rome got control of himself.

"All right, Yancey. I want you to do something."

"Sure, anything."

"You got some paper and a pen?"

Yancey pointed to the dresser. "In there. Belongs to the landlady."

Rome moved to the bureau and pulled open the drawer. Beneath two soiled work shirts were a few yellowed sheets of writing paper. He also found a metal-tipped pen and a bottle a third full of ink. He set the items on top of the table in the center of the room. Then he caught the chair with his boot tip and jerked it forward. "Sit down."

Yancey sat, fidgeting with his underwear.

"You're going to write what I say. Pick up the pen. You can write, can't you?"

"Yeah, I went to school in Indiana when I was a kid."

"Don't waste my time. Write this. *I, Cole Yancey . . .*"

The pen scratched laboriously. Yancey hunched over the table, peering at each word.

"*. . . killed Job Thompson outside of church tonight on orders from my boss, Bruce . . .*"

"Not so fast, will you?" Yancey whined.

"Shut up and keep writing. *Bruce Gashlin.* Got that?"

Yancey nodded.

"Date it and sign your name."

Yancey obeyed, then pushed the paper away from him. Rome picked it up, scanned it briefly, and put it down again. "Not just the initials. I want your whole name."

"I always use my—" Yancey stopped, looking again at the gun. He wrote out his full name.

Rome was reaching for the paper, feeling satisfied, when the door opened abruptly. Bruce Gashlin stood there, his clothes dirty and sweat-stained from hard riding. His fingers curled around the doorknob. His husky face remained calm, but his blue eyes narrowed just a bit.

"Well!" He laughed gently. "Mr. Rome, I didn't expect you." He noticed the gun immediately, closing the door and stepping into the room. Rome's backbone tingled. A new factor had entered the situation. It was now no longer just Rome against Yancey.

Rome indicated the paper on the table. "I've got a nice confession from Mr. Yancey about Job Thompson's murder. It implicates you."

A tiny superior smile edged Gashlin's mouth. His fingers dipped into the pocket of his checked waistcoat, and he pulled out a cigar. "Unfortunately, we couldn't do a thing at the railroad camp since you'd already gone. Anyway, your boss Hamilton had plenty of men with rifles. I just wanted to have a talk with Cole here. I didn't think you'd be on the scene."

"I'm leaving," Rome told him. "But I think the sheriff will be looking for you in a little while. I'll be with him. I want it to be legal."

Gashlin shook his head. "The paper won't stand up in court." His fingers dipped down into the waistcoat again. Rome observed him carefully. Controlled as it was, Gashlin's tone still revealed more than a trace of anxiety. The paper could finish him, and he knew it.

"I'll take my chances," Rome said. "And get your hands up where they belong."

Gashlin shrugged. "I only want to light my cigar."

The fingers reappeared, holding a pepper-pot derringer.

Rome tried to move fast. He swung the pistol toward Gashlin, but the other man slid the tiny gun across the table. "All right, Yancey." The youngster's eyes flared wildly as the derringer fell into his lap. He fumbled for it.

Rome swung his gun back again, the finger whitening on the trigger. He had no time, and Yancey was back in power, his young eyes full of kill-lust as he brought the derringer up from beneath the table. Gashlin was smiling; Yancey's face broke into its idiot grin. *He had no time. . . .*

A ragged burst of piano music came through the window, cut off abruptly by the thunder of Rome's gun exploding three times. Yancey dropped the derringer on the table with a loud thump, then sat back, his eyes bulging. Blood poured out of the hole Rome had blown in his neck. Slowly, he toppled to the floor.

Rome whirled. The last fragments of the confession were curling into black ash. Gashlin tossed the match onto the table. He kept smiling. "Do you want to kill me, too, Mr. Rome?"

From the first floor, the drunken landlady began to shout. Rome cursed and ran for the door. He did want to kill Gashlin, kill him where he stood, but he had to get away. The foundation had fallen, the bottom had tumbled out, and the hole had grown death-deep. He was caught now, more than ever.

He crashed against the landlady coming up the stairs, knocking the lamp out of her hand. There was a rattle of glass, then a leaping of flame as she screamed again. He bolted through the door and vaulted onto his mount, digging his heels in savagely. He thundered away through the darkened streets, out toward the end-of-track. Behind him, hoarse shouting filled the night. The moon had vanished; the world lay dark as he rode.

The gun, the law of the gun, he thought. You couldn't outwit it, you couldn't beat it. In the end, it trapped you; you returned to it, and it destroyed you.

He had actually killed a man. The hoofbeats echoed it. *Killed a man, killed a man, killed a man . . .* The wind screaming in his ears sang it to him. Nothing remained but force, animal force. He knew it was wrong, but the other way had failed.

The end-of-track camp lay in darkness. The guards challenged him and he called out to identify himself as he rode past. He ran up the steps of the office car, pushed the door open, and faced Ben Hamilton, his heart beating furiously, his mind whirling.

"I killed Yancey, Ben. I shot him, I killed him, I couldn't help it. . . ."

His nerve broke, and he sank onto the chair before Hamilton's desk. He cradled his head on his arms, letting the dry sobs shake him, letting the strained emotions break loose.

He was no gunslinger. He was no fast-draw man. He worked for the railroad. He had a job. But they were killers. Ruthless . . .

He worked for the railroad . . . my God . . . the railroad . . . the wheels . . . round and round . . . killed a man . . . and round . . . killed a man and round and round . . . killed, killed, killed . . .

It took Ben Hamilton nearly an hour to quiet him down.

When Rome began to talk coherently once more, Hamilton drew the story from him.

Rome felt a sense of calm slowly returning. The familiar interior of the old car with its closed-in atmosphere of protection soothed his nerves. "I'm just not the man to handle a gun like that," he said wearily. "I thought times were changing. I thought you could work out differences in other ways."

"Back East, maybe. The country out here's slow to change. You ought to know that."

"I'm a killer," Rome said, as if he hadn't heard the other man.

Hamilton jabbed a finger at him. "The important thing is to get out of sight. We'll fix a place for you to hide in one of the boxcars. Then we've got to get the Kansas & Western rolling through Warknife."

Rome nodded. "Maybe these'll help." He fished the three papers from Gashlin's office out of his pocket, shoved them across the desk, and explained briefly what they were and how he had gotten them.

Hamilton read them, then laughed.

"By God, this may be our break." He got to his feet quickly. "Come on, let's get you under cover. They may be looking for you soon."

It was cold in the boxcar, cold and dark. He slept huddled among some old blankets Hamilton had collected in the camp. The first night he rested fitfully, lying awake for hours listening for the drum of hoofs in the distance. The night air remained still.

When dawn gashed the east with gray streaks, he realized they wouldn't be coming. The Thompson killing still stood; they would be hunting for him on that count. But Gashlin probably figured Yancey could be forgotten. There were a hundred others like him to be bought anywhere in the West.

Toward noon, while Rome hunched in the boxcar playing solitaire with a worn-out deck furnished by one of the Polish section hands, he heard the sound of horses. He slid the door open a fraction of an inch, peered out and saw a big man, evidently the sheriff, with a party of horsemen from War-knife drawn up in front of the office car. They were conferring with Hamilton. Presently, they rode out again, back toward the town.

Hamilton made his way across the sprawling camp to the boxcar. "Looking for you," he reported. "About Thompson. Told them you'd gone—lit out of here last night after we saved you from stretching the rope. They don't seem to feel too bad about it. They've quieted down, and the sheriff doesn't like lynchings. They figure somebody else will catch up with you."

"What now?" Rome asked quietly. He gestured at the boxcar's interior. "Do I have to stay cooped up in this damn place when I should be out clearing myself?"

Hamilton's eyes bored into him. "Can you do that?"

There was silence for a moment. Then Rome shook his head. "Gashlin's free and I've got nothing on him."

"Nothing but those papers. They aren't incriminating, but they may help."

"You got an idea?"

"Yeah," Hamilton said. "Right now, you wait." Without another word, he stalked back across the camp. After Cookie brought Rome his noon meal, he saw Hamilton ride out in the direction of Warknife.

Wait. . . .

The hours stretched on, dull, colorless, relieved only by an unwanted nagging fear about which he could do nothing. He was trapped. He had no alternative but to wait, as Hamilton had said. Even then he didn't have an idea in the world of how to clear himself. Maybe he would have to ride out permanently. With a sick feeling, he realized that he might always be a hunted man. Something had to break . . .

Ben Hamilton returned right at sundown, riding directly to Rome's car. He was grinning as he swung up, passing Rome a cigar. "This is it, boy! I think we'll be laying track within two days."

"What happened?"

"I took the papers to the sheriff."

"What for? They won't put anybody in jail."

"That's true. The sheriff himself told me he can't touch any of the ranchers, or Gashlin. The papers are strictly legal. But he didn't like the idea of the ranchers double-dealing Warknife like that. A lot of people really do want the railroad. Now the word's going to spread."

It spread rapidly; Rome heard it secondhand from the men who came back after an evening in Warknife. The town was reacting; rising on its haunches; wondering, voicing questions, even hurling accusations. As individual citizens had once fused into a single mass of hatred directed at Rome, now they were uniting against the trickery of a few. They began to wonder about Gashlin's statement of Rome's attempted bribery.

"Everybody, and I mean everybody, knows about them papers," one of the men reported. " 'Course, with Job Thompson dead, there ain't much said against him. But the others are getting laid low. The small ranchers didn't have any idea those three and Gashlin was sinking their chances of shipping beef by rail."

The voices rose, became angrier. The news carried back to the dim, lonely boxcar where Rome waited.

"Gashlin's about five hundred percent more unpopular than before. People don't like being shoved around because of him . . . they're starting to cuss the stink—and him."

Rome felt small satisfaction. Maybe the rails would

stretch out. Maybe the Kansas & Western would roll. But Job Thompson's killing remained bloody on his hands.

Three mornings after Hamilton took the papers into War-knife, more riders came to the camp. After they left Hamilton didn't appear, so Rome made his way to the office car. Hamilton was busy at the desk when he entered.

"Dammit, Mark, you're not supposed to be roaming around. Somebody might ride in here any time and spot you—"

"I just wanted to find out what those men were doing here."

Hamilton grinned. "The whole town's busted wide open. Drew and McMaster gave back the money Gashlin paid them and tore up the papers. Cathy Thompson plans to do the same. It appears she didn't have any idea that old Job was part of a deal involving bribery."

"That means something—"

"You're right it means something. Gashlin's sore as hell." Hamilton fingered the green metal cash box on top of the desk. "But I bought the right-of-way through all three spreads. Public opinion just got too strong. I heard those three families were almost social outcasts. Like they had leprosy or something. We're going through, starting now."

That made Rome feel better. The wheels were turning again. New life was being pumped into the Kansas & Western. He glanced out the window and saw it. Men bustled about busily. Track foremen were assembling their crews; flatcars were being loaded.

"I think maybe we've got this thing licked," Hamilton said at last.

"I wouldn't count on it a hundred percent."

"Why not?"

"Gashlin will still try to stop us. And this time it won't be with paper deals. He'll use guns and dirty tactics. We ought to expect it and get ready."

Hamilton studied him. "We will. Maybe it'll be a good thing. In one way it scares the hell out of me—we're cutting our time pretty thin as it is. But maybe we can draw Gashlin into the open and get rid of him once and for all.'' He paused. ''The situation's backwards now. Gashlin's out, we're in. He'll fight for sure. But we're in.''

''All except me,'' Rome said quietly. ''I swear to you, Ben—somehow I'll get that Thompson thing cleared up.''

''Your chance'll come.''

Rome nodded. ''Right now I want to work.''

''All right. We're going to hit this thing hard. Day and night. I'll put you on nights.''

''I want to be out on the track. I want to help put those rails down myself, Ben.''

''Good enough. Only don't expect to do that all the time. We may need extras in everything, foremen, engineers. We'll be working on a rough schedule.''

''Suits me.''

Hamilton slapped him on the shoulder. ''Get back to your damned boxcar and wait till dark. Then you can get busy.''

Rome thought of Gashlin all afternoon, wondering how and when the strike would come. When he got hold of him . . . well . . . He thought about that a lot. The bitterness feeding in him, gnawing at his mind, changed him. All he wanted was Gashlin before him and a gun in his hand. Rome wondered if he would be strong enough to keep from murdering the man the first time he laid eyes on him, the first time he was unprotected.

Noise filled the camp. Whistles shrilled and flatcars began to move up the line about a quarter of a mile, pulled by the small switch engines. Hoarse shouting echoed everywhere. Smoke wisped in the sky, and soon from the west came the clang of hammers.

At four o'clock a storm came smashing down from bloated gray clouds. At six, in the rain, Rome was swinging a hammer, driving in spikes. Behind him the switch engine bored a yellow tunnel of light through the downpour, wreathing the working men in a ghostly aura.

The rain kept coming down, soaking into the parched

ground. Hamilton drove the men, working them twenty-four hours a day. Rome's muscles ached almost unendurably when the dawn came, but he went back to his duties after a two-hour rest. His clothes didn't dry out. His head swam, and when he slept again, he swung a hammer in his dreams. He knew he was getting sicker, but he didn't care.

The Kansas & Western was going through. . . .

They drove the rails across Drew's spread, then McMaster's, then through Warknife. Rome stayed completely hidden the night they laid track through the town. The next day they were beyond the eastern outskirts and he was eager to work again. He argued with Hamilton and finally won, working through the day, too, stopping only about seven hours for sleep when he got too feverish.

They cut timber and built the trestle over the cut on Thompson's spread. Once at night, working under the eye of the locomotive behind them, Rome saw Cathy Thompson watching on horseback, Hamilton beside her. He kept his head down as he slammed another spike home. She didn't matter. Even Gashlin had been wiped from his mind. The world consisted of the rails and the ties, the spikes and the watching yellow eye marking progress through the rainy darkness.

Men began to drop. The ones remaining worked harder than ever. The dispensary in the rear of the office car never closed, and the supplies of medicine dwindled. The men were sick, but a restless energy drove them on. Hamilton was often among them, swinging a hammer, cursing, as wet and as sick and as tired as they were. But, like them, he was proud of what they were doing, and it showed. It kept them going.

Nine days after they started work they were back on schedule and almost to the far boundary of Job Thompson's ranch. Rome went back to the main camp east of the recently constructed trestle, trying to find some warmer clothes. The air had grown cooler, turning the wet ground into thick mud.

Rome was in the mess tent, downing a cup of hot, acidic coffee when one of the foremen came in and spotted him. "Hey, Mark—they're short of iron up ahead. We're loading a couple of flatcars. Can you take them up?"

Rome nodded and finished his coffee. He tramped through the drizzle toward the snorting switch engine. "Steam's up," the foreman called as Rome climbed into the cab.

He edged the throttle back, his hands moving with skill over the controls. The railroad man's sense of precision, his sensitivity to the massive iron locomotive born of instinct as well as practice, took hold. Smiling, Rome leaned out and watched the track ahead.

The wheels turned, hissing, clacking, rattling off their song of triumph. They weren't beaten. They were rolling west again. They were going through. He felt elated, even with the residue of fever and sickness to dull his senses.

He wasn't making over eight miles an hour. But that was all right. The trestle would be coming up soon, and he hadn't far to go after that. Just being in the cab, feeling the engine under his hands, made him feel immeasurably better. He thought suddenly of Cathy and wished that she were with him.

The seemingly endless rain slanted down through the headlight, cold and dreary. Rome didn't care about the rain anymore. He jerked the cord, listened to the whistle scream its cry of conquest. He wiped his forehead and smiled again.

A quarter of a mile east of the trestle, Gashlin struck.

The riders came out of the murk, half a dozen of them. They followed the train at a fast gallop. Rome whirled, jerking out his gun. He could make out the figure of Gashlin, leading the riders.

The locomotive rolled past a small gang of workers who dodged to avoid the oncoming horses. One of the riders shot at the railroadmen; Rome saw two of them go down. Then the locomotive swung around a bend. Rome hoped fervently that the men would summon help.

The train was rolling through the uncleared timber, the trestle coming up soon. Rome crouched in the cab with the pistons making a thundering sound beneath him. The wheels clacked as the riders swung onto the last flatcar one by one. Their guns were out as they advanced toward the cab through the rain. Gashlin carried a large dark parcel.

"Stop the engine," he shouted to Rome over the roar. "Stop it on the trestle!" Rome triggered a shot and the attackers ducked. Rome spied a couple of rough, unfamiliar faces in the gloom. Gashlin had evidently added a few professional guns to his force. By the hellish glow of the firebox, Rome could see that Gashlin's face was anxious. His back was to the wall. . . .

Rome debated the situation for an instant. They were not firing now but stalking cautiously because they wanted the locomotive halted on the trestle. Rome guessed what the parcel contained. Dynamite.

It would be a crippling loss: a valuable switch engine, and, more important, a key trestle that would take time to rebuild. They might never finish on time, and Gashlin would keep his business. . . .

"Stop this thing!" Gashlin roared, his voice ragged with desperation.

Carefully, Rome took aim and began firing. He slipped along the side of the tender, triggering his shots over the top. He had to time it carefully now, very carefully. Gashlin must be realizing that he couldn't stop the train; he shouted orders to his men and they began firing from the flatcar nearest the tender.

One by one, Rome shot them down, all except Gashlin. It was a new sensation, feeling the power of the weapon in his hand. He took his time with four, only wounding them. The fifth clutched his stomach and screamed, his body arching backward and pitching from the flatcar, lost in the darkness and the rain.

Gashlin remained. He was crawling down the opposite side of the tender, hidden from view. Rome edged his way back into the cab, his nerves strained. Fear gnawed the pit of his stomach. He pulled the throttle all the way out and felt the locomotive shiver. Imperceptibly, it picked up speed.

He waited.

Gashlin appeared at the far corner of the tender and hurled the package toward the boiler opening. Rome stepped out of the shadows, grabbing for it. His fingers strained for it, and he wanted to scream with rage when he missed it; he felt the thing brush past his fingertips as the locomotive rocketed onto the trestle.

Gashlin was struggling to get a pistol out of his coat. The dynamite went spiraling into the maw of the firebox. Acting more by instinct than from thought, Rome ran forward, smashing into Gashlin and pushing him backward off the train. Rome tumbled with him for seemingly endless seconds, down and down, through rain and blackness.

Rome thought, My God, we may be falling into the cut, we may . . .

He hit the ground and felt his body vibrate with the jarring pain. The locomotive rolled a thousand feet beyond the trestle, the last flatcar careening wildly, before it blew to pieces.

Rome flattened himself on the sodden ground, hiding his face. Heat and steam and tiny shards of metal stung his back. He lay there, his heart thumping rapidly while the reverberations died away. Then he staggered to his feet and surveyed the situation.

The trestle remained intact with only a few lengths of rail ruined. The switch engine had disintegrated. The flatcars lay on their sides, rails and ties spilled onto the shoulders of the roadbed. Rome peered at them in the murk and then he thought of Gashlin.

Gashlin lay half a dozen yards away, face up, unconscious. Rome knelt near him, taking a match from his pants pocket. Then he realized that he still held his gun in his left hand. He shifted it to the right, then stuck it in his belt, laughing at his own clumsiness. He finally got the match lit and cupped his hands around it, shielding it from the rain.

He stared at Gashlin. The man's face was bearded and weary-looking. The strain must have worn him to nothing. His business sliding out from under him; making this one attempt to save it . . .

Suddenly Rome thought of Job Thompson. Anger flooding over him, he pulled his gun. Standing up, he pointed the barrel at Gashlin's head, his finger tightening on the trigger.

He stood that way for a long moment, the rain whispering down 'through the timber surrounding him. Then he scowled. Slowly he pushed the gun back into his belt. Bending down, he hoisted Gashlin's unconscious form onto his shoulder and began to trudge westward.

Ten minutes later he met a handcar coming toward him from the end-of-track. Thankfully he dumped Gashlin's body onto the car and huddled down beside it. One of the railroadmen pumped the car back west while the other workers trudged to look over the wreckage.

In the lighted work area, where men labored in the flaring glow of lanterns hung on poles beside the track, Rome met a tired Ben Hamilton. Quickly he explained what had happened. As he was finishing the story, the sheriff rode in.

"This here's Mark Rome," Hamilton said.

The sheriff reached for his gun. Rome, faster, already had him under his sights.

Easy, Sheriff," Rome said. "I want to get this cleared up as much as you do. That's Bruce Gashlin on the ground. He just blew up one of our switch engines and tried to dynamite our trestle on top of it. He killed Job Thompson—that is, Cole Yancey did, on his orders."

"I don't figure it," the sheriff replied. "Not any of it."

"Wait till he wakes up," Rome said. "Things'll straighten out then."

At least he hoped they would. He was counting on Gashlin being the opportunist in any situation.

In the rain, Rome shivered. A ring of men had gathered,

watching intently. Hamilton ordered them back to work and they tramped away through the mud. Slowly, Gashlin stirred on the ground, opened his eyes. The first thing he saw was Rome's gun.

Next his gaze fastened on the sheriff. He tried to get to his feet, slipped in the mud, and sank to one knee.

"Get up, Gashlin," Rome said.

He tried again, swaying until he made it.

Rome weighed his words with care, hoping he had judged the man correctly. "We've got you dead to rights for dynamiting the engine and for having Job Thompson killed. You can take your chances and keep quiet, or you can spill the whole thing and maybe you'll get off easier. Prison's better than a rope."

Gashlin didn't wait five seconds; he told his story. Rome noticed that his eyes moved continually as he did so. Stalling for time?

At the end, the sheriff fumbled to pull manacles from his pocket.

Rome was watching for the play. It came as the sheriff stepped between him and Gashlin. There was a flurry of movement. Hamilton shouted, and the sheriff jerked aside, howling in pain, clutching his hip. Teeth bared, Gashlin faced them, the knife shining for a moment until the rain washed the blood off. The sheath under his arm had a broken lace and dangled loosely at his belt.

Gashlin's arm started back, his eyes filling with hate for Rome. The arm lashed upward; Rome pulled the trigger once; the knife dropped.

Gashlin toppled forward. His arms moved out feebly in an effort to stop the fall. The last chance, Rome thought sourly. Gashlin fell facedown in the mud, quivered, and flopped over onto his back. His face hardened into a mud-daubed mask.

Hamilton was helping the sheriff. Rome tossed his gun away, feeling incredibly tired.

"Go to bed, Mark," Hamilton said over his shoulder.

Rome nodded dumbly, rubbing his eyes. The collective exhaustion of the last few days hit him all at once, but he made it to one of the tents. Somehow he managed to find blankets and a dry spot on top of some pine boards.

When he woke up nearly twenty hours later, the railroad had moved on.

It continued to move, after time for the men to rest. During that interval, Rome saw the sheriff, answered a few last questions, and rode out of Warknife, a free man.

He stopped at the Circle JT. Mrs. Thompson welcomed him quietly, then left him and Cathy alone in the parlor.

"Well, you'll be moving on, won't you?" she said.

He nodded. "Guess I will."

She touched his arm. "To say I'm sorry isn't enough."

"You don't have to say anything, Cathy."

"Do you think"—she hesitated—"you'll ever get railroading out of your blood?"

"Someday, maybe. A man has got to settle sometime. The railroad will need an agent here to handle all the cattle shipments."

"It would be a good place," she agreed, and he smiled inwardly. Intuitively, silently, an understanding had sprung up between them. The old affection could be rekindled. . . .

"But I've got to do this job first," he told her. "I've got to see the Kansas & Western finished."

"I know. I'll still be here."

"Then I'll be back. It's a promise."

He kissed her in the doorway of the ranch house. She clung to him for a moment, then gently pushed him away.

"Go on, Mark," she said quietly. "The railroad's waiting."

He squeezed her hand and walked to his horse. He waved as he rode out of the yard.

The country was tinted with the light of early evening, and somewhere to the west men labored and cursed to meet the deadline. Slowly, inevitably, the bands were joining the oceans, and he was part of that conquest of immense distance. The iron horse. The eternal pioneers moving forward, sometimes clumsily, haltingly, but still forward.

Spurring his mount, he rode toward the burning ball of the sun, to where the end-of-track lay waiting.

About the Authors

Bill Pronzini has written numerous Western short stories and such novels of the old west as FREEBOOTY and THE GALLOWS LAND. He lives in San Francisco, California.

Martin H. Greenberg has compiled nearly 100 anthologies, including westerns, science fiction, and mysteries. He lives in Green Bay, Wisconsin.

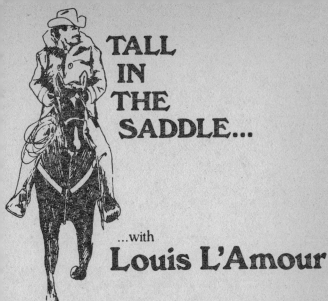

TALL IN THE SADDLE...

...with

Louis L'Amour